MW00438645

# GAMBLING with the ENEMY

Toni Leland

*Gambling with the Enemy*
©2005 Toni Leland

All rights reserved. No part of this book may be reproduced or transmitted in any form or by any means, electronic or mechanical, including photocopying, recording, or by any information storage and retrieval system, without permission in writing from the publisher.

ISBN 1-887932-40-2
Library of Congress Catalog Number: 2005902567

This book is a work of fiction. Any references to historical events, real people, or real locales are used fictitiously. Other names, characters, places, and incidents are the product of the author's imagination, and any resemblance to actual events or persons, living or dead, is entirely coincidental.

Printed in U.S.A.

Parallel Press is an imprint of the Equine Graphics Publishing Group

# *Acknowledgments*

If nothing else, this book taught me that the craft of writing is 30% inspiration and 70% research. Without the diverse group of willing individuals to help me through all the stuff I didn't know, you wouldn't be reading *Gambling With the Enemy*.

Many thanks to: Officer McElhaney of the Zanesville Police Department; the Cincinnati FBI Field Office; Peter Cultice for a peek into the mind of a lawyer; Barbara for her knowledge and experience in the economics of horse farm management; my patient critique partner, Janet; and my gambling gurus, Bob and Art.

I owe a serious debt to the eagle-eyed advance readers who spared me the embarrassment of typos and plot inconsistencies: Holly, Robert, Ellen, Art, Marilyn, Janet, and Carolyn.

As always, thank you, Bob, for putting up with this madness.

*Dedicated to the men and women*
*who have given their lives*
*in the fight against terrorism,*
*and*
*to those who continue the battle.*

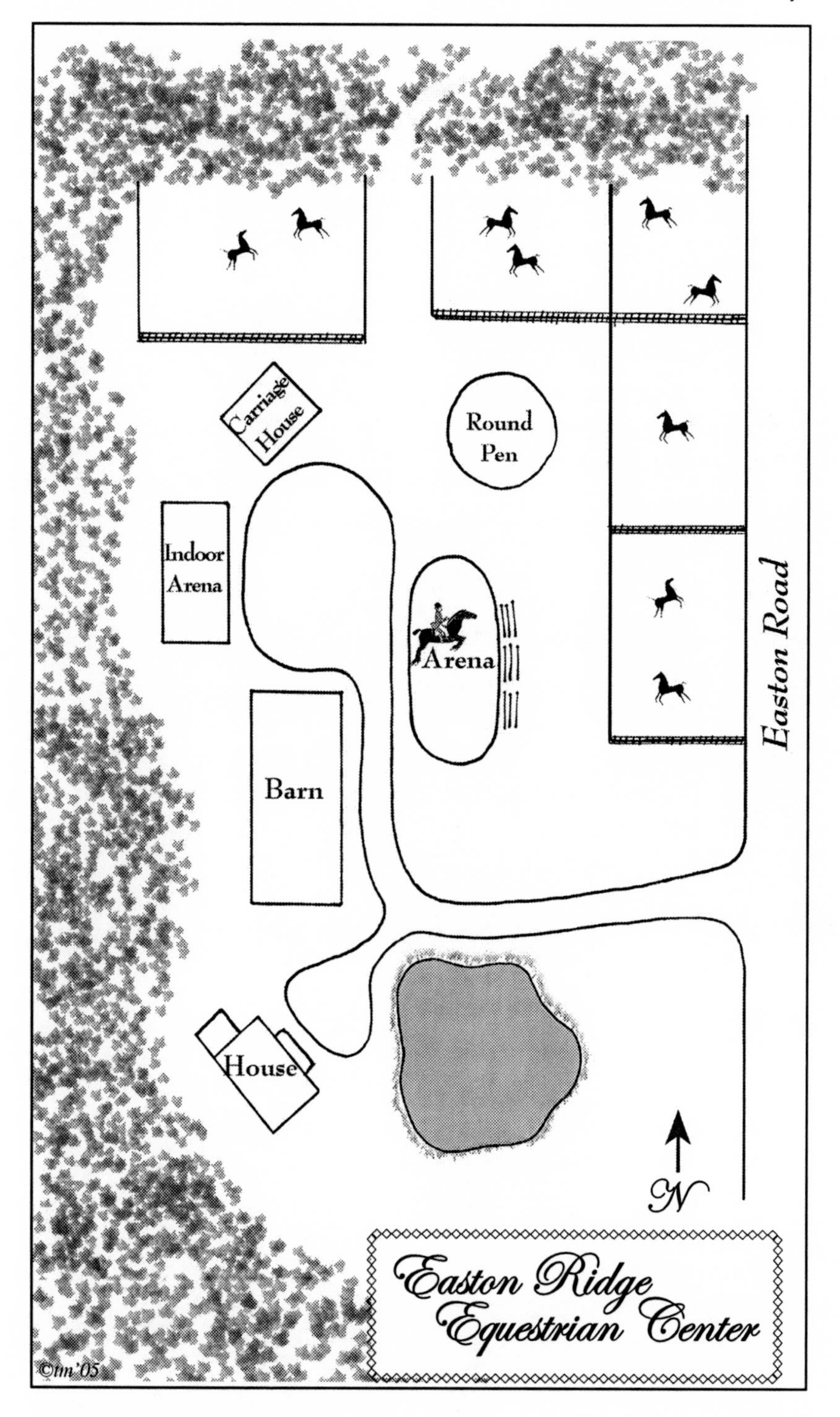

Carriage House
Round Pen
Indoor Arena
Arena
Barn
House
Easton Road
N
Easton Ridge Equestrian Center
©tm'05

## Arabic Glossary

Arabic is a beautiful and musical spoken language, with many dialects and forms of address; however, it is difficult to convey the rhythm and sound in writing.

For the interested reader, the following words and phrases are those used in the everyday life of Middle Eastern people.

*Allaah* – God

*Insha'Allaah* – God willing

*Allaahu akbar* – God is great

*Ma'assalama* – goodbye (Go in peace)

*Shukran* – thank you

*Yalla* – hurry

*quyeese* (m) /*quyeesa* (f) – good

*Ana behibek* – I love you

*Habibi* – my darling, sweetheart

*umm* – mother

*hijaab* – Muslim woman's headscarf

*subha* – prayer beads

*muezzin* – the crier who calls the faithful to prayer five times a day.

# *One*

Jessica stared, momentarily stunned by the exotic woman standing in the doorway. Skin the color of a cinnamon latté, a serene expression, large dark eyes fringed with long black lashes. A pale yellow scarf covered her head, the ends draped over one shoulder and secured with a gold brooch. An equally lovely young girl pressed against the woman's side, and Jess formed a mental image–the two, wrapped in silk and flowing chiffon, silhouetted against an ancient pyramid. So out of place in a horse barn.

Faith Angelo followed the newcomers into the small office, and Jess immediately noticed her partner's rigid features. An uneasy murmur threaded through her chest.

Faith gestured toward the young girl. "This is Dania. She wants to take riding lessons."

The strained tone of voice sent another blip across Jess's mental radar, but she rose quickly and moved from behind the desk.

"Hello, Dania."

The child stared at the floor, murmuring an unintelligible response.

Jess extended her hand to the woman. "I'm Jessica Rayder. Welcome to Easton Ridge."

"I am Zada Abbass Mahfood."

The woman's handshake was gentle and quick, her palm soft and cool. Several gold rings adorned each hand.

Jess smiled. "Would you like to tour the barn and meet the horses?"

Mrs. Mahfood turned to Dania and murmured a quick question in a musical language. The child nodded.

Zada's lukewarm smile emphasized the awkward atmosphere. "Yes, that would be fine."

Faith leaned against the doorjamb, well behind the visitors. She caught Jess's eye and frowned, shaking her head vigorously.

Jess kept a neutral expression. "How did you hear about us?"

A hint of Britain breezed through Zada's perfect English. "My husband heard that your facility is very good, then last year, we met the famous Faith Angelo at the Silver Classic."

Jess smiled. "You've made a good choice. Follow me."

Out in the barn aisle, she turned to Dania. "Where do you go to school?"

The girl didn't answer, instead, turning dark eyes up to her mother's face.

"Dania attends the Muslim school outside Hartford."

Abandoning attempts to break through the girl's shyness, Jess started the barn-tour spiel.

"We have twenty-two horses here." Moving along the bank of solid oak stalls, she explained the routine. "Students are expected to learn how to care for their horses. The wash rack is over there, and this is the crosstie area where we groom." Dania seemed anxious about the idea, and Jess smiled. "We have a lot of fun here. We put on schooling shows, and we travel to organized events in other towns. We have several students your age."

Dania nodded solemnly.

Jess led the visitors through the north doors and into the sunshine. "During good weather, we use the open arena for lessons and shows. We have an indoor arena for winter work, though it needs some repair right now. Last year's blizzard caved in one corner of the roof." A band tightened around her chest. "We hope to be able to use it again by November."

Faith spoke up. "When did you want to start? I'm kinda bu–"

Jess threw her a warning look, then smiled at Dania. "You could start today, if you'd like."

The girl's huge eyes glowed and she nodded enthusiastically, her small pretty face beaming from the frame of her white headscarf.

Faith's shoulders slumped, and she gestured toward the far end of the barn. "Okay, let's go find a pony that's just right for you."

Relieved, Jess turned to Zada. "I think that's our cue to get lost."

Confusion darkened the woman's eyes, and Jess hastened to reword the comment. "I mean, let's go back to the office and take care of the paperwork. I can answer any questions you might have."

Zada threw an uneasy glance at her daughter's retreating back, then followed without a word. In the office, she settled into a chair, smoothed her skirt, then folded her hands in her lap. Discomfiture sharpened her remarkable features, and Jess attempted to reassure her.

"She'll be fine, Mrs. Mahfood. Faith is wonderful with kids. Has Dania ever ridden a horse?"

"Once. We visited a farm in Massachusetts, and paid for a pony ride. She loved it."

Jess carefully kept her expression neutral. How would Faith be able to teach the unresponsive and over-protected girl? More important, how would Dania fit in with the others? A small ripple moved through Jess's chest. Kids could be so cruel to one another–they'd eat this little mouse alive.

A few minutes later, Zada handed over five crisp hundred-dollar bills. Jess forgot her concern about the girl's timid personality, and pushed a sheet of paper across the desk.

"Here's a list of things you'll need to buy for Dania. We have frequent schooling shows here at the farm during the year. Lesson money is due on the first of every month. Do you have any questions?"

"Yes, may I stay and watch Dania when she takes her lesson?"

"Of course! We love parent involvement. Let's go see how they're doing."

Zada's features relaxed and she rose to follow Jess. In the aisle, Dania's excited voice rang out from the crosstie area.

"*Umm! Umm!*"

Excitement colored every unintelligible word she babbled.

"English, *Habibi*. You must speak English when you are here."

Zada bobbed her head in apology. "Sorry, she forgets."

Dania's exuberance bubbled. "This is Pete. Miss Faith says I may ride him every week! *Insha'Allaah.*"

Jess grinned and shook her head. *The universal addiction of little girls.*

Late that afternoon, Faith dropped into the chair by the desk and let out a long sigh. "Man, I'm glad the day's over."

"How did Dania's lesson go? She's awfully quiet. I can't imagine how you'd be able to interact with her."

"Quiet? You have to be kidding! She never stopped chattering the whole time she rode the horse. The lesson went fine, except the mother hovered around, acting real protective, like she thought something might happen to the kid."

"It's probably a cultural thing. I'm sure Middle Eastern children aren't raised the way we were."

A shadow changed Faith's delicate features. "I'm kinda sorry I met them–I never dreamed they'd really show up for lessons. I feel creepy having foreigners hanging around here, especially A-Rabs."

"C'mon, that's not fair. You're judging them just because they look different than us."

"Well, ever since 9/11–"

Jess jumped up and scowled. "No, I don't want to hear that stuff! And don't think I missed your attempts to discourage them. Faith, we have a serious financial vacuum right now, and their money is as good as anyone else's. So get over it."

In the sudden quiet, Jess considered the essence of the brief disagreement. Both she and Faith had grown up in the melting pot of New England, and never gave a second thought to the diverse mix of people in the region. Though the devastating attacks on America had thoroughly shaken them both, with time, Jess had moved back into the familiar security of everyday life.

Apparently, Faith had not.

Ж

# *Two*

A hollow knock shuddered through the steering column, and Jess quickly switched off the radio and glanced at the dashboard glowing in the dark like the control panel of a jetliner. Holding her breath, she listened in the silence as the big Freightliner diesel moved slowly along the winding road, hauling its precious cargo through the night. The headlights illuminated an eerie tunnel of trees ahead, and the hair on the back of her neck prickled. *Not a good place for a breakdown.*

She glanced over at Faith's features, angelic in sleep. They'd had a good show and her partner certainly deserved a catnap.

A moment later, Faith woke with a start, then yawned. "Mmm. Boy, I'm tired." She chuckled. "Are we there yet?"

Jess's nostrils curled and, for an instant, she mentally denied the odor. She sniffed again, but the smell had faded.

Faith peered at the digital clock on the dash. "Where are we?"

"About an hour fr–"

A loud clank made them both jump. The truck vibrated with the repercussions, then the agonizing screech of metal against metal echoed in the night air. Another indescribable crunch, and the truck jolted to a stop.

Jess clenched the steering wheel. "Shit!"

"Jessie, what *was* that?"

"I don't know, but it wasn't good." She opened the door, recoiling at the blast of muggy night air that pressed into the cab. "You go back and check the horses."

She fished a flashlight from under the seat, then walked around to the side of the hood. Clutching the light between her chin and shoulder to free up both hands, she fumbled with the temperamental latch, but it wouldn't budge. A second later, she stared in numb disbelief, knowing it didn't matter whether she looked at the engine or not. In the pale yellow beam of the flashlight, a perfect rosette of metal peeled back around a gaping four-inch hole in the hood.

Faith's hysterical shriek shattered the night.

"Oh, my God! Come quick!"

Jess sprinted toward the trailer access door, adrenaline flooding her system. Inside, Faith pointed her flashlight beam at a bay gelding in the end stall. He leaned against the partition, his left hind leg cocked, the hoof barely resting on the floor mat. A long, bleeding gash slanted across his hock, and dark pink flesh curled back to expose glistening white bone.

"Turn on the lights, Faith, and get the first-aid kit."

The interior of the six-horse trailer brightened, and the other three horses shuffled and snorted nervously. Jess lifted the lock pins on the partition, then swung the heavy metal panel into the next empty stall, and secured it to the wall.

"Untie his head and hold him. I need a closer look."

Keeping an eye on the nervous gelding, Jess inched forward to examine the nasty wound. A minute later, she straightened up and sighed.

"The cut looks worse than it is. The bleeding's stopped, but I'll bandage him anyway."

Faith sounded forlorn. "Lexie will be devastated."

Jess closed her eyes briefly. *Of all the horses to get hurt, wouldn't you know it'd belong to a client?* Pushing away the enormity of the problem, she concentrated on wrapping the hock, taking care not to wind the gauze too tightly.

When she'd finished, she rose and moved to the horse's head. He'd settled down a little, and the wild look had disappeared from his eyes. She smoothed her hand over his neck, and patted his shoulder.

"It's okay, Jazzy. We'll get you fixed up in a little bit. Good boy." She turned to Faith. "Get me a tube of bute–we might as well reduce the pain."

The temperature spiked inside the truck cab, and Faith fanned herself with a rumpled show program. "What's wrong with the truck?"

"I'm no mechanic, but from the looks of the hole in the hood, I'd say we threw a rod."

Faith nodded blankly. "How long do you think we're gonna be sittin' here?"

Jess focused on the tiny numbers fading from the screen of her cellphone. "The guy said forty minutes. That probably means at least an hour." She shook her head and sighed. "This'll cost a fortune. Two tow trucks and an emergency vet call."

Faith's brow wrinkled. "Why two trucks?"

"One to haul the trailer back to the farm and another one for the truck."

"Oh." Faith brightened. "Well, at least it didn't happen on the way to the show. . ."

Jess tuned out the attempt at optimistic chatter, and struggled to contain her emotions. She gazed through the windshield at a thatch of tree branches hanging over the road, bathed in the pulsing orange of the emergency flashers. A deer materialized from the edge of the woods and drifted across the road, apparently unafraid of the silent hulk of metal. Headlights glowed around a curve ahead, and a small car hurried past. The distraction gave panic an opportunity to slip in and take control, and Jess's throat tightened. Tears burned against her lids and she blinked furiously, but no amount of self-control could keep the months of financial worry from rolling in like a high tide.

"Jessie, are you okay?"

Drawing a deep, shaky breath, she nodded, struggling to regain her composure–be the rock that Faith always depended upon.

Faith patted her arm. "It's not like we had an accident, or something *really* disastrous."

Jess's usual I-have-this-covered attitude disappeared, and her deep frustration surfaced. Months of grappling with the impending doom of failure stoked the fires, and an angry blaze roared out of control.

"Faith, this *is* a disaster! Do you have any idea how much this tow will cost? How much a new engine will cost? How much it'll cost to have Doc Stevens out in the middle of the night on a weekend?"

Faith blinked in stunned surprise. "Don't we have insurance?"

Jess's small bit of control slipped away. "No! I had to let the roadside insurance slide. The engine warranty expired last month. And *we're* responsible for client horses when we haul them."

The harsh words hung on the thick air, more ominous for having been spoken out loud, and her angry tears finally spilled over.

Faith slipped her arm around Jess's shoulders, hugging her tightly.

"Jessie, it's going to be okay, really. My God, I've never seen you like this."

The warm air again intensified the faint odor of alcohol, and Jess recoiled from the sympathy, glaring at her life-long best friend.

"We've never been in such deep trouble before! Where the hell have *you* been? Have you forgotten we lost six students because of the blizzard? That's three grand a month! Don't you think that had some impact on our finances?"

Pain flickered in Faith's blue eyes, and Jess felt like a heel, but the suspicion that her partner might be drinking again quickly replaced the empathy. At that moment, Jess's fractured state of mind couldn't abandon the chance to bring someone else in to share the blame.

Suddenly, brilliant headlights and a strange glow from revolving emergency lights illuminated the woods. A large commercial tow truck pulled in front of the rig, and a smaller dually parked farther up the road.

Jess reached for the door handle. "We'll talk about it later."

Samir Mahfood removed the wrapper from a plump cigar, and inhaled the heady aroma of fine tobacco. As he performed the comforting ritual of preparing to smoke, the low voices of his companions mingled with the conversations of other café customers and the muted background noise of the casino.

A stocky man with a neatly trimmed beard tapped the ash off a cigarette. "Samir, your business is doing well?"

"Very well. I am waiting for a shipment from Egypt, beautiful carpets. This week, *Insha'Allaah.*"

Samir smiled, watching the first satisfying plume of smoke curl away from the glowing tip of the cigar as he listened to his friends. They were so easily entertained by the ordinary things that men around the world discussed when they gathered together. As usual, the conversation eventually turned to the latest unrest in the Middle East, and his pulse quickened. Another triumph for Allaah was in the wind. He could feel it.

The tone of the discussion changed abruptly, became sharp and angry, bringing Samir's attention back to the group. His friends peered intently at a television newscaster, whose earnest voice sent a chill of anger racing through Samir's chest.

*"Racial profiling took a new and frightening step this week. In Boston, Ahmed Mussawi, a U.S. citizen, was informed that his bank account had been closed, leaving him with no access to the funds. Other banks are following suit, a questionable decision based on the FBI's attempts to stop the flow of money to terrorist groups, both here and abroad. . ."*

The outraged rumblings of Samir's companions further incensed him, but he remained silent. Since the attacks in New York, the shadow of discrimination hovered over his countrymen, his friends, his family. What did it matter that he'd lived in America for almost twenty years? Been a good citizen, a hard-working businessman?

He puffed on the cigar and willed away his tension, watching the television screen through narrowed eyes. *These Americans do not understand with whom they are dealing. Allaahu akbar.*

ӾӾ

# *Three*

In the thin light of dawn, Jess sifted through a stack of bills on her desk, trying to decide which ones would go unpaid as a result of the three-hundred-dollar towing fiasco. Fatigue ached through her bones, but her brain felt surprisingly clear. They hadn't rolled into the farm until after midnight and, by the time the horses were unloaded, and Jazz Man's hock was x-rayed and stitched, it had been almost three-thirty.

She gazed at the green accounts ledger, softly tracing the silver stamped letters with her fingertips. "Easton Ridge Equestrian Center." A dream come true, but teetering. Telling Faith about the financial situation took some of the edge off Jess's self-imposed isolation, but didn't solve anything.

She flicked off the lights, and wandered out into the barn aisle. A throaty nicker drifted through the quiet air, and Jess grinned as a soft white muzzle poked through the bars.

"Good morning, Miss Casey."

Jess gazed fondly at the hunter pony that had taken her through puberty and into high school, giving her the self-confidence to be the best jumping student at Westover. At least, until Faith Angelo showed up.

Jess slid the stall door aside and stepped into her favorite world, a universe where carrots and love were the only demands made on her. The graying chestnut mare chuckled softly, eagerly nuzzling pockets for hidden treats. Jess's problems faded as she offered the golden nuggets.

"*You* are a little piggy-wig!" She stroked the mare's smooth neck. "You know, it's a good thing Faith was so nice, because *I* certainly wasn't about to make friends with her."

Casey dozed off, her aged body relaxing under Jess's gentle touch and soft voice. Jess closed her eyes tightly, remembering a scene seven years ago. Beautiful Faith with bloated face, dull eyes, unkempt hair and clothes. How could things have changed so horribly? Charm and talent dissipated into an alcoholic fog.

Now, it seemed that Faith's demons had returned.

The young girl's anguished wail sent a painful shot through Jess's chest.

"Lexie, calm down. He'll be okay, he just needs some time to heal."

Distraught, unreasonable teenagers were Faith's department, but Jess struggled to get the girl to stop crying and listen. A minute later, Lexie's mother came on the line, and Jess gulped at Doris Troy's frosty tone.

"Jessica, how could this happen? We put that horse in your care. This was Lexie's year to go to Brandford. *Now* what?"

Jess fought the inclination to snarl a sarcastic reply. Doris was opinionated, intrusive, and unforgiving. But rich.

"Doris, Jazz should be fine in a couple of weeks. Lexie can ride one of our jumpers in the meantime."

"And the vet expense?"

Jess feigned confidence she didn't feel. "We'll take care of it."

Faith stepped into the office, and her optimistic expression turned Jess's stomach to jelly. There'd be no easy way to soft pedal the financial situation. She took a deep breath and plunged in.

"We're on the verge of bankruptcy."

Faith's eyes widened and she gasped. "Jess, please tell me you're exaggerating."

Jess shook her head and held out a handwritten letter. Faith sat down next to the desk, and scanned the sheet of paper.

Her voice dropped to almost a whisper. "Two weeks? Why would he *do* this? Three months isn't *that* far behind, is it?"

"Frank's been really good about it, but he wants the rent every month, and on time." Obviously, Faith had no idea what being three months delinquent really meant. "He knows we're having money problems and, understandably, he's trying to protect himself from larger losses."

Faith didn't respond, and Jess leaned back in the chair. "We were doing okay 'til the bottom dropped out of the lesson program."

"But most of the kids are back now–doesn't that help?"

"Yes, but four months without that income put us way behind. We can't possibly catch up 'til the end of summer." She sighed. "And, we *have* to get the truck fixed or we won't be able to take students to any horse shows."

"How much will *that* cost?"

"I'm waiting for the garage to call with an estimate, but I'd guess a new engine will cost about eight grand."

"Oh, man! How are we gonna pay for *that*?"

Jess shook her head, her heart heavy with sadness. "I have some old savings bonds I'll cash in."

Faith's features crumpled. "Aw, Jessie. . .not the ones your grandpa gave you every year?"

"Yeah, but this is no time for sentimentality. I'll go to Hartford first thing in the morning." She leaned forward. "Do you think Bill would help out a little? Temporarily?"

An angry glint flashed in Faith's eyes. "I doubt it! He's not too crazy about me being here. Says I should stop trying to live in the past." Her lower lip quivered. "No one's more self-righteous than a reformed drunk."

"Are you two still going to AA meetings?"

Faith shifted in the chair and fiddled with the hem of her shirt. "Of course."

Jess sensed a lie, but decided to let it pass. She picked up another sheet of paper.

"I've listed all our monthly expenses and marked the critical ones. We *have* to feed the horses, keep them shod, and pay for vet care. The public liability and vehicle insurance are mandatory. So is the lease payment. The only possibilities I see are canceling the mortality insurance on our own horses, and laying off the barn help–unless we can attract about six more students like Dania Mahfood by the end of the week." She handed the expense sheet to Faith. "We could also waive our own salaries until we get caught up."

Faith stared at the page and her voice cracked. "We spend

eighteen thousand dollars a *month* just to operate?"

Jess couldn't hide a grim smile. "Do the math. We have twenty-two horses here."

Faith's shoulders drooped and a forlorn expression darkened her face. "Jessie, we *can't* lose this place. I've never been happier."

Jess walked down the quiet barn aisle, thinking about her long friendship with Faith. Until recently, their "little girl plans" had been successful. Easton Ridge had the distinction of being one of the most sought-after riding stables in the area, mostly thanks to Faith's reputation as a former show-jumping champion.

Jess flipped a light-switch, and the honey-hued knotty pine walls of the trophy room glowed warmly. A large glass-fronted disply case commanded attention. Behind the paned doors, soft light glinted off shiny silver trays, bowls, and loving cups, sparkled through crystal mugs and glasses, and illuminated myriad other prizes won by both women. Beside it, a dark cherrywood cabinet housed a riot of brilliantly colored rosettes and ribbons. At one end of the room, a photographic gallery covered the wall–a lifetime of achievement.

A yellowed newspaper clipping featured the two of them, standing proudly beside their horses, each holding a gleaming trophy. The grins on their young faces told the story, but gazing at the pictures, Jess felt the familiar childhood stab of envy, followed by guilt. Why should she deny Faith her fame? She'd earned it. But the brief stellar career had died, crushed by tragedy and, finally, obliterated with booze.

Sorrow filled Jess's heart as she flicked off the light and left the carefree days of childhood behind.

ꭗ

# *Four*

The Hartford skyline came into view, rising to greet Jess like an old friend. She cruised slowly past the former offices of Carson & Banks, the brokerage firm where she'd made incredible amounts of money with her sharp analytical skills and daredevil risk-taking. Compared to the newer structures that had grown up in the adjacent blocks, the stone walls of the Kline Building looked dingy and out-of-date. The investment company had moved to a strip mall on the upscale west side, and several small retail shops had taken up residence in the once-elegant edifice. Jess allowed herself a smug smile. Gut instincts and detailed market scrutiny had driven most of her transactions while she was actively brokering, and she'd felt the imminent dot-com collapse well before it happened.

The car wound upward through the concrete spiral of a parking garage, and minutes later, Jess descended the odorous stairwell, recoiling at the strong smell of urine at each landing. She emerged onto the sidewalk, and took a deep breath. The muggy, stale city air pressed against her lungs. On the corner, Old City Bank stood guard over Market Street. Jess pushed through the massive revolving doors, and stepped into the cavernous lobby. The vaulted ceiling muffled all sounds, creating a hushed and secretive atmosphere. *Give me my village bank any day.* She obediently moved through the empty rope maze toward the cashier counter, then presented her safe-deposit key to a teller.

Inside the vault, a mosaic of steel squares filled two walls, floor to ceiling. The heavy plate glass door closed silently behind the retreating teller, a muffled hum the only indication that the lock had engaged.

Staring at the small metal box, Jess felt like a thief. Grandpa would be so disappointed to know his gifts would be used for something as mundane as paying bills. She took a short breath, then opened the lid. A faded black velvet case lay in the bottom of the box. Tears burned her eyelids as she stroked the soft fabric before opening it to gaze at her mother's gold retirement watch. It would be Jess's only remaining legacy when she left the bank.

Faith stood beside the desk, arms crossed over her well-endowed chest, a frown meshing her fine eyebrows into a single line. "You *have* to be kidding! Can't we wait until after the schooling show? I need the extra help."

Jess tried to keep exasperation from coloring her tone. "I told you–if we're going to fix this problem, we have to take drastic measures. You and I can clean stalls."

"We could ask the boarders to do their own."

Jess shook her head fiercely. "No, we can't let the customers know the situation–that would really be the end. You know how rumors fly."

Faith glowered. "Some fancy operation *this* turned out to be!"

She flounced out of the room, and Jess bit back a nasty retort. Faith's aggressive attitude was completely out of character. Jess shook her head at the probability of yet another problem on her plate.

She paged through the accounting ledger. They'd had a fair month, and maybe without the expense of three stable hands, she could scrape together the rest of the past-due lease payments. A quick glance at the calendar revealed that time was not on their side.The phone shrilled and she cleared her throat.

"Easton Ridge, Jessica Rayder."

A minute later, she wanted to disappear forever. "Thanks, Doc. See you in a while."

She found Faith in the feed room, writing up a grain order.

"Are you ready for this? Jazz Man has a hairline fracture just below the hock."

Faith's jaw dropped, and dismay clouded her face. "Holy Cow! *Now* what?"

"You tell *me*. I can't believe I have to call Doris with this news."

Jess ran her finger along the edge of a grain bin. "Any chance Lexie could ride Manifesto?"

Jess held her breath. Faith never allowed anyone to ride her show horses.

Faith tilted her head. "Why can't she ride Danny?"

Jess exhaled slowly, controlling her temper. "Okay. Just thought I'd ask. By the way, I've ordered the show lunch from the A&P deli. I can pick it up at seven on Saturday morning."

"The A&P? What happened to Anne's Catering?"

"Too expensive. I'm skipping the tent, too."

"You really *are* putting us on a budget. Maybe you should take up playing poker again." Faith smiled sheepishly. "Sorry I shot off my big mouth a while ago. I know you're just doing what's needed."

Jess nodded, but didn't smile. "I need all the support you can give me."

"Did you get to Hartford?"

"Yeah–did you talk to Bill?

Faith shook her head, her tone evasive. "He came home late. I was asleep."

Jess had a brief image of the arrogant realtor Faith had met at an AA meeting two years earlier. To Jess, they'd seemed an unlikely match, but he'd provided Faith with much-needed emotional support, so Jess had reserved judgment.

She nodded, quelling the impulse to press the issue. "Maybe you can talk to him tonight."

Faith grunted and turned her attention back to the clipboard without responding.

Jess left the feed room and headed down the aisle toward the stalls at the north end of the barn. A tall gray Anglo-Arab gelding bobbed his head and snorted.

"Hey, Danny, how's my boy today?"

The horse whinnied enthusiastically, and Jess chuckled as she slipped a halter over his ears. Ten minutes later, she buckled her riding helmet, and led the horse out into the sunshine.

Nothing lifted her spirits quicker than a good ride. The strong rhythmic movements of Steely Dan's body rippled through her legs, making her own body flow with his. She trotted him along the rail, feeling his energy and enthusiasm. His steady trot thumped in the soft dirt, and he snorted at the small puffs of dust. Jess urged him into a canter, and the air ruffled through his black mane. A thrill moved through her. *Just like the old days.* Danny picked up speed and collected himself before lifting effortlessly over the first jump. Jess became one with the horse, and all her dismal thoughts and frightening problems disappeared.

Anxiety gnawed through Jess's gut and a band tightened around her chest. For the past few hours, she'd thrown herself into the organization and management of the upcoming schooling show, edging all other problems from her conscious thoughts. Now, the landlord's letter lurked like a tiger, ready to pounce and tear out her throat.

She skimmed the words. "*. . .hate to do this. . .can't let more time go by. . .need full payment in two weeks. . .*"

She'd have to call him and ask for more time.

Several clients were late with their board, and the monthly bills were accumulating. A cold lump formed in the pit of her stomach as she slid a letter opener along the edge of the credit card statement. She knew the balance would be high, but she gasped anyway. Over eleven thousand dollars. She'd been in denial, coasting on credit and over-confidence, sure that any day, things would change. And they certainly had.

"Frank? Jess Rayder. . .Yeah, things are starting to pick up. Listen, I'd like you to come over when you have some time. I have a partial payment for you, and I want to discuss our situation."

The elderly man's voice sounded warm and friendly. "Sure, Miss Jessie. I can stop by tomorrow."

"Thanks, Frank. I appreciate it. We'll get square with you, I promise."

She hung up the phone and stared at the stack of mail. Tap-dancing had never been her long suit, but lately she was getting awfully good. A car door slammed, and she glanced out the window. Doc Stevens opened one of the compartments on his mobile clinic truck, and began gathering what he'd need to cast Jazz Man's leg.

Feeling like she might throw up, Jess reached for the phone to call Doris Troy.

# *Five*

Jess pushed through the heavy glass doors of the Seven Rivers Casino, suddenly wondering if her spur-of-the-moment decision to get away for a while was just a little indulgent. A good meal and a change of scenery seemed like a good idea, but more than that, she simply wanted to do something *she* could control.

She sucked in a deep breath, trying to adjust to the deafening clamor of raucous laughter, hundreds of loud voices, slot machines, and money rattling into metal trays, punctuated every few minutes by an obnoxious bell clanging the news of a winner. Faith's taunt echoed in her head. Poker playing had always been strictly recreational, and with great confidence in her skill, Jess usually came out on top. But she'd never viewed the talent as a way to make a living, or solve problems. Her father's warning drifted into her thoughts. "*Don't play if you can't afford to lose.*" She pulled a wad of bills from her purse and stuffed it into her pocket, remembering her saucy retort. *"Daddy, I never lose."* Okay, so this idea was a little risky, but the alternative was worse.

"May I help you?"

A tall, slim black woman stepped up close, her friendly wide smile producing crinkles around her large brown eyes. She wore a tailored gray suit, and a name badge identifying her as "Elvora, Player Development Manager, Seven Rivers Casino."

Jess squinted at the nametag, and the woman chuckled. "Sounds really important, huh?"

Jess grinned. "Yes. . .I'm looking for the poker tables."

Elvora pointed toward the far corner of the casino. "Right over there, honey. You have a great night."

Samir moved across the casino floor toward the café, thinking about his daughter's excitement over her first riding lesson. Both his wife and Dania were delighted with the new adventure and, for this, he thanked Allaah. Glancing over the captive crowds at the gaming tables, he felt contempt for the lack of self-discipline that ruled gamblers. His gaze stopped abruptly, focusing on a poker table at the perimeter of the room. *That is one of the riding instructors. I am sure of it.*

Intrigued, he moved closer, staying well out of the woman's line of sight. He'd thoroughly researched Easton Ridge, and knew many details about the two women, but not this. For the next twenty minutes, he watched her play–aggressive and self-assured, almost cocky. And very skilled. But something else simmered beneath her confident exterior–intensity with a nervous edge. Samir recognized the body language of a driven human being. If she had come to the casino to have fun and relax, she wasn't doing either.

For the next two hours, Jess played carefully, keeping her bets reasonable, and winning most of the hands. Confidence took charge and she made progressively larger bets. As the stakes rose, so did her winnings.

The dealer announced a fifteen-minute break for the shift change, and Jess leaned back in the chair and gazed at the three stacks of chips in front of her.

A deep voice cut through her concentration.

"You're certainly having a great night."

An attractive man settled into the chair beside her and smiled. His short-cut silver hair contrasted sharply against his tan, and startling violet-blue eyes sparkled with unabashed interest.

Jess's cheeks warmed, a new and unnerving sensation. "I hope this little break doesn't mess things up."

He chuckled and offered his hand. "Howard London."

"Hi. I'm Jessica Rayder. You from around here?"

"Nope, Coeur d'Alene, Idaho. And you?"

"Right here in Connecticut."

From the corner of her eye, she caught sight of a new dealer heading toward the table. She looked at her chips again, her thoughts already moving back to the game.

The handsome stranger didn't seem to notice. "Thought I'd come out and see what all this Indian casino uproar is about." He looked around the room. "Impressive."

Irritation prickled across Jess's shoulders and she forced a smile. "Well, looks like we're in business again. Nice talking to you."

He grinned and stood up. "Have a good night."

He sauntered away, a confident set to his broad shoulders, and Jess blinked, startled by the distraction. Since when did *she* notice men? Since never. Who had the time or energy?

Turning her attention back to the table, she saw the new dealer talking to Elvora. The black woman glanced at Jess and smiled broadly, then walked away as the dealer locked in his cash box. Jess counted her chips, and surveyed the players. During the last few hands, those who'd remained in the game were cautious with their bets.

Her killer instinct emerged and, by eight o'clock, she'd more than tripled her money. She scooped up the stacks of chips.

"You all finished, honey?"

Elvora's velvet voice rippled with interest, and Jess grinned.

"Yes, I think I've made enough enemies for one night."

A wide smile brightened the woman's face. "You ever want into a serious game, you give me a call. You're dangerous, girl!"

Brushed steel doors closed with a soft whoosh behind her, and Jess padded down the silent hotel hall toward her room, thinking about Elvora's offer. Interesting idea, but out of the question.

In the nicely-appointed room, she gazed at her reflection in the mirror and thought about handsome Howard. *A yahoo from out in the middle of nowhere, in a strange place, looking to get laid.* A pleasant way to oblivion?

She grinned at her freckled twin in the mirror. "Yeah, right!"

Jess had always gotten by on brains, not looks. The attention of a handsome man was pleasant, but also a little disconcerting. She eyed her strawberry blonde hair corraled behind a headband. Gray eyes gazed back at her from behind pale, almost invisible eyelashes.

She sighed and turned away. "Horses are more dependable

than men."

Thirty minutes later, she perused the menu posted outside the Monaco Steakhouse.

"Hello, again."

Howard London's disarming smile sent a disconcerting ripple through her stomach.

A hesitant expression crossed his face. "The food here is great. Why don't you join me? Seems silly for each of us to use up a whole table."

She smiled. "I agree."

They followed the maitre d' to a table in the corner and, after the first awkward minutes, Jess relaxed. She hadn't been in the company of an interesting man in a long time, and this one was especially intriguing.

He lifted his Scotch. "Here's to big wins."

Jess chuckled. "Hear, hear." She took a sip of wine. "What do you do in Idaho?"

"I own a hunting and fishing lodge–a big boy's playground."

"The casino must be a huge contrast to that."

He grinned. "Yeah, but sometimes I just have to get back to the hubbub of the East Coast."

"You're not from Idaho?"

"Hell, no! The lodge is my retirement. Don't get me wrong–I love it, but sometimes, I need a break from all those outdoor types."

Jess sliced off a piece of steak, then gave him a sidelong glance. He didn't look old enough to be retired.

"What did you retire *from*?"

"Law. New York City firm. Nearly killed me." He chuckled, then put down his fork and squinted at her. "Okay, now you know all about *me*. How about some information about you?"

"I own a riding stable."

He leaned forward, his eyes twinkling. "That sounds intriguing. Tell me more. How did you get involved in riding?"

Jess laughed. "*Very* long story. My partner and I took lessons together when we were kids. Faith was fantastic, I was an also-ran." Hearing herself say those words out loud sent a sharp pain through her chest. "Then during college, I didn't have much time for riding."

Howard raised his eyebrows. "You need a college education to run a stable?"

"No, I had another life before this one. After I got my MBA, I built a career as an investment analyst with a firm in Hartford. I left just before the dot-com debacle."

He sat back in his chair and grinned mischievously. "Ah, that explains it–you're *some* poker player. Not many women play the game."

The deep red merlot caught the reflection of the lights as Jess took a sip, and warmth spread through her throat.

"My dad taught me when I was twelve. We played for hours, betting M&Ms, and laughing a lot. He was such a tease."

She paused, momentarily overwhelmed by the memory. A quick glance at Howard's face brought her back to the present.

"Anyway, I got pretty good at the game, and managed to keep myself in spending money all through college."

Howard chuckled. "I imagine the college boys didn't appreciate being beaten by a girl."

"You got that right."

"So you just decided to open a riding stable?"

"No, it's not quite that simple. My marriage broke up about the same time I quit my job. I decided I'd do something with my life that would make me happy. I had plenty of money from my investments and the divorce settlement, so I took the plunge. Returned to what I loved as a kid."

"And?"

Jess cocked her head. "Are you *really* interested in all this stuff?"

"Absolutely. I love knowing what makes a beautiful woman tick."

*You big liar.* She smiled and looked away, embarrassed by his flattery, but loving the sensational ripple moving through her chest.

"I began looking for my old friend, Faith. To be successful in the riding lessons game, you need to have a hook, something that makes your program stand out. Her name and reputation would be our ticket to success." Jess shook her head and took another sip of wine, then threw Howard a rueful look. "I found her in a broken down horse-farm in Rhode Island."

His eyes narrowed. "I take it she hadn't been as successful as you?"

"It wasn't really her fault. At the peak of her jumping career, she took a bad spill during a major competition. She only broke her arm, but her horse shattered both forelegs and was destroyed on the spot." A chill ran across Jess's shoulders. "In the arena, in front of thousands of spectators."

"God, that sounds awful!"

Her voice dropped to a whisper. "It was. . .our horses are like family. Faith had been riding that one for ten years."

Howard's tone softened. "What happened?"

Jess heaved a big sigh. "She never recovered–left competition, took one trainer job after another, gradually moving down the ladder. When I found her, she was a drunk."

"Oh man, I'm sorry I asked."

"No, it's okay. Anyway, I told her what I wanted to do, and she was thrilled. When we were kids, we plotted constantly about how we'd open our dream stable someday. So Faith started attending AA, while we looked for property and bought equipment and horses. Within six months, she was dry, and on the circuit, wooing clients. The rest is history."

"Sounds like something out of a movie. . .Would you like some dessert?"

"No, thanks. I'm going to call it a night. I have to get back to the stable early tomorrow."

She reached for her handbag and Howard's warm hand covered her wrist.

"Please, Jess, let me get this. I haven't enjoyed myself this much in a long time."

His eyes reflected such sincerity, she couldn't argue. "Thank you. Me neither."

Once he'd paid the check, awkwardness crept back into the atmosphere and Jess rose from the table.

Howard jumped up. "I'll walk you to the elevator, then I'm going to play a little roulette before I hit the hay."

As they moved down the concourse, Jess smiled privately at

how nice it felt to be "escorted home." She threw a sidelong glance at the striking man beside her and wondered, for just a moment, what a relationship with him would be like.

Howard caught her scrutiny. "What?"

Her face warmed. "Oh, uh, I was just wondering–you never told me what kind of lawyer you are."

"Criminal Law." He dipped a hand into his pocket and brought out a business card. "If you ever get out to Idaho, call me. I'll give you a tour of beautiful Lake Coeur d'Alene."

# *Six*

Jess closed the accounting ledger with a snap. *One small step at a time*. She tucked a stack of hundred-dollar bills into an envelope, then closed her eyes and exhaled. The excursion to the casino had been a little scary, but she'd won enough to give Frank a fair partial on the lease payment.

She examined the financial sheet she'd prepared for the landlord. *As long as I appear to be making an effort, he'll probably work with me*. Tires crunched in the gravel outside, and she peeked out the office window. Frank McCarney, local wealthy eccentric, stepped down from the cab of his faded red 1963 Chevy pickup.

Jess waved from the barn door, grinning as the old geezer tipped his straw farmer hat and started toward her on wobbly bowed legs. The jokes around the village were unfounded–Frank was as sharp as they came, but the packaging was deceptive.

"Hi-ya, Frank! Warm enough for you?"

"Mornin', Miss Jessie." Rheumy blue eyes glanced at the sky. "Weather'll be changin' soon. My knees're achin'."

Jess led him through the barn. Across the aisle, Faith was showing three youngsters the proper way to cinch a saddle. She looked up and grinned.

"Hi, Frank! Ready to go for a trail ride?"

He chuckled and waved, his wrinkled face reddening with the attention. He looked around, taking in everything as they moved down the aisle toward the office.

"Looks good. You're keepin' the place up nice."

"Go ahead and sit down, Frank. I want to show you something." She handed him the financial sheet. "Here is a list of our current students and income. As you know, the blizzard last winter gave us quite a setback."

Frank slipped on a pair of reading glasses, and peered at the figures.

Jess continued. "Last weekend, the truck engine blew and I had to use some of our cash for the tow and repair." She flinched inwardly at the lie. "But, as you can see, in a month or so, we should be in good shape."

He threw her a sharp look over the top of his glasses. "Tough to be in business with no financial cushion."

His expression sent a flicker of apprehension through her mind, but she hurried on to the next part of her plea.

"I know, but we're gonna get past this." She held out the envelope, willing her hand to stop trembling. "Here's twenty-five hundred dollars toward what we owe you. Would you give me some more time?"

Frank took the packet, gazed at it for what seemed like a long time, then tucked the envelope into his pocket.

"Yeah, I can do that. I like you girls, and I know you're workin' hard to make a go of this place, but I gotta tell ya–I got people bangin' my door down to sell this property. It's worth a lotta money–not that I need it–but business is business."

He rose and pulled his hat down over his wispy gray hair. "I'll give you three more weeks. After that, well–"

"Frank, you have my word. You'll get your money by then."

Jess stared at the driveway after Frank's old truck disappeared. *Three weeks. Sounds like a lot of poker games.* Amazed she'd even considered such a solution, she shook her head and started down the aisle toward the wash rack. She stepped over a puddle of soapy water, then stooped to retrieve a hoof brush. Faith looped a hose into neat coils, then straightened up and brushed her dark brown hair away from her face.

"Whew, bathing ten horses is a lot of work."

Jess nodded absent-mindedly. "Frank's given us some additional time. If we're lucky, we'll get some new prospects at the show on Saturday."

"How'd your conversation with Doris go?"

"As you'd imagine. She made a veiled threat to move Lexie to a stable in Ridgefield. I just hope she doesn't start talking to the other parents and organize a mass exodus."

"Dammit! Who the hell does she think she is?"

"The rich lady who pays her board bill in advance and shells out money hand over fist, that's who."

Faith shook her head, then grinned. "Speaking of money, Dania's coming for another lesson tomorrow, and Mama Mahfood wants to go horse-shopping on Sunday."

"Boy, *that* was fast!" Jess winked. "Just make sure it's an expensive one–we could use a big commission."

"I've set up two appointments. We'll go to Naomi Morton's first, then down to Ridgefield. I'm sure we'll find something that costs a lot."

Jess watched Faith's face. The telltale bags under her eyes were a worrisome omen.

"Did you ever get a chance to talk to Bill?"

Faith threw her a guilty look. "Uh, no. . .we had a little argument. The timing's not right."

"Okay, no problem."

"So? How *was* he?"

"He, who?"

Faith grinned wickedly. "Don't try to kid *me*! Gone overnight? You've got a boyfriend, now give."

Jess wasn't in the mood for Faith's nonsense. "I do not."

"Then where'd you go?"

Jess's muscles tensed, irritation crawling into her reserve. "New Haven. Did you get the show release from Dania's mom?"

Faith looked puzzled. "I gave it to you yesterday, just before you left."

Jess shook her head. "Oh, yeah. Guess I'm getting forgetful in my old age."

"I don't think your age has anything to do with it." Faith stepped up close, her face bright with curiosity. "Are you going to tell me about him?"

Jess looked away, then an idea popped into her head. *Why not? She'll never meet him. . .he lives in Ida-Godforsaken-ho!*

"His name's Howard, he's a retired lawyer. It's nothing serious."

Faith squeezed her arm. “I’m so glad you’ve finally found someone. You work too hard.” Her eyes twinkled. “So when do I get to meet mystery man?”

Jess groaned. “Give it a break, will you?”

# *Seven*

On Saturday morning, Jess was up and dressed by six. Across the lane, students warmed up in the practice ring, and the parking lot already held a few cars.

Faith's voice crackled through the phone. "Are you gonna get here soon? I could use some help."

"Good grief, I haven't even had breakfast yet. What's your–"

"Don't waste time bitching, just get over here!"

The line went dead, and a sickening feeling filled Jess's gut. This was *not* the morning to have a meltdown. As she headed toward the barn, the air still felt cool, but a clear blue sky promised uncomfortable warmth by midday. Faith appeared in the doorway, her features deeply lined with tension, her red-rimmed eyes blazing with hostility. She strode toward Jess like a steamroller.

"It's about *time* you got here!"

"What in hell is the matter with you? Calm down."

Faith burst into tears, and Jess stepped forward to hug her friend.

"What's wrong?"

Faith struggled to extricate herself from the embrace, angrily swiping at her eyes.

"Bill. . ." She gulped back a sob. "He left me." She dissolved into tears again.

"Aw, honey. . .I'm sorry. Want to talk about it?"

"No, he's a jerk. I'm glad he's gone." She wiped her eyes, and smoothed a hand over her hair. "C'mon, we have a show to put on."

Jess followed, deeply disturbed by Faith's roller coaster

emotions, and wondering if her friend had really headed down the wrong path again.

Inside the cool barn, little girls scurried around, fastening riding helmets, giggling and giddy with excitement. Jess grinned, remembering how she and Faith had done the very same things, so long ago. She glanced toward the crossties where Faith held the rapt attention of the older girls. She seemed to have recovered, for the time being. Jess focused her thoughts on business to keep her mind off the conversation they'd have later that day. She couldn't let it go any longer.

A parade of luxury cars glided into parking spots, and emptied their well-dressed occupants while Jess watched. In the space of a few years, Easton Ridge Equestrian Center had become the elite place to prepare youngsters for a career in show jumping, and today's audience reflected that reputation. Jess spotted several new faces scattered through the crowd, and hoped they were prospective clients.

A glistening black Mercedes appeared, its smoky windows adding a mysterious touch. The door opened and a striking, dark-skinned man stepped out. He wasn't tall, but his self-assured body language made up for his short stature. He smoothed his suit jacket, and walked toward the spectator section. *Dania's father, of course.* Jess watched for a few minutes, examining his exotic features and noticing the sharp contrast to the WASPy crowd.

Zada wiped the folding chair with her handkerchief, then Samir sat down and glanced around the crowded spectator area. *Yes, these are very rich, very important people. This is good.* He'd made the right decision about where Dania would take riding lessons.

Zada pointed to an area beyond the arena, where several youngsters perched on their horses, waiting for the event to begin.

"See the lady over there? The one with the dark hair? That is Faith Angelo. She is very nice. Dania likes her."

Samir nodded, but said nothing. He still thought the notion of horseback riding was a foolish one, but Zada had been determined.

She spoke again. "There is another lady, Miss Rayder, the manager. I do not care for her. She is hard."

Samir thought about his discovery earlier that week. *Hard, yes, but also very sharp, very intelligent, very driven.* The loudspeaker echoed, sparing him from the necessity of small talk with his wife.

Faith stood in the center of the arena, holding a microphone.

"Good morning, and welcome to Easton Ridge Equestrian Center. Our show today is the first public event for some of our young riders. They will have a chance to demonstrate what they've learned. A schooling show is organized like a real horse show, except the riders do not compete against each other, only against their own skills–a little bit like a recital. All riders will receive ribbons for their accomplishments. Thank you all for coming, and I hope you enjoy the show."

Zada's voice rose with excitement. "Look, there's Dania! Doesn't she look beautiful?"

Samir turned his attention from the arena, and his heart swelled with love for the dark little girl sitting proudly on her pony. She looked calm and confident in her riding outfit, a purchase that had displeased Samir. He objected to the idea of his daughter wearing trousers. He did not want her to be anything like the brazen American girls in their immodest clothing. However, Zada had finally convinced him that the costume was a requirement for riding horses. As a compromise, Dania had been made to promise she would not parade around in any public place in the skin-tight riding breeches.

Zada rose and headed toward the refreshment table, leaving him alone with his thoughts. He let his gaze wander over the crowd again, then turned his attention to the huge barn. The well-maintained white building had dark brown trim around the doors and windows. On the roof, a cupola formed a sharp outline against the sky, topped by a running-horse weathervane, frozen in mid-stride and motionless in the quiet air. Sorth of the barn, a small house sat at an angle, facing a large pasture fenced by weathered split-rail oak. A large pond sparkled in the sunlight, the water moving in swirls behind the ducks and geese scattered over the surface.

Samir focused on the activity around the barn entrance for a moment, watching the instructor help a rider into the saddle. He briefly scanned the area for Zada, then turned his attention back to the property. Behind the main barn, a new-looking single-story building with several wide doors and many windows looked as though it might house an indoor arena. A huge blue tarp covered one corner of the roof. Just beyond the structure sat an old-fashioned four-door carriage house, with what appeared to be living quarters over the vehicle storage area. A wooden staircase rose on both sides of the building to a wide veranda that undoubtedly provided an expansive view of the property.

Applause interrupted Samir's concentration, and he looked back to the arena as a horse and rider left the ring.

Zada settled down beside him. "Dania is next."

He accepted a plastic cup of steaming coffee and glanced at his wife. Her lovely face was flushed with excitement, and he smiled fondly.

"*Habibi*, maybe you should take riding lessons, too."

She giggled. "I cannot help it, Samir. She is so happy."

Nostalgia softened her features, and Samir patted her hand. He felt sad that she'd had such a difficult time adjusting to life in the United States, even though she'd been with him many years. Though he'd been successful in continuing the traditional oriental carpet business started by his father, their lifestyle was simple and restrictive, compared to that of Zada's youth. Here, she confined herself to the small Muslim community, resisting the luxuries and opportunities available to her, always living with the onus of being a foreigner on American soil, and wearing it almost like a badge. Occasionally, her strong nature rebelled, and she would ask him to take her home to her family in Yemen.

Anger rose in his chest. He desperately wanted to make things right for her, and for Dania. He slipped a hand into his pocket and grasped the *subha* hidden there, his fingers moving methodically over the prayer beads as he silently asked for patience.

ꭗ

# *Eight*

Jess grinned at Dania perched on her pony.

"Ready to show off?"

The girl's pretty features crinkled into a charming smile that turned up the corners of her exotic eyes, giving her the look of a pixie. Jess still couldn't get used to the appearance of the black riding helmet over the white headscarf. The child stood out like a sore thumb amongst the other kids, and Jess's initial concern for her welfare had been correct–the students basically shunned the young foreigner.

Faith finished adjusting Dania's stirrup, then patted the horse's shoulder. "Okay, now you go out and show everyone what a talented rider you are."

Jess followed them out into the sunshine, and took a spot on the rail next to Faith. Dania entered the arena, and trotted her horse around in a tight circle.

Faith shook her head. "Boy, no one would ever believe that girl's only had three lessons."

The horse straightened out and headed toward the first obstacle–cavaletti poles spaced fifty inches apart. Dania gathered the reins to guide her pony over the pattern. Jess watched, marveling at the girl's grace as she executed the obstacle with studied concentration.

Faith stepped back from the rail as Dania finished the beginner course. "I think she could really go places. I'm going to start preparing her parents for that prospect."

Jess glanced at the Mahfoods, leaning forward in their seats, pride brightening their faces as they watched every movement their daughter made.

"I doubt you'll have any trouble convincing them."

Listening to the animated chatter of the older girls while they cleaned up their horses, Jess had to suppress a grin. Easton Ridge's star students were critiquing the jumps.

"Lex, I think that oxer was a little higher than usual. I mean, like, Tipper almost didn't clear it. Did you have any trouble?"

"Yeah, but I thought it was just 'cause I'm, like, riding a different horse. Let's ask Faith."

Jess stepped out of the tack room and chortled. "Early in the season, girls. . .it's not the jump *or* the horse."

Beth was defensive. "But, Jess, I've *never* had any trouble before!"

Jess smiled indulgently at the girl's petulant expression, remembering her own youthful excuses for messing up. She understood these two youngsters perfectly.

"Don't worry–you're both headed for Brandford and you know it."

Beth's face relaxed and she grinned. As the two girls walked away, eagerly discussing the biggest show of the season, Jess's smile faded. A lot could happen before Brandford.

The remaining spectators were gathered around the food table, enjoying the bright sunshine and listening to the students recount every jump, or quiver of a horse's back.

Jess headed toward Zada and her daughter. "Dania, you did a great job!"

The girl responded with a dazzling smile. "Thank you, Miss Rayder. I cannot wait until I have my own horse. I know I will be able to ride *much* better!"

Zada's laugh rang with delight, then a wistful look crossed her face. "A girl and her horse are a team, much better at everything they do. It was the same when I was a young girl."

Jess couldn't hide her surprise. "You ride?"

"I learned when I was younger than Dania. I attended a private school where they had a fine stable of excellent horses."

"How exciting! Do you still ride?"

A veil dropped over Zada's eyes, and her tone cooled.

"No. I am a married woman now."

"But you're in America! You can do any damned thing you want to!"

Zada's expression sent a chill across Jess's shoulders.

"Miss Rayder, America is *your* country–not mine." She turned to Dania, whose demeanor had become subdued. "Go change your clothes. Here comes Papa."

"Miss Rayder? I am Samir Mahfood, Dania's father."

Jess offered her hand. "Nice to meet you, Mr. Mahfood."

He gazed at her with hooded dark eyes, his expression pleasant, but somehow intrusive. "Please, call me Samir."

He turned to Zada and spoke quickly in Arabic, gesturing toward the car. She bowed slightly, then hurried after her daughter.

"Miss Rayder, I would like to discuss my Dania's riding lessons. Do you have some time?"

"My Dania is doing well, yes?"

Samir settled into the chair, taking care not to rumple the back of his suit coat. He smiled at the plain-faced woman sitting behind the desk.

"*Very* well. She has a natural talent for riding, and Faith is quite excited about her progress."

Samir's chest swelled with pride. "My wife is very happy with this. She does not have many social activities, except with the other wives from the mosque."

The familiar shadow of wariness on Jessica Rayder's face reminded him that his ethnicity and religion were hot topics in world news. He quelled the rush of irritation that threatened to upset his purpose in the conversation.

"During the lunch break, I walked around your beautiful property."

Her features tensed a little. "Yes, we were fortunate to find it."

"And you are prospering with the riding lessons?"

"We've worked hard for our success."

Samir nodded, considering how best to proceed.

"My wife has always loved horses. I am thinking about buying a farm for her, to give her something to occupy the time."

"It's very expensive to operate a horse farm."

"It could be no more than any other business, could it?"

"I think you'd be surprised. We've grown quickly in the past two years, but all it takes is one expensive disaster to–" She looked startled and abruptly stopped talking.

"What do you mean, disaster?"

Her eyes reflected the blunder, and she stammered. "Oh, nothing serious. . .you know, just a series of small things, cash flow. . ."

He smiled, seeing her discomfort. "Ah, yes, of course."

Jess stood up. "If you do decide to buy a place, I'd be happy to answer any questions you might have about operations."

"*Insha'Allaah*. Thank you."

A feeling of purpose came over him, and his hand slipped into a pocket, seeking the prayer beads. *There is a chink in the wall. An opportunity.*

The last jump had been broken down, the bright orange cones stacked neatly by the fence, and the food and debris cleared away. Faith flopped onto one of the folding chairs in the spectator section.

"I am *so* tired! These kids keep getting younger and younger."

Jess chuckled. "Only last week, you told me you weren't too old to compete anymore."

Faith rolled her eyes. "Yeah, well, that was then, this is now."

In the companionable silence, Jess thought about her near-blunder with Samir Mahfood. How could she have been so careless? Clients had a nasty habit of abandoning stables in financial trouble. She shook her head. And the damned fool seemed to think running a farm was no big deal.

Faith broke the silence. "What did you think of Dania's father?"

"I only talked to him for a few minutes. He's okay, I guess."

"Well, he makes *my* neck-hairs prickle." Faith stared at the ground for a moment. "He obviously rules the family with an iron hand. Dania is a different child when he's around. . .And Zada! I thought she was gonna grovel in the dirt, right there at the food table." She shuddered. "I can't imagine being so oppressed."

Jess nodded, thinking of the unfortunate conversation with Zada about riding. Some things in the world would never change, but both she and Faith needed to have some compassion and understanding.

"You know, I didn't think about it, but after 9/11, they must feel a little nervous about looking like the enemy."

Faith stood up and stretched. "Whatever. Dania's father gives me the creeps. Thank God, I only have to deal with Zada on this shopping trip."

Jess took a deep breath. "What really happened with you and Bill?"

Faith stared at her for a minute, obviously trying to come up with something plausible. Then, her shoulders drooped.

"We've been going round and round for a while. He wants me to get a *real* job. This isn't the first time he's moved out." She sounded unsure. "He'll probably come back. He usually does."

Faith's movements seemed wooden as she tried to act nonchalant. Jess had no solid proof that Faith had slipped back into her former self-destructive behavior, but the suspicion was growing by the day. How best to bring it up?

)(

# *Nine*

The next morning, Jess heaved a load of horse apples into the wheelbarrow outside the stall door. Picking stalls was therapeutic–no concentration required, just the mechanical, assembly line movements needed to sift through the sawdust. Uninterrupted time to think.

She was still kicking herself for her indiscretion with Samir. Add Doris Troy's chilly attitude at the show, and Jess might be faced with a sudden cash drain. Lexie seemed fine with riding Danny, but Doris had commented that he was an awfully large mount for such a small rider, and didn't present a very flattering impression. Jess jammed the fork into the sawdust. *Cripes, we hand over a sixty-thousand-dollar horse to a kid, and Doris is worried about aesthetics.* Another load of manure landed in the cart, and she set the fork aside. At least during the hectic week before the mishap, she hadn't gotten around to canceling the insurance on Danny. *Thank God for small favors.*

She stepped out into the aisle and glanced at her watch. *Where the hell is Faith? I've finished almost half the stalls.* She wandered into the office, and had just poured a cup of coffee when she heard Faith's voice in the barn. She set the cup down, and strode out into the aisle. Faith's hair looked uncombed, still secured with the same headband she'd worn the day before. Large sunglasses obscured most of her face. *Oh, hell.*

Jess cleared her throat loudly. "Well, nice of you to drop in."

"I overslept. You, on the other hand, obviously got out of bed on the wrong side."

Faith brushed past, shrugging out of her cardigan, and Jess

smelled stale liquor in the wake. *Okay, enough is enough.*

"Knock it off. You're hung-over, aren't you?"

Faith whirled around, her jaw set, her lips forming a hard, thin line.

"You just can't let it go, can you? I have a cold, and I overslept. Period."

She turned and stormed into the feed room. Bin lids banged and cabinet doors slammed. Anger and sorrow curled through Jess's chest. She couldn't let even their long friendship jeopardize Easton Ridge.

She moved quietly into the doorway. "We need to talk seriously."

"About what?" Faith kept her head down as she measured out grain.

"Why are you drinking again? You've been dry for so long."

"I had two beers last night on the way home. What's the big deal?" She straightened up and put her hands on her hips. "You're worse than Bill."

"I hate who you turn into when you drink–I don't even know you. Is this why Bill left?"

"Who knows? Who cares? Just let me get my chores done. I'm meeting Zada and Dania at noon."

"No, you're not. You're going home. I'll finish up here."

Faith snatched off the sunglasses and glowered with bloodshot eyes. "What the hell does *that* mean?"

"It means you're in no condition to be around clients. We can't afford to lose the Mahfoods because of your lack of self-discipline. I'm sure you know Muslims don't drink. Do you think they'd appreciate having you around their daughter in your current state?"

Faith stood stock still, her expression frozen into a mask of indignation and, for a moment, Jess thought the battle might continue.

Faith slipped the sunglasses back on. "Fine."

She walked out the door, and Jess let out the breath she'd been holding. They'd have a real conversation about it later.

"Faith sends her apologies. She's sick today." Jess grinned at Dania. "You'll just have to settle for me."

Dania looked dubious, and a flicker of annoyance passed over Zada's features, but she said nothing. After everyone settled into the farm van, Jess headed toward Waterbury. Her passengers were quiet, only murmuring to each other in their own language.

*This ought to be fun.* She cleared her throat, determined to do the best she could.

"Naomi Morton raises some of the finest sport horses in New England. I'm sure she'll have something perfect for you, Dania."

In the rearview mirror, Dania's dark eyes were unfathomable pools that gave no clue to what she might be thinking.

Zada spoke. "We want the best for our daughter. Money is not a problem. I hope you will keep that in mind."

*Hallelujah!*

Twenty minutes later, Jess pulled up in front of a white farmhouse flanked by two large red barns. Horses grazed in several pastures, separated by neat New England stone walls. A large pond shimmered beyond one of the barns. Jess imagined the scene blanketed in snow–a real life Currier & Ives.

Naomi Morton had been in the horse business a long time, and her reputation for honesty and quality stock gave her an edge over dozens of other breeders in the region. If Zada couldn't find the "very best" here, Jess was in trouble.

Naomi came out to meet them, her solid body a testament to the hard work of caring for horses.

Her sun-baked face crinkled into a smile. "Hi-ya, Jess. Nice to see you." She turned to Dania and offered a hand. "I'm Naomi. You must be the famous rider, Dania."

The girl colored, and a pleased smile spread across her face as she took Naomi's hand. "Yes, Ma'am."

Naomi chuckled. "None of this Ma'am-stuff, call me Naomi. Okay, let's go look at horses."

She turned on her heel and marched toward the nearest barn. Zada and Dania followed her, and Jess brought up the rear, relieved that Naomi had taken charge. Jess wasn't much of a saleswoman–that was Faith's department. Thinking about the situation again, disappointment filled her heart. What would happen if Faith couldn't, or wouldn't, climb out of the pit this time?

Naomi brought out a small chestnut hunter pony, similar to

Dania's schooling horse.

"Checkers has a fine competition record. He's done it all, and has the ribbons to prove it. He's a good, sound mount for a beginner."

Zada shook her head firmly. "We want a more refined horse, one that will complement Dania's riding form. Do you have any mares?"

Jess stared in disbelief, and Naomi shook her head.

"I do, but I don't recommend putting an inexperienced rider on a mare. They're unpredictable and moody during the breeding season, which just happens to coincide with show season."

Zada's jaw hardened. "I rode mares as a young girl, and didn't have problems."

Naomi's features tightened into a somewhat patronizing expression. "Did you compete with your horse?"

Realization softened Zada's tone. "No, I only rode for pleasure. What else do you have?"

Naomi put the pony back into his stall, then walked down the aisle to another. Zada murmured something to Dania, then threw a quick look at Jess, who felt completely inadequate at that moment.

Naomi returned, leading a large Dutch Warmblood. His sleek coat was the color of a vintage penny, and he wore four, almost perfectly matched white socks. Dania's eyes lit up and Jess groaned inwardly. *Oh, Lord. I recognize that horse. He's fabulous, but much too strong for her.* At that instant, Jess wished she hadn't sent Faith home.

Naomi stood the horse up to show off his fine body. "This is Buus Ravensburgen. His barn name is Buster. He's one of my own bloodstock, and has made me proud on the intermediate jumping circuit. He's a gentle, willing gelding with a lot of talent." She smiled at Dania. "From what I hear, you'll be needing a horse like this soon."

Zada turned to her daughter. "Do you like him, *Habibi*?"

Dania moved toward the horse, her large eyes wide with delight. "Oh, yes, *Ummi*!" She looked up at Naomi. "May I pet him?"

"Of course. In fact, you'll need to take a ride on him before I'll let you make a decision."

Buster dropped his large head and sniffed Dania's shoulder, then nudged it. She giggled happily and stroked his soft muzzle. Then, to Jess's astonishment, she planted a soft kiss on his nose. Buster nickered deep in his throat, and bobbed his head.

A match made in heaven.

Jess listened to Zada and Dania talking in the back seat. The words were a jumble, but held an unmistakable undercurrent of excitement and happiness. She glanced at the signed contract on the passenger seat. Eighty thousand dollars for a first horse. Unbelievable.

"Miss Jessica, I will bring the down-payment in the morning. Is that convenient?"

"I'll be there."

Dania piped up. "Will I have Buster for my next lesson?"

"I'm not sure, Dania. We have to get him vet-checked and insured before Naomi will release him. I'll try to get everything finished by Thursday."

She met Zada's eyes in the rearview mirror and saw the message: make it happen.

Ӿ

# *Ten*

Samir watched two hefty black men hoist a twenty-foot cylinder wrapped in heavy brown paper, then march down the loading ramp, carrying the object as though it weighed nothing. They dropped it carelessly onto the concrete floor, then returned to the truck. Samir eyed the parcel, then turned his attention back to the deliverymen. Exhaust fumes drifted through the open loading bay, burning Samir's nose while he concentrated on keeping his impatience under control.

The men made several more trips in and out of the dark cargo compartment, then the last cylinder hit the floor. A small red dot glowed from the filthy wrapper, and Samir's pulse jerked. He quickly signed for the delivery, pulled down the huge door, and flipped the switch on the exhaust fan. He hurried past the stack of carpets without a glance, and poked his head through the curtained entrance to the front of the store.

"Hasim! I am checking the new delivery. I do not want to be disturbed."

A minute later, he dropped to his knees beside the roll with the red mark. He ripped off the covering, and the carpet unrolled, spilling an exquisite, intricate pattern of rich reds and greens across the gray concrete.

"Ahhh, beautiful!"

He ran his hand lightly over the dense, velvety surface, feeling the quality of the tight weave crafted by skilled artisans. Throwing a quick glance toward the door to the shop, he struggled to flip the heavy carpet over to locate the label of authentication. Carefully snipping the tiny threads that held the tag to the backing, his thoughts raced. Suddenly, his breath came in short puffs and joy coursed through his heart. There it was–the message he'd yearned to see these past twenty years.

Zada's elegant gold Lexus disappeared down the driveway, and Jess turned back to her desk to gaze at the fat envelope. Eight thousand dollars in cash. Enough to make a serious dent in the debt–but not hers to spend. The commission on an eighty-thousand-dollar horse would be around twelve grand, but came out of the final payment, six months down the road. She sighed and tucked the envelope into the back of her locking desk drawer.

As she turned the key, Faith stepped into the office. Deep creases traced her once-beautiful skin and her red-rimmed eyes were puffy.

Jess held back a gasp. "Are you all right?"

Faith slumped into the chair. "I guess." She gazed at her hands for a minute. "Jessie, I'm really sorry about yesterday. I can't believe I'm so messed up. I have no business taking my problems out on you. It's not your fault."

Jess leaned her elbows on the desk. "Faith, you can lick this. You did it once, you can do it again. I'll help. You know that." She hesitated. "Did Bill come back?"

Silence, then a ragged sigh. "No, I think I pushed him past the limit. Guess I got what I deserve."

Jess wanted to soothe Faith's pain, but knew better. Facing up to one's own actions was the first step in recovery from alcohol abuse, and well-meaning friends who treated the process lightly only worsened the situation.

"Faith, listen, we have a lot on our plate right now. I want you to promise you'll pick up the phone and call me if you feel the urge to have a drink. We have to stay focused, or we'll lose everything we've both worked so hard for."

Faith's lower lip quivered and her eyes glistened. "I promise. Thank you for not throwing me out."

Jess moved around the desk to hug her friend. "Honey, I'll never abandon you, no matter what happens."

Jess played the message again. "*This is the Hartford Women's*

*Clinic calling for Jessica Rayder. Please call Dr. Frame's office as soon as possible."* She stared at the small red light on the answering machine in the kitchen. *Now what?* She'd had her annual exam the previous week, just before the horse show. *Probably some mix-up with the insurance.* While she finished making a sandwich, elevator music trickled through the receiver, and her thoughts moved on to the upcoming horse show, and all the things she still needed to do.

After five minutes on hold, the doctor came on the line. Jess instantly recognized the studied reassurance in his tone.

"Jessica, your mammogram has some questionable areas. I want you to come back for a repeat film."

Heaviness pressed against her chest and she took a deep breath. "What does 'questionable' mean? Cancer?"

"Not necessarily. The anomalies could be technical error, or underexposure, but since this is your baseline test, I want to double check. A tumor doesn't necessarily mean malignancy, so don't worry until we find out more. Hold on while I transfer you to the x-ray office."

Jess nodded silently and, a few minutes later, made an appointment for Wednesday. She put the phone down, feeling the tremor in her stomach. *Stay calm. He's just being thorough.*

Several of Faith's advanced students were entered in the Hunter Jumper Silver Classic on the coming weekend, and Jess's responsibilities included all the show paperwork. She buried herself in the details, building a barricade against the dark shadow of personal turmoil. The photocopier hummed and clicked, scanning and printing registration papers, health certificates, and parental consents for the minor exhibitors.

"Miss Jessica?"

She jumped, sending a stack of papers fluttering to the floor.

Samir hurried forward, dismay widening his eyes. "Oh, my! I am *so* sorry!"

Jess caught her breath. "I guess I was daydreaming or something. I didn't hear you drive up."

He began gathering up the scattered papers, his smile brightening his brown face and making his dark eyes sparkle. For a moment,

Jess noticed his swarthy good looks, like those of the swashbuckling heroes of old adventure movies.

He handed her the rescued pages. "Next time, I will honk the horn, as we do in my country." He chuckled. "There, we honk at everything, and at nothing."

Jess turned off the copier, then faced him. "What can I do for you this morning?"

"I have been thinking about Dania's lessons. I have always thought it was foolishness, this desire to ride horses. She is so young, and there are many things she must learn to do before she becomes a grown woman."

Jess's heart sank. *He's going to pull her out.*

He gestured expansively. "But I have seen how happy she is, and my wife's pleasure, as well. I want to be more involved, be a part of their happiness."

Jess quietly exhaled her relief. "That's good. We believe students have a better chance at success when their parents are involved. You're most welcome to come to Dania's lessons."

An embarrassed smile crept over his face. "That's not exactly what I had in mind."

"*You* want to take riding lessons?"

He laughed. "No, no. I would just like the opportunity to be around the stable, and enjoy the relaxing atmosphere." His expression grew pensive. "I have spent my life in America building a business, making a place for my family in this wonderful country. I have taken no time for myself, made no room for play–only work, work, work. I want to change that."

Jess suppressed her astonishment. "Samir, you're welcome to visit any time."

He bobbed his head and smiled broadly, his white teeth gleaming. "*Shukran!* Thank you! Thank you very much!"

An hour later, Jess watched the Mercedes glide down the driveway. She'd given him the deluxe barn-tour, and he'd seemed genuinely interested in the horses and the work routine. His enthusiasm for spending his leisure time at the barn puzzled her, but relief that Dania would continue to fill the stable coffers was her prevailing emotion.

"What did the A-Rab want?"

Jess looked up at Faith and scowled. "Stop calling him that! He just wanted to tell me what a great job we're doing." A shiver of anger moved across her shoulders. "You have to knock off the prejudice crap."

Faith shrugged as she moved into the office. "Sorry. When will Dania's horse be delivered?"

"As soon as I get him insured. Maybe by Friday, I don't know." She shook her head. "He might be too strong for a beginner. We'll have to see. Oh, by the way, I'll be out of the office Wednesday morning. Can you manage on your own?"

Faith bristled. "What's *that* supposed to mean?"

Jess closed her eyes. "Faith, it means nothing. Lighten up."

That evening, Jess curled up on the couch in front of the television, attempting to numb her brain with the inane problems of the shallow characters on the screen. It didn't work. After twenty minutes of playing out every possible scenario about the x-ray appointment, she pushed the worry away to contemplate the envelope hidden in her desk. If she could double that money, all their problems would be solved. A thump ran through her pulse. After her doctor appointment, the whole thing might be academic.

She poured a glass of wine, and wandered out to the porch to think. The public poker tables at the casino weren't the answer. She needed a big game, and a little time. She stared into the dark. Elvora had already given her an open invitation–why not?

ЖK

# *Eleven*

In the early morning light, Samir cruised slowly along the access road around Easton Ridge, memorizing the rustic countryside. The area was isolated, yet only minutes from major highways and transportation centers. A number of cars and trucks passed, headed in the opposite direction, and a large SUV roared up behind him, then swept past and disappeared around a curve. *A little congested, but still a good location.*

His thoughts turned to Jessica Rayder. A strong, independent woman, yes, but beneath the brittle exterior, he sensed panic. Her eyes held the wary look of a bird with a broken wing, waiting to be taken at any moment. If he could learn the source of her fear, it might strengthen his position.

Faith's voice echoed outside the office door. Jess quickly placed the accounting ledger over the down-payment money, and pasted a bright smile on her face.

"All done with lessons?"

"Yeah, but I must have been having an off day. I didn't have much patience with the older girls. I really shouldn't need to remind them about things they learned years ago."

Jess nodded, uncomfortably aware of the hidden money. "Maybe they're just nervous about the show. When are you leaving for Springfield?"

"Thursday at six. I want to get in early so the horses have time to rest from the trip."

"Okay. I'll meet you up there around noon."

Faith left the office, and Jess scooped up the money and stuffed it back into the envelope, doubt suddenly crashing in on her. *I have no business even considering this idea. This is not my money. What if I lose it?*

Casey was the last horse to come in for the night, and she trotted along briskly, bobbing her head in anticipation of dinner. Jess smiled, loving the familiarity of the evening routine. The old mare hurried to her feed bucket, and buried her nose in the fresh grain. Jess leaned on the stall door, relaxing into the serenity of the moment.

"Hello?"

*What the hell is he doing here this time of night?* She composed a smile, and turned to greet Samir, then almost laughed, but managing to curb the impulse in time. The proper businessman–always elegantly suited, white-shirted and necktied–wore stiff new blue jeans, a western shirt with pearl studs, and loud yellow snakeskin cowboy boots, complete with silver tips. The only thing missing was a Stetson.

Jess struggled for the right thing to say, but the words still came out wrong.

"Samir! Are you going to a rodeo?"

His happy expression faded into wide-eyed confusion. "Rodeo? Uh, no, I came to help with the chores."

Remembering his astonishment that she and Faith were doing all the barn work, she smiled, a little ashamed, but genuinely grateful.

"Thanks. We can *always* use some help."

The stench of urine-soaked stall bedding clung to Samir's clothes, and permeated the interior of the Mercedes, masking its usual rich, leathery smell. He concentrated on the road, pushing away the disgusting odor and images of the afternoon's unpleasant activities. Allaah had given him a direction and a purpose, and Samir was a most willing servant.

His cellphone chimed, then his pulse quickened at the voice he hadn't heard in over two years.

"Samir, my old friend. I have news. Two fine carpets will be delivered to you next week. They are very expensive, and will require special handling. Store them in a protected place."

Samir smiled. "I have the perfect spot. I will take good care of them."

"Excellent. Good-bye, my friend. *Allaahu akbar.*"

Later that afternoon, Samir's cellphone vibrated on the desk. He quickly set aside the daily accounting reports, and glanced around to see if anyone was nearby.

The caller's brusque tone rumbled through the receiver. "Dirk Dickson here."

"Ah, yes. Good afternoon. How are you today?"

"Didja wanna chat, or do ya want the info?"

Samir frowned. *Americans are so rude*. "Yes, please. What did you learn?" He listened, nodding slowly. "Mr. Dickson, would it be possible for you to continue your observation?"

"Sure, for another three hundred bucks."

"It is no problem. I will meet you at the casino tonight, same place."

Samir set the phone aside and nodded. The details were coming together nicely. Not only did the horsewomen face possible eviction, but apparently Miss Jessica also had some health problems. As he'd suspected, she was under a great deal of strain.

ℵ

# *Twelve*

Jess shivered in the tiny cubicle. *Why do they keep these places so damned cold?* She pulled at the paper gown, trying to cover herself. The sharp odor of disinfectant tickled her nasal passages, further elevating her anxiety. Suddenly, the dressing room curtain whisked aside, and she jumped.

"Okay, Miss Rayder, I'm ready for you."

The plump technician waddled down the hall and into a small room, dominated by a floor-to-ceiling x-ray machine. She consulted a piece of paper, then gestured at Jess.

"He wants the right side. Slip off your gown and step up close to the machine."

Jess's skin pimpled in the chilly air, and she flinched as the technician positioned the breast on the cold metal film plate.

"Let me know if this gets too tight. I wanna make sure we get it right this time. . .I caught some flak for the last one."

A motor hummed and the upper plate of the machine began to descend, connecting with Jess's soft flesh, pressing it hard against the bottom plate. Her eyes teared and she clenched her jaw.

"Take a deep breath and don't move."

Frozen into the frightening moment, her thoughts raced. What if she *did* have cancer? What would her future hold?

The pressure released, and the technician touched her shoulder. "You can put the gown back on, but wait in the dressing room 'til I check the film."

Alone again with her thoughts, self-pity moved through Jess's mind. She had no family, no close friends, other than Faith. No one to miss her if she died. The thought stung like a slap, and she straightened up on the bench and angrily squared her shoulders. She would *not* get all worked up before she had a reason.

The curtain parted and the technician's round face peeked in.

"You can get dressed. The doctor will call you after the radiologist reads the film."

Jess didn't feel like returning to the farm right away, so she headed north along the Farmington River. The heavily populated urban areas of Hartford and New Britain sprawled in all directions. Connecticut's close proximity to New York City kept the economy booming, and the residents well-heeled, but within a few miles of those outer edges of humanity, the countryside changed to dense forest and rolling hills. Small pockets of poverty still nestled in these rural areas, evidenced by the occasional small run-down farm, or house trailer in an overgrown yard filled with rusted cars and trucks.

She followed the winding road through the country, and finally pulled into a small picnic site beside the Nepaug Reservoir. Beneath the shady canopy of oak trees, she gazed at the sunlight reflecting off the water, and wondered about the future.

Two hours later, Jess strode through the entrance to the casino, and scanned the sea of gamblers, searching for Elvora's pleasant brown face. As if by ESP, the casino manager appeared beside her.

"Good afternoon, Jessica. Here for the night?"

"Not this time–actually, I came to see *you*."

Elvora's brown eyes twinkled. "I'm listenin'."

"You said you could get me into a high-stakes poker game, a private one."

"What a coincidence. . .I'm putting together a game for the weekend after next. You'd be a good addition."

Jess hesitated. The game would almost coincide with Frank's deadline. She'd be cutting it close.

"Would you arrange that for me?"

"Sure, honey. Give me a call at the end of the week, and I'll set you up with the details."

"Thanks, I appreciate it."

Elvora smiled. "I don't mean to get personal, but for this game, you might want to dress up a little bit." She winked. "And try a little makeup. I think you'll feel more at ease with the other players in the group."

Jess's idea of dressing up consisted of good black slacks and a clean blouse. She cocked her head. "You mean, a *dress*?"

"Yup, preferably something classy. These are very wealthy folks."

"Okay, if you say so."

Jess moved across the casino floor, shaking her head. Irritation replaced perplexity. What did her appearance have to do with how well she played cards? She passed a small cocktail lounge, and someone laughed loudly. After a cursory glance, she did a double-take, and stopped to stare. Anger roiled through her chest. In a corner booth, Faith's boyfriend held hands with a young blonde woman.

Without a thought of whether she had any right, Jess strode up to the couple, and laced her arms across her chest.

"Well, I see it didn't take you long to get over Faith!"

Bill looked startled, then his smooth personality kicked in. "Excuse me, but is that any of your concern?"

Jess relaxed her stance a little. "Yes, it is. She's a shambles."

He looked away. "You got that right."

His companion rose and excused herself, saying she'd be back in a minute.

Bill scowled up at Jess. "You have a helluva lot of nerve, you know."

"Bill, what happened? You guys were doing so well."

His brusque manner faded, and a glimmer of sorrow passed through his eyes.

"I love her more than anything in the world. I wanted to have a future, a family, but apparently she doesn't want the same things. I can't spend my life waiting for her to climb out of a vodka bottle."

Ж

# *Thirteen*

By the time Jess arrived at the Eastern States Exposition Center the following day, the exhibitor parking lot was jammed with trucks, trailers, campers, and cars. The huge fairground was home to hundreds of events every year, and horse shows filled a large portion of the schedule from April through September. Animal barns, outdoor arenas, exhibition buildings, and a huge coliseum sprawled over a hundred and seventy-five acres. The background clamor of neighing horses, shouts and laughter, the muffled public address system, and muted music filled her with the familiar excitement of competition.

The Easton stalls were located in the large barn close to the coliseum. As Jess approached, Beth and Lexie were leading their horses toward the practice ring, their young voices bubbling with enthusiasm. Jess smiled. *Nothing ever really changes in this business.*

Faith stood in the grooming stall with Dania.

"Oh, good! You're here. The bedding order got fouled up and I'm short. Would you go over and take care of it?"

"Sure." Jess looked at Dania. "Are you excited about your first real show?"

The girl's face glowed, bringing out her youthful beauty. "Yes!" Her expression instantly clouded. "But I wanted to ride Buster."

Faith chuckled. "Dania, you need to spend some time getting used to him before you ride him in a show." She gave Jess a pointed look. "We need to talk."

Jess's stomach jigged. "I'll go take care of the bedding."

Hurrying across the grounds to the show office, she tried to calm her jittery pulse. This Buster-thing could get her into real trouble.

Twelve little girls composed Dania's hunter class. Jess stood beside Faith at the rail as they watched each rider go through the course. Dania made her warm-up approach to the first obstacle, and Jess held her breath as the small girl guided the pony through the course. Faith exhaled sharply as Dania finished and trotted through the out-gate.

"I'm telling you, Jess, she is *so* good. If her parents would allow it, she could go on to become a national champion, compete at Rolex–maybe even train for the Olympics."

Jess chuckled at Faith's enthusiasm and confidence in her students. Dania wasn't the first Easton Ridge rider who'd been groomed for bigger things.

The background noises faded and Jess gazed at the scene, feeling like an invisible spectator. How would she make it through the day? Through the week? Doctor Frame's words echoed through her head, and her throat tightened. The cloudy mass on the x-ray was no technician's error and, though the doctor was optimistic, Jess shivered at the looming prospect of a biopsy the coming week. Until then, she'd have to wrestle the demons in her brain and the pain in her heart.

*Life's a bitch, and then you die*. Her pulse skipped. This wasn't amusing. What had she done to deserve all this trouble? Anger replaced the fear. Not a damned thing, and if anything else went wrong in her life, she'd be doing chores on the funny farm.

Howard London's handsome face drifted into her thoughts and she closed her eyes. If she got through this alive, she'd make a trip to Idaho. Time to get a life.

She pushed away the morbid thoughts and scanned the grandstand, looking for the Mahfoods. The two Middle Easterners stood out against the background of pale spectators surrounding them, and Jess wondered if they felt out of place. Then she remembered Zada's terse comments about America. *I suspect they are painfully aware of the emotions running high in this country.*

Faith whooped loudly and waved her arms. "Go, Dania!"

The child trotted her horse over to the ring steward to accept a third place ribbon. She flashed a beautiful smile up at her parents and, at that moment, she was just another little girl in love with horses.

Twenty minutes later, Jess listened to Dania's affectionate conversation with her pony as she wiped sweat from the saddle area. The scene reminded Jess of her own first time in the ring.

Faith's low voice pierced the nostalgic moment. "Follow me. I want to ask you something."

*Uh-oh, here it comes.*

They moved out of earshot of the students.

"Naomi called last night and wanted to know when she'd get the down-payment on Buster."

The challenge hung in the air, and Jess's heartbeat skipped.

"I deposited the cash, and meant to write a check, then I got really busy and plumb forgot about it. I'll do it as soon as I get home." She smiled confidently. "She's not worried, is she?"

"No, but Dania is, and I suspect the next thing will be Mama Mahfood breathing down my neck. I'm telling you, Jess, that humble act beneath the headscarf is really phony–why do the men make them wear those things, anyway?"

"Faith, the men don't have anything to do with it. Muslim women cover their hair as an act of faith. The scarf is called a *hijaab*, and is *not* required." She touched Faith's arm. "These are normal people, just like you and me."

Faith shrugged and looked away. "I suppose, but I can't help it." Her gaze snapped back and a frown creased her forehead. "Since when do you know so much about Muslims?"

"When the Mahfoods first came to the barn, I thought it might help to know a little bit about their culture. I did some research on the internet."

Faith gave her a blank look. "Hmph. Oh, by the way, we have a new stall cleaner."

Jess jammed her fists onto her hips and glowered.

"What's the matter with you? We just let everyone go 'cause we can't pay them."

Faith glared back. "If you'll let me finish? This woman wants riding lessons, but doesn't have the money, so she offered to trade work for them. Her name's Mona Johnson, and she lives just down the road. She can come in every morning for a couple of hours."

Jess felt foolish. "Oh. Sorry."

"I hope you get over your bad temper soon. We're into serious show season, and I could use your help." Faith stepped up close. "Are you sure you're okay? I mean, *really?*"

Her sad expression made Jess feel like a rebellious child rejecting genuine concern.

"I'm fine."

Her abrupt tone hit its target, and Faith's sympathetic expression disappeared. She nodded curtly, then walked back toward the stalls. Jess watched her for a moment, pain clamping down on her throat. Why couldn't she open up and let Faith in?

Thinking about her imminent shopping trip, Jess watched the cars and trucks weave through the growing traffic. She knew she wasn't glamorous, but it had never bothered her. In the past, when she and Faith had attended the fancy post-Brandford parties, she'd pulled out a dated black dress from the back of her closet, and called it good. Now, recalling the expensive attire of the other women at those events, she grimaced. She'd probably looked about as appealing as a teen-aged boy dressed up in one of his father's old suits.

*I'll stop in West Hartford, see if I can find something suitable.* She shook her head, amazed she was even considering such an idea. A shopper, she was not. She pulled into the Westfarms Mall and stared at the entrance to the Ann Taylor store. *Prepare for battle.*

ⅩⅩ

# *Fourteen*

Jess accelerated and moved into the thickening commuter traffic, then turned on the CD player. Easy jazz surrounded her, and she leaned back in her seat to think about the future, whatever it might be. Howard's tan face and dazzling smile jumped into her thoughts, and her pulse skittered. Suppose, when this was all over, she pursued a relationship with him? She could easily control it, given the geographical distance between them. The daydream moved to long walks in the woods, romantic nights in front of a fire, steamy sex under–

A piercing wail suddenly battled with the smooth notes of a saxophone. She looked in the rearview mirror and her stomach twitched. *Damn!* Behind her, state patrol headlights flashed blindingly. She glanced at the speedometer, took a deep breath, and steered the car to the side of the highway. In the rearview mirror, she watched the trooper get out of his car. He was young and slim, and his uniform shirt molded perfectly to his chest. He settled the distinctive wide-brimmed hat carefully over his blonde crewcut, then started toward her.

His blue eyes were friendly. "Afternoon, Miss. May I see your license and registration?"

Up close, he wasn't as young as she'd thought.

"Was I speeding, Officer?"

He grinned. "I don't know. . .*were* you?"

She laughed. "I don't think so."

"Are you aware that one of your turn-signal lights isn't working?"

*He stopped me for a burned-out taillight?*

She shook her head. "No. I wonder when *that* happened."

"I'll be back in a minute. Please stay in the car."

A few minutes later, he reappeared and handed her papers through the window.

He had a nice smile. "I'm not gonna cite you, but you do need to get that light fixed."

She glanced at his nametag. "Thank you, Officer Carter. I'll do that as soon as I get home."

His gaze drifted to the jumble of bridles on the passenger seat, and his expression brightened. "You have horses?"

"I own a riding stable. I'm on my way home from a show."

The trooper relaxed onto his elbows, settling in for a chat. "You know, my little girl wants to take lessons. We've been thinking about it. . .Where's your place?"

"In Whigville."

"Hey, you're right in my neighborhood. We live in Canton. You have any openings? Maybe I'll drop by some weekend, let Kristy watch a lesson."

"That's a good idea. Easton Ridge Equestrian Center on Easton Road. You can't miss it."

Trooper Carter straightened up and thumped his knuckles twice against the car door. "Well, Miss Rayder, you have a nice day. And don't forget that taillight."

Jess entered the barn and sprinted for the phone.

"Jessica? Howard London from Idaho. Remember me?"

A shock of pleasure careened through her chest. *Do I ever.*

"Yes, of course I remember you. What a nice surprise. How *are* you?"

"I'm good. Business is hectic, but that's normal this time of year. How about you? Keeping all those little girls happy?"

Jess laughed, surprised at her pleasure in hearing his voice. She'd often wondered if she'd ever see him again.

"Oh, yes–it's the way we keep our pocketbooks filled."

His wonderful deep laugh boomed through the receiver. "Well, surprise–I'm calling from Hartford."

Her stomach jumped, and prickles of anticipation crawled over her skin. "What are you doing *there*?"

"I had some business to take care of in New York. I really love the great outdoors, but I'm a city boy, at heart. Sometimes I just have to get back to the chaos of the bright lights to remind me how lucky I am to be away from it." He laughed. "Isn't that absurd? Anyway, I thought I'd hit the casino before I head back to the wilds. Wondered if you might join me for dinner Saturday night."

Five minutes later, Jess hung up the phone, feeling like a schoolgirl with her first prom date.

Jess slid the barn door closed, and started toward the house, a new bounce in her step. A familiar black Mercedes turned onto the lane, and she halted in mid-stride, irritation spoiling her happy mood.

Samir honked and pulled over. He grinned as he climbed out of the car.

"See? I didn't frighten you this time."

She smiled thinly. "What's up, Samir? I'm really beat."

"Yes, I'm sure you are, but I want to discuss something important."

"Could it wait until tomorrow?"

His smile faded. "No, I think time is not on your side."

Something in his tone sent fear through her chest. "What do you mean?"

He gestured toward the barn. "Could we go inside to talk?"

She turned and retraced her steps, uncomfortably aware of the man beside her. Maybe he wanted to talk about Dania's new horse. She could bluff this one–no problem.

A minute later, he leaned forward in the chair. "I know you are having financial problems here, and I would like to help."

Jess bristled. "I don't know what you're talking about. We're doing quite well."

"Jessica, I have been in business a long time. I see the signs." He waved a hand expansively. "Surely, you do not want to lose all this."

*How could he possibly know anything about the farm's finances?* She refocused on his words.

"I do not want you to lose it, either. My Dania and Zada are so happy to come here, and I enjoy being here, as well."

"We're not going–"

He held up a hand. "Let me help you. I have an idea."

She sank back into the chair to listen.

"Two of my nephews are attending college here in the United States. They will return to Yemen in the fall, but they need something to do until then. If they came to work for you for the next two months, that would help, yes?"

"Samir, you don't understand. I can't afford–"

He raised his hand again. "I will pay their wages. I want to help." He chuckled. "Besides, they need something to keep them occupied, and I think I am not cut out for the country life, after all. My nephews will be more suitable."

Jess's brain slipped into gear. *More foreigners. Faith will go ballistic.*

"That's very generous of you, and we can certainly use the help."

Samir relaxed and sat back. "Good. It is settled then."

A string of red beads materialized in his hand, and his fingers moved rhythmically across each one. His dark eyes glittered above a tentative smile.

"How are you feeling?"

Jess felt ill. "I'm fine, thank you. Now, if you'll excuse me, it's been a very long day."

He rose and smiled. "Do you need assistance here tomorrow morning? I could come, if you like."

Her smile felt wooden. "No, that won't be necessary, but thank you. I'll see you at the show."

He bowed politely. "*Insha'Allaah.*"

Sleep wouldn't come, despite Jess's exhaustion. The unsettling conversation with Samir played over and over through her head and, with each repetition, she found different rationales for his comments. Why had he asked her how she felt? Was there a message there? Was she being paranoid? She'd been so distracted for the past few days. Had she been careless with information again? *I have to regain control of my life.* She squeezed her eyes shut. *Assuming I'm going to live.*

ӾӾ

# *Fifteen*

On Saturday morning, Jess pulled the plastic film away from the charming dark green dress. The frock had simple lines, a scooped neck, and long fitted sleeves. It looked rather plain on the hanger, but she remembered her stunning reflection in the dressing room mirror. The dress didn't cling, but touched her in all the right places, making her straight body look mysteriously curvy. The perfect color brightened her hair and drew some of the sallow shades from her skin.

Her gaze drifted down to the black sweater she wore, and followed the contours of the knit as it draped across her breasts, a part of her that might be hiding a horrible secret. Dr. Frame had tried to reassure her that the biggest percentage of breast masses were non-malignant, but she still couldn't shake the fear. The biopsy on Monday morning would reveal her future. Until then, she *had* to think about other things to keep her emotions under control.

Her throat tightened. Maybe she'd wake up and find that the past six months had simply been a bad dream. She took a deep breath, willing herself to concentrate on a positive and bright future. Howard's call had sparked an enthusiasm she hadn't felt in years. Since the divorce, she'd shied away from any attachments that might derail her goals. Idaho was three thousand miles away–how much safer could she be?

At noon, chores finished and car packed, she picked up the freeway and headed north to Springfield. Once the car slipped into the stream of traffic, her thoughts turned to Samir's proposition, and his comment about running out of time. He was definitely beginning to make her nervous.

Back in the hubbub of horse show, Jess studied the array of brightly-colored ribbons hanging over the entrance to Easton's stalls. Faith's kids were having a great show, the kind of positive publicity that could attract new clients. Jess gazed at the banner across the aisle. "Faith Angelo at Easton Ridge Equestrian Center." Jess's own skill as a horse trainer, her good eye for performance prospects, and her excellent business acumen were important, but Faith's national reputation was the glue that held it all together.

By two o'clock, the Easton students were finished with classes, and Jess headed south, her thoughts centering on the promise of the poker game. *Time to get aggressive. Either that, or rob a bank.* She chuckled at the ludicrous idea, recalling a news story earlier in the year about some looney-tunes woman who'd managed to pull off three bank robberies in one afternoon. *I'm not that desperate. Yet.* Her thoughts refocused on Samir. Why was he so interested in helping her? It seemed unlikely that he was so wrapped up in his family's recreational activities that he'd go to the trouble of trying to help solve someone else's financial woes. The logical client response would be to move the student to a different stable. And why had he made a point of telling her he knew they had money problems?

Jess laughed at her image in the mirror. "You are *so* inept!"

She leaned closer, struggling with a mascara wand that had just escaped from her eyelashes. Huffing with exasperation, she snatched up a tissue to capture the brown glob clinging to one eyebrow.

"I can't believe women do this every day."

A minute later, she stepped back to check the effect of her efforts. The woman staring back at her didn't resemble the one who'd inhabited her body for so long. The touch of color on her cheeks and lips defined her features and, even though she'd had a hard time with them, the eye shadow and mascara made her look quite glamorous.

By the time she'd fiddled with her uncooperative hair, zipped into the green dress, and slipped into a pair of heels, her palms felt clammy and her breath came in quick little snatches. *This is ridiculous! Why am I so nervous?* A touch of doubt flickered into her thoughts, and the ever-present black cloud of anxiety fed her sense of impending doom and helplessness.

Jess stepped from the elevator into the cavernous lobby of Seven Rivers Casino, then moved across the marble floor to the center of the large hall, where a magnificent fountain sculpture commanded the entryway. A life-size bronze Indian warrior stood beside a tumbling waterfall, his arms raised to the sky, the serenity of prayer etched into his strong features. The soothing sound of running water enveloped Jess in a quieting sense of solitude.

"Jessica?"

A flutter moved in the pit of her stomach, she turned, and the flutter leaped into a frenzy. Howard was even more attractive than she remembered. A navy blazer hung from his square shoulders, a crisp contrast to his sharply creased chino trousers and pale blue button-down shirt. A red-and-grey striped tie drew attention upward to his tanned face and sparkling blue eyes.

He stepped forward, a wide smile brightening his face. "Man, you look *gorgeous*!"

She squirmed with embarrassment and pleasure. "Thank you. I, uh, don't have much occasion to dress up."

He squeezed her arm. "We should definitely fix *that* problem! Where shall we eat?"

They strolled leisurely through the beautifully landscaped courtyard in front of the casino and hotel, and a few minutes later, Jess gasped at the breathtaking view from the glassed-in elevator that crawled up the outside of the twenty-story building.

Howard whistled softly. "I can't believe this place, out here in the middle of nowhere, better than any of the Atlantic City resorts, and it's a helluva lot classier than most Las Vegas casinos."

"Do you spend a lot of time gambling? You seem to know all the big names."

He laughed. "I don't really come to gamble, more for the resort atmosphere, the pool, different scenery. These places are such a bargain because they offer good prices, nice hotels, cheap meals, etcetera, hoping you'll spend your money at the tables."

"Do you gamble at all?"

He grinned. "Yeah, sometimes I play the roulette wheel, and

I like blackjack." His expression sobered. "But I have a pact with myself that I won't jeopardize my retirement at the gaming tables. I worked too hard to get where I am now."

Jess swallowed the lump rising in her throat, guilt edging into her chest. In contrast to Howard, she was prepared to literally gamble with the farm, take a chance on everything *she'd* worked so hard to achieve. But what alternatives did she have?

Howard opened the menu. "This looks as good as my favorite New York City restaurant."

A few minutes later, he raised his glass. "To a great evening with a beautiful woman."

Jess blushed and took a sip of wine, and felt the harsh reality of her life ebbing away.

Howard talked about his lodge in Idaho, explaining that during the better part of the year, business was brisk at the fishing and hunting preserve. The winter months were slower, since few tourists cared to brave the harsh winters in the mountains of western Idaho.

"We still get a few die-hard tough-guys that want to hunt for elk, so I stay open year-round."

Jess set her glass down and leaned forward. "Do you ever miss practicing law?"

"Once in a while, but not often. It's a tough job with a lot of stress." He shook his head. "And I hate to lose a case, but occasionally that goes with the territory."

His manner was sincere and forthright, so different from the edgy, nervous horse-industry professionals Jess was used to being around. She nodded solemnly. Howard shrugged off the beginnings of a serious mood, and grinned.

"Anyway, I keep my license current, just in case I get tired of good-ol' boys with guns." He cocked his head and squinted at her. "So, how come we always talk about me? I want to know more about you."

"There's nothing terribly interesting to tell. I just work and keep the place running. We never thought Easton would become so successful, but we aren't complaining."

She hoped her bravado sounded convincing.

Howard nodded. "I guess being in the right place at the right time with the right skills is paramount for success. I know *I* sure lucked out."

Jess enjoyed watching his face as he talked, the way his trim moustache twitched with each word, and the amazing dimple that punctuated one cheek when he grinned.

He gave her a mischievous wink. "How about taking me to see this fancy place of yours?"

She blinked, caught off guard. "Sure, that would be great sometime."

"No, I mean tomorrow. Sunday's your day off, isn't it? I don't have to leave until about four–it'll only take me a few hours to get home."

"To *Idaho?*"

He grinned. "Yeah, I have my own little plane."

A jumble of thoughts raced through Jess's head. Faith and the horses would return sometime late in the morning. It probably wasn't a good time for a tour, but what the hell.

She smiled. "Okay, it's a date."

He rose from the table. "Interest you in a nightcap?"

She glanced at her watch. "It's way past my bedtime. I'd better say goodnight." She looked up and smiled, suddenly feeling shy. "But thank you anyway."

He offered his arm. "I'll escort you to your room."

Jess's fingers slipped over the smooth surface of the gabardine coat sleeve, the simple gesture feeling so intimate. His warmth pervaded the layers, seeping into her skin, and sending her thoughts in a new direction.

They stopped at the door to her room.

Howard's tone was offhand. "Are you seeing anyone?"

"Good grief, no! I haven't had time for a social life since Easton opened. "*Oh, that sounded great!*

Howard lifted her chin and searched her eyes for a moment. "Looks like I have a lot of work to do." He grinned, then brushed her cheek with a kiss. "'Nite. See you bright and early."

Jess closed the door behind her and leaned against it, her heart thumping, her head filled with disappointment. She sighed. *About what? The fact he was a gentleman?* She certainly hadn't sent any signals telling him she wanted otherwise.

"Fool!"

She pushed away from the door and tossed her handbag on the dresser. In the mirror, a rosy flush colored her cheeks and her usually dull eyes sparkled.

"New game plan. Tomorrow I'll make sure there's no doubt in his mind."

## *Sixteen*

In the brilliant morning light, Jess's romantic pie-in-the-sky dreams seemed unrealistic. A twinge of sadness moved through her chest. No matter how much she wanted to follow her yearnings, she couldn't think about personal involvements until she knew where her life was headed. She sighed and walked outside to wait for Howard. The sun warmed her shoulders and she took a deep breath of fresh air. Maybe she should make up an excuse to cancel his visit to the farm. A minute later, he emerged from the hotel, and a stir of excitement sent the dismal thoughts packing.

His rich baritone thrummed through the cool air. "Good morning! Is this a fabulous day, or what? Are you hungry? There's a little doughnut shop down the road."

His obvious pleasure in simply being alive sent a warm flush of optimism through her head. Maybe all her problems would sort themselves out, and she'd have the chance to explore her new feelings.

A few minutes later, Howard beamed across the café table. "I really enjoyed last night." A small, foolish smile rippled his moustache. "Made me feel young again."

Jess pushed everything out of her mind but the moment. "I know, me too."

Howard gaped at the barn. "This is fabulous! I never dreamed a riding stable could be so elegant."

Pride warmed Jess's cheeks, and she chuckled. "It's not that fancy. This place looks like hicksville next to some of the facilities in Westchester County. But we couldn't afford the rent in that area, so here we are."

*Right. And even in the low-rent district, we got into trouble.*

She shook off the negative thought and, giving her best impression of a tour-guide, took Howard through all the various parts of the huge barn. An excited nicker echoed from a nearby stall, and Jess laughed.

"Meet Casey, my very first horse."

Howard's hands settled onto Jess's shoulders, his warmth a startling reminder of her simmering fantasies.

His deep voice whispered close by. "You're lucky to have such a wonderful life."

He smoothed one hand over the mare's back, and Jess's throat tightened painfully at the gentle gesture. The comforting quiet of the barn formed a cocoon around them, and she felt as though her heart would break for wanting things to be different.

She cleared her throat, breaking the silence. "Okay, next stop on the tour is the brag room."

The soft lights in the trophy room illuminated the array of ribbons and awards on display, giving the room the look of an art gallery. Howard whistled under his breath.

"Wow! Are these all yours?"

"Some of them are mine. Most of them belong to Faith, or our star students."

He moved to the wall of photographs and, a moment later, pointed to the newspaper article.

Jess chuckled. "That was a long time ago. We had some great times."

"Do you still ride?"

"Almost every day. It keeps me somewhat sane." She motioned toward the door. "That's all for the barn. Come on, I'll show you the rest of the property."

Howard exhaled sharply as they trudged across the gravel. "Man, you need a golf-cart to get around this place."

"Nah, we're tough. Besides. . ." She threw him a sly look. "All this walking helps us keep our youthful figgers."

Howard's frank perusal of her body became an instant reminder of her hidden secret. The specter of breast cancer sent a shudder of despair through her heart.

He cocked his head and squinted one eye. "Have you ever been out West?"

She shook her head.

"Well, let me tell you, riding stables out there are really basic. You could teach those folks a thing or two about how to put one of these places together." He grinned. "Maybe when you're rich and retired, you could leave all this behind, come out West and start over."

Another fantasy. Looming death or physical disfigurement, bankruptcy, the shattered dreams. It was all too much, and pain clamped around Jess's throat. She blinked furiously at the tears suddenly gathering behind her eyelids. Howard moved closer and grasped her shoulders, his eyes dark with concern.

"Jess, I'm here if you need to talk to someone."

The sincerity in his voice sent the waiting tears over the edge. The urge to step into his arms and feel the solid comfort of his sympathy almost overwhelmed her.

She stepped back and shook her head. "I can't. But thank you."

He nodded, disappointment shading his features. "I have to go. I have a take-off slot at four."

"No time for a tour of Whigville?"

"Not this trip. . .Next time?"

His intense gaze made her stomach jig. *Please, let there be a next time*. Before she could respond, a truck and horse trailer turned into the driveway. *Dammit!*

He turned toward the sound. "Customers?"

"No, it's Faith. She's been at a horse show in Springfield."

The truck rolled to a stop beside them, and Faith jumped out, her face flushed. Jess's thoughts raced. *There's a real possibility for disaster here*.

Faith grinned. "Good morning! Ready to help unload horses?" She faced Howard and stuck out her hand. "Hi, I'm Faith Angelo. I'm sure Jessie has told you all about me."

"Howard London. Yes, she speaks very highly of you."

Faith threw Jess a wicked look, then turned her attention back to Howard. "Well, it's nice to finally meet the mystery man who's been keeping her so busy."

Jess nearly fainted. *Oh God, Faith. Shut up!* A furtive glance at Howard revealed a cool demeanor, as though he thought nothing seemed unusual.

"Yep, that's me. . .and a tough job it is!"

Jess's smile felt wooden. "Howard's in a hurry to get to the airport. I'll be over to help you in a minute."

Faith waved and climbed back into the truck. As the rig moved away, Howard took Jess's hand.

"You gonna tell me what that was about?"

She stared across the pastures, aware of his warm fingers threaded through hers.

"I'm really sorry. That was so embarrassing."

He squeezed her hand. "Well, I guess if I'm the secret boyfriend, I'd like to know how much fun we've been having."

She turned and searched his face. His gentle expression gave her confidence.

"Faith's been pestering me about being away overnight that weekend we met. She was sure I had a boyfriend. I didn't want to tell her where I'd been, so I finally just said my friend's name was Howard." She quickly added, "I didn't elaborate, or make anything up. I just wanted her off my back. . .I'm really sorry."

He leaned over and kissed her cheek.

"I'm flattered. I'm just sorry it isn't all true." He opened the car door and climbed in. "I'll call you next time I'm going to be out this way." The dimple deepened into his tan cheek. "Or, you could call *me* the next time you're in Idaho."

Faith leaned against the trailer, arms crossed. "Gee, Jess, you never told me how good looking he is."

Jess kept her emotions hidden. "If you'll think about it, I never told you *anything* about him."

A flash of pain moved across Faith's features, and Jess immediately regretted the snide comeback.

"Aw, Faith. I'm sorry." She stepped over and squeezed her friend's shoulder. "I'm sorta new at this boyfriend thing. Forgive me?"

"Yeah, but you're sure jumpy and irritable lately." Faith sighed, then gazed directly into Jess's eyes. "Do you want to talk? Jess, we've always talked about *everything*. What's changed?"

Swallowing the thick lump in her throat, Jess tried for a smile. "Nothing's changed. I'm fine. Howard's a great guy, and I enjoy his company, but I don't see having anything permanent with him."

A horse whinnied impatiently from inside the trailer. Faith looked unconvinced, but seemed to know the conversation had ended. She slid the latch on the trailer door and dropped the ramp.

"Okay. Come on and help me get these horses unloaded. I'm bushed."

Jess settled into her bed, weariness rolling through every muscle. She wanted to sleep, but feared closing her eyes. If she slept, the night would disappear, and morning would come too soon. Her future would be unveiled in a few short hours and, suddenly, the prospect of that knowledge terrified her.

The strain of dealing with raw emotions–Faith's, Bill's, and her own–claimed her, and she buried her face in the pillow and prayed for the first time since she'd been a little girl asking God for her very own horse.

# *Seventeen*

Samir sat in his tiny office, gazing at the photograph of his wife and Dania smiling back at him in the dim light. In the showroom beyond the curtain, Hasim and a customer discussed the durability of a Turkish Anatolian carpet. The day had dawned like any other, but at ten o'clock that morning, Samir's life had taken a new direction, a path for which he'd been preparing his entire life.

He left the shop through the rear entrance, and started down the street. A few blocks ahead, the minarets of the mosque towered over the surrounding buildings. On the heavy midday air, the soulful wail of the *muezzin* drifted, sweet and promising, calling the faithful to prayer. Samir's heart filled with joy and his fingers feverishly worked the strand of red beads as he strode toward the mosque.

He'd finally received The Call. His mission was clear: he would be an instrument of Allaah's will.

The fog drifting through Jess's head made it hard to concentrate. Jumbled images whirled through her thoughts as she struggled to open eyelids that seemed to weigh five pounds each. She finally succeeded, then flinched at the brilliant light. *I'm freezing!* Gentle hands quickly tucked the blanket close around her body, and she realized she'd spoken out loud. In the haze, Dr. Frame's pleasant face shimmered into focus, and Jess's memory sharpened.

"Can you hear me, Jessica?" He smiled. "You're going to be just fine. No cancer. The mass is benign."

A trickle of hot tears rolled down her temples, and she sank deep into her relief, welcoming the heaviness crowding in. She closed her eyes and drifted again. *Thank you, God.*

When she awoke later, the fog had disappeared. She gazed at the ceiling in the small recovery room, and began to chart the future. Every thought was crystal clear, and Faith headed up the list of priorities–she *had* to go back to AA. It would not be an ultimatum, but Faith would understand the ramifications of refusal. The business could not afford the liability of an alcoholic in charge of children. Period. And without Faith, there would be no Easton Ridge.

A chubby woman in pale pink scrubs appeared next to the bed. "I need to check your blood pressure. How are you feeling now?"

"When can I go home?"

The nurse didn't respond, her eyes focused on the apparatus. A moment later, she pulled the stethoscope from her ears and smiled.

"As soon as the doctor signs you out, probably another hour or so."

She breezed out of the room, and Jess's thoughts returned to reality. The private poker game would be the big fix, and not a minute too soon. A tremor of excitement ran though her chest–part pleasure, part anxiety–but mostly, the challenge of the chase.

Late that afternoon, the taxi turned into Easton and Jess gazed through the window, surveying her domain with new resolve. In the practice ring, Faith watched two riders move smoothly around the perimeter. By the barn door, another youngster adjusted stirrup leathers. Jess felt energized and optimistic. *She* was in charge of the future, and nothing would keep her from fulfilling that destiny.

Early the next morning, Jess sorted through the payables and receivables, making notes and trying to develop a realistic budget. Outside, a car door thumped, and she glanced at her watch. Faith seemed to have gotten herself back on track the past several days, coming to work clear-eyed and energetic. A good start, but not a victory. Jess shook her head sadly. The ongoing battle of a recovering alcoholic.

Faith strode into the office. "Whoa! *You're* certainly an early bird!"

"Gotta get those worms. How did things go yesterday?"

"Just fine. Naomi delivered Dania's horse. What a fabulous animal–he came off that trailer and made himself right at home."

Jess nodded. "He might be a handful, but you should have seen the connection Dania made with him. Love at first sight for both of them."

"Did you ever mail that deposit check to Naomi?"

Jess's stomach dropped. "Huh? Oh, hell, I completely forgot about it." She busied herself closing the ledger and tidying a stack of invoices. "What'd you tell her?"

"That you'd call her. . .She wasn't real happy about leaving the horse here with no security."

Jess heard her own defensive tone. "Jeez, Faith, it was an oversight. I'll take care of it."

Faith's tone softened. "Jessie, are you going to tell me what's going on? Unexplained day off, coming home in a taxi. . .Did you think I wouldn't notice?"

Jess closed her eyes and exhaled slowly. "Two weeks ago, I had an abnormal mammogram. The doctor wanted to do a biopsy–that's where I was yesterday."

The silence felt suffocating. Faith stared across the desk, a parade of emotions passing over her features.

"Why didn't you tell me?

"I dunno. Maybe I thought saying it out loud would make it real."

Faith rose from the chair, her chin quivering, her injured tone finding its target. "I guess our friendship *didn't* survive the test of time."

"Aw, Faith. . ."

Jess watched her partner stalk out the door. Would it do any good to go after her? Try to explain why she'd felt compelled to keep the horror and fear inside? *Do I even know why?* Had she so little confidence in Faith that she couldn't lean on her, even a tiny bit?

In moments, Faith's voice shattered the painful musings.

"Jessie!"

She jumped up and raced into the aisle. Faith strode toward her, flanked by two figures. Against the bright backlight of the open doors, Jess could see only silhouettes. A second later, she stared at two strange men.

Distress showcased Faith's features. "These men say you hired them."

Dark skin, deep emotionless eyes, black hair, expressionless faces. Neither man spoke, just stared at her, waiting.

"Oh, I'm sorry, I forgot to tell you. These are Samir's nephews. They'll be helping out for the summer."

Confusion passed through Faith's eyes and her brow wrinkled slightly. "I thought we weren't hir–"

"I'll tell you about it later." Jess nodded to the men. "Welcome."

The shorter of the two spoke in clipped words. "I am Hafez al-Nabi." He gestured to the heavy-set man beside him. "This is my cousin, Mustafa al-Ani."

"I'm Jessica Rayder. I'll show you to your quarters, then Faith can give you instructions for the morning chores."

She turned quickly to avoid Faith's still-questioning gaze, and the men followed her down the aisle toward the door. She crossed the gravel parking strip that separated the barn from the carriage house, then unlocked the door to the former servants' quarters. She wrinkled her nose at the musty odor wafting out of the long-closed room.

Hafez looked wide-eyed. "Is wonderful!"

"I apologize for not being ready. Samir didn't tell me you'd be arriving so soon. I'll be back in a few minutes to make up the beds."

Hafez smiled widely, revealing yellow teeth with gaps. "Do not trouble yourself. We need only a blanket to be comfortable."

Jess nodded and headed back toward the barn. *Samir must be the only one in the family who's well off.*

Faith met her at the door to the tack room. Her eyes still reflected anxiety, but anger now colored her high cheekbones.

"What's going on? Why are you being so secretive?"

"Faith, I *told* you, I forgot." Jess's own irritation began to surface. "I had a lot on my mind, and I can't exactly refuse free help, can I?" She opened the storage closet and pulled down two blankets. "Samir is sponsoring them for the summer, and they needed something to do. He's paying their salaries."

An ugly expression distorted Faith's fine features. "What's the deal? We're suddenly overrun with A-Rabs. First the Mahfoods, now this. I don't like it."

Jess slammed the blankets down on top of a tack trunk, and whirled to face her partner. “Faith, knock it off! Since when did you start being so prejudiced?”

The color drained from the pretty face and Faith’s voice hummed with hatred. “Since three thousand people died on 9/11 because of these assholes.”

# Eighteen

By one o'clock, a headache throbbed through the base of Jess's skull. The scene with Faith played over and over, and Jess's despair took hold. Had it only been twenty-four hours since she'd made optimistic plans for the future? She–who would be Faith's salvation–had screwed it up royally with her damned independent, I'm-in-charge streak. She sighed. Let a few hours pass, then find Faith and apologize, maybe even come up with some plausible reason for her own bizarre behavior.

The telephone intruded on the dismal thoughts, and Elvora's smile sparkled through her words.

"We're all set for Saturday night. How about you?"

"Absolutely. Tell me where and when, and I'll be there."

"Meet me at seven by the fountain in the lobby, and I'll take you up to the suite."

"How many will be in the game?"

"Six altogether. These are big mucky-mucks, including a Saudi Arabian sheikh."

Something clicked in Jess's brain. Was she imagining it, or was her world suddenly peppered with Middle Easterners? She shook off the thought. Apparently she'd just never noticed them until the Mahfoods came into her life.

"Genuine royalty? What's his name?"

"Mohammed. Real original, huh?" Elvora chuckled. "But you wouldn't believe how much money the sheikh's advance group is spending on this little jaunt."

Jess's mental wheels spun. *That's okay. I'm not intimidated by anyone.*

Elvora's tone softened, taking the edge off her next words. "I hope you found a dress. . .foreign men like pretty women. You might have quite an advantage."

A second later, Jess hung up the phone and snorted. "Like I need one."

A sharp rap on the doorjamb preceded a wiry woman with chin-length brown hair and sharp features. She looked to be in her early forties.

"Jessica? I'm Mona Johnson." Her firm handshake matched her self-confidant posture.

Jess smiled. "Come on in and sit down. I understand you're going to trade slave labor for lessons."

Mona sat down next to the desk and crossed her legs. She had a pleasant smile, and her husky voice hinted at a lifetime of cigarettes.

"Yeah, I'm a substitute teacher in the afternoons, usually one or two days a week at the elementary school in Burlington. Just barely a living, but it gives me some time to myself."

Jess laughed. "And you want to spend that time cleaning stalls?"

"No, I want to spend it learning to ride. All my life, I've wanted to ride horses, but the circumstances were never right. Now they are."

The woman's expression revealed the depth of her dreams, and Jess felt surprise at her own response. *How many little girls end up as lucky as Faith or me? Apparently, not many.*

Mona filled out the employment forms, then rose. "I'll be here at five tomorrow morning. See ya."

Twenty minutes later, Zada Mahfood stepped into the office, followed by a young boy and a dark-skinned woman carrying a baby girl.

"Good afternoon, Miss Jessica. I apologize for interrupting your work." She gestured toward the other woman. "I've brought my friend, Nadia Mohammed, to watch Dania's lesson."

Jess's voice cracked when she spoke. "Mohammed?"

Zada smiled. "You know the name?"

"Ah, well, it sounds familiar."

The other woman chuckled softly. "Yes, it is a name such as

your Johnson or Smith."

Zada patted the boy's shoulder. "This is Ibrahim. He wants to ride horses, just like Dania." She cast an indulgent smile on the handsome little boy, whose arrogant expression sent irritation crawling across Jess's shoulders.

Mrs. Mohammed spoke, her tone respectful. "Samir speaks highly of your riding stable. It would be an honor to bring Ibrahim here for lessons."

Jess's thoughts raced. Good fortune had definitely returned to Easton Ridge. Three free pair of helping hands and another rich riding student. Top it off with a good night at the poker table, and Jess could relax back into the life she loved. Maybe even take a little trip to Idaho.

Half an hour later, she stuffed Nadia Mohammed's five hundred dollars into the envelope with the down-payment money.

Jess stepped into the tack room. "Faith? Can we talk?"

Faith kept her head down, concentrating on the bridle she was cleaning. "Sure. What about?"

Jess sat down on a tack trunk. "I'm sorry I didn't talk to you about my health. I felt so overwhelmed with the financial thing, it was more than I could handle at the time. I didn't want to try answering questions until I had answers. It had nothing to do with our friendship, believe me."

Faith set the bridle aside and tilted her head. She gazed at Jess for a few moments, then nodded.

"I guess I can't blame you. I haven't exactly been a rock of strength myself lately."

"How *is* everything? Any word from Bill?"

Jess cringed inwardly at yet another secret she'd kept from her friend.

"No, I'm concentrating on getting straight right now. When the time is right, I'll talk to him." She rose and carefully hung the bridle on the hook, and her voice cracked. "He was so good for me, so loving, promising a future together, a family."

Jess's heart ached while Faith haltingly continued the confession.

"The first time I slipped off the wagon and treated myself to a glass of wine at a party, he grabbed my arm so hard it hurt, and steered me out onto the patio. Wanted to know what the hell I thought I was doing. Then, he snatched the wineglass and threw it into a shrub."

Jess felt as though she were looking into a raw, oozing wound. "What happened?"

"The booze made me cocky, I got snotty, and the evening dissolved into a quarrel. The next morning, I had a horrible hangover, and vowed not to let it happen ever again." She shook her head. "Famous last words."

Jess rose and reached for Faith's arm. "When I woke up in the recovery room, and found out I wasn't going to die, you were the first person in my thoughts. You are more important to me than you could possibly know. You owe it to yourself to get straight and continue with your success here at Easton. I'll be right beside you if you falter. I promise."

# *Nineteen*

The next morning, Jess awoke to the sound of sparrows chirping outside her window. She stretched and yawned.

"No stalls for me today!"

What a luxury to be up early with no pressing responsibilities. She carried her coffee to the porch, and settled into the swing. The fresh scent of newly mown grass and honeysuckle floated on the cool morning air. A crisp blue sky carried wisps of contrails, drifting into zigzag patterns high above the earth. Only the soft whine of a jet airplane on its approach to Bradley International disturbed the silence.

Gazing across the field at the barns bathed in the first pale peach-colored rays of sunrise, Jess couldn't conceive of living anywhere else. She moved her fingers over her chest, gingerly touching the still-sore spot beneath her right nipple. Resolve edged into her thoughts, shaping a plan, and solidifying her strength. She could do this. She *would* save Easton.

A movement caught her eye, and she watched two figures moving briskly toward the main barn. *Good, the nephews are starting early.* She watched them disappear into the dark entrance. She turned at the sound of a truck coming up the drive and, a few minutes later, Mona strode into the barn. *Guess I'd better get my own butt in gear.*

The barn was humming with activity by the time Jess arrived. Hafez worked his way down the aisle with feed tubs, while Mustafa washed and refilled water buckets. Jess watched them for a moment, pleased by their diligence.

Five minutes later, she frowned at Faith's scrawl, rambling

across a scrap of notepaper on the desk. *"Naomi hasn't received that check yet."*

"Damn!"

The crumpled note bounced off the rim of the wastebasket. She needed to avoid a confrontation with Faith until after Saturday, then first thing Monday morning, she'd personally take the cash to Naomi. Until then, she'd have to tap-dance. Timing and skill were the only things that would keep disaster from winning.

Taking advantage of the privacy of the early hour, she logged onto the internet and began searching for rehabilitation programs. As she read various sad case histories, and tales of success, Jess became more determined to stay on top of her friend's alcohol problem. But when everything was back on track, she would definitely take some time for herself. She grinned at the blue computer screen, and quickly typed in a search.

"Whoa!" she whispered.

Over fifty hits featured Howard London, and she began clicking on links. Thirty minutes later, she sat back in wonder. High profile cases, astonishing verdicts, New York's darling. Her backwoods lawyer was some piece of work. More reason to get her life in order.

She unlocked the desk drawer and removed the bulging envelope. Her fingers trembled a little as she counted the down-payment money, reassuring herself she had enough to play serious poker.

Mona stepped through the door. "Morning!"

Jess nearly jumped out of her chair and Mona grinned.

"Sorry, didn't mean to scare the hell out of you. Which horses go out today?"

Jess tried to act nonchalant. "Mmm. We'll have to look at the lesson schedule."

Mona strode up to the desk, giving Jess no time to hide the cash. "Wow! That your mad money?"

Jess rose and glanced down at the stack of bills as though it weren't important. "I wish!" She moved away from the desk and stood in front of the planner on the wall. "We have lessons all day. Faith will have to tell you which horses stay in."

"Okey doak. . .I see you have some new barn help."

"Yeah, college students with time on their hands."

Mona grunted, then disappeared through the door. Jess exhaled sharply, quickly stuffing the bills back into the envelope, then into her shoulder bag. Her clanging heartbeat began to slow. *This money is determined to get me into deep trouble.*

Jess spent the afternoon working with two young hunters she'd purchased as school-horse prospects the previous fall. Both horses had muscled up under her conditioning program, and she felt confident they'd be ready for students by late fall. Seated atop a chestnut Thoroughbred, Jess's problems faded like a bad dream. She urged the horse into a canter and took him over three consecutive jumps. He was well-collected, but his landings were a little rough.

Faith leaned on the rail and chortled.

"He looks real good, Jessie. Kinda hops there at the end, though. We'll have kids popping off like bread from a toaster."

Jess laughed. "You read my mind. Could you work him over fences a couple times a week? Smooth him out a little?"

"Sure, but it'll have to wait 'til after my clinic on Saturday."

A car pulled up in front of the barn, and two little girls spilled out.

Faith sighed. "Well, back to the salt mines."

Later that afternoon, Faith dropped into the chair by the desk. "I can't believe the Classic is only three weeks away." She closed her eyes and exhaled. "One farm show and Devon are all we have left between now and then. I hope these kids keep up their dedication."

She opened her eyes and frowned.

Jess tensed. *Uh-oh. Here it comes.* The phone rang and she snatched it up like a drowning man grabbing a lifeline.

"Easton Ridge Equestrian Center, Jess speaking." Her stomach pitched at the voice on the other end of the line, and she glanced at Faith, now examining her fingernails.

"Yes, Naomi, I understand. The only thing I can figure is it got lost in the mail."

Faith sat forward, eyes narrowed, and Jess assumed her best poker face.

"Right. If you haven't received it by Saturday, give me a call and I'll write another one and deliver it in person. . .Yeah, don't you hate it?. . .Okay, thanks for calling. Bye."

She hung up. "Can you believe it? Damned post office keeps raising the cost of stamps, but can't even deliver a simple letter to the next county." She rose from the chair, changing the direction of the conversation. "You ready for your jumping clinic on Saturday?"

"Yeah, I have–"

A sharp rap on the doorjamb preceded Frank McCarney's voice.

"Miss Jessie? You girls busy?"

"Hey, Frank, what a nice surprise! Come on in."

She smiled and gestured toward a chair, but an uneasy stir moved through her innards. The landlord had never dropped by unexpectedly.

He moved into the room a couple of feet, and shook his head. "I don't mean to keep ya, but I want to talk to ya about the rent."

Jess steeled herself. "We still have almost a week, Frank."

"Yeah, I know, but truth is, I'd like to know if you're gonna be able to get current. Someone is keen on the property, and he's lookin' at some others, too. I'd hate to lose him if you're not–"

Jess took two steps toward the old man, using her six-inch height advantage to strengthen her position. "Frank, I don't have to talk to you about this until next week. I said we'd have the money, and we will. Shit, I can't believe you're doing this."

His wizened features hardened, his eyes glittering with indignation. "No need to be vulgar, Missy. It's just business." He turned toward the door. "I'll see you on Monday."

Jess stared silently at the empty doorway. Behind her, Faith's voice squeaked.

"Jessie, why would he *do* that? What *are* we going to do?"

Samir said goodnight to his group of friends at the casino. On the drive home to Hartford, his thoughts centered on Easton Ridge. Hafez and Mustafa had settled in and were learning the routine at the barn and, so far, everything had gone smoothly. He considered the location of the riding stable and its adjacent protected forest land. Hafez's detailed description of the buildings and access confirmed Samir's assessment–the farm was perfect.

He lit a cigar, then sat back and reconstructed his earlier conversation with the landowner. The old man had been reluctant at first, professing loyalty to the two women, but everyone had their price, and he was no different. An offer of double rent, paid a year in advance, had gotten his attention, especially when Samir shared his suspicion that the horsewomen were in deep financial straits. Even so, anger crawled through Samir's gut. McCarney's overt displeasure about dealing with a foreigner minimized Samir's satisfaction with the conversation.

# *Twenty*

Jess stared out the bedroom window into the black void she'd watched for most of the night. Her body ached for sleep, but her brain wouldn't let go. *Thanks a lot, Frank.* Faith had vowed to start looking for a loan immediately, and Jess had struggled to keep from revealing her own plans for saving the business. The black sky turned gray, and she rolled out of bed. With any luck, by this time tomorrow, she could tell Frank to kiss her ass.

Stepping out onto the porch, she shivered at the chill in the morning air. A tiny patch of clear sky hovered directly overhead, but on every horizon, mounds of heavy black clouds lurked, waiting to sweep across the land. She retreated into the kitchen and turned on the television. The too-perky weather girl chirped her ominous forecast: *"We'll see gale force winds by this afternoon, with heavy rain and the possibility of damaging hail in some regions. . .Looking at New York City, we–"* Jess pressed the power button on the remote, and tossed it onto the counter.

"Great. I suppose I'll end up slogging through this mess to get to the casino tonight."

A glance through the window confirmed it. The cloud ceiling had dropped, giving her an eerie, caged feeling. She shuddered at the prospect of driving all the way to the northeastern part of the state through a serious thunderstorm. Maybe it would clear off by the time she was ready to leave. Within minutes, the sky darkened dramatically, triggering the barn floodlights. A vicious wind sprang up, and the small decorative birch trees along the driveway contorted into dangerous angles. Ten minutes later, a sheet of rain pounded against the window.

The storm reached its zenith around noon, and Jess stared out the window at Mother Nature's fury. "I'm *not* driving in this! I have too much at stake to be frazzled when I get there."

A few minutes later, she had the Hartford limo schedule and, knowing the poker game could last into the wee hours, booked a room at the casino hotel. Nervous energy coursed through her body, intensified by a poor night's sleep. She couldn't remain idle. A stack of unopened mail caught her eye, and she carried it to the couch, determined not to dwell on the upcoming evening.

The mélange consisted of bills and junk mail, catalogs and trade magazines. A postcard fluttered to the carpet and she retrieved it with curiosity. *I don't know anyone who travels.* The shiny card pictured a rustic lodge, nestled amongst evergreens. In the upper corner, "Coeur d'Alene Refuge" was printed in heavy white script. Her heartbeat skipped. She quickly turned the postcard over, and eagerly scanned the precise handwriting. *"Jess, just thinking again about our great evening together. Hope you can get out to Idaho one of these days. Fondly, Howard."*

"First thing on my list, honey."

XX

# *Twenty-One*

Hot water streamed over Jess's shoulders, easing the tension that had been building all day. She inhaled the dense steam, energized by the power of the moisture. A shiver of anticipation raised gooseflesh on her arms. Her initial apprehension over spending the evening with royalty evaporated, the concept so unfamiliar that she couldn't feel anything but curiosity about what Sheikh Mohammed might be like. Vivid images of scowling, dark-skinned men wearing flowing white robes galloped through her head on snorting Arabian stallions–the only connection she could make to the term "sheikh."

It *had* occurred to her that she might be the only woman at the table, and she didn't know if that was good or bad. In the past, she'd found most male poker players to be influenced by her gender. The egotistical types were usually annoyed at the effrontery of a girl thinking she could take their money, but the majority of men let their own hormones interfere with their card-playing skills. On the other hand, if tonight's group was composed of all Middle Easterners, the cultural issues might work against her. She'd just have to wait and see.

An hour later, she stepped back from the mirror, satisfied with the way she looked. She'd taken her time with the eye-makeup, enhancing her gray eyes with soft brown shadow and mascara. Tiny specks of silver sparkled in the blush across her cheeks, and soft peach lipstick gave her mouth a fuller, more feminine appearance. She stared at her reflection, wondering again why her appearance mattered in the scheme of the evening.

Jess gazed at the fountain sculpture and smiled, thinking of her first meeting with Howard in the very same spot.

"Good evening, Jessica. You look wonderful tonight." A wink accompanied Elvora's wide smile. "You'll be the belle of the ball."

They moved toward the rear of the casino, skirting the chaos on the main floor, then followed a uniformed man down a quiet hall. He unlocked a private elevator, and they stepped inside. As the small cubicle rose through the innards of the building, a shot of adrenaline careened through Jess's system and her stomach twitched unpleasantly. Her entire future depended on this one night–she could make no mistakes. She took a deep breath and exhaled slowly, willing the unsettling buzz to disappear.

The elevator gears whispered on the air for only a few moments, then the doors slid quietly aside. Jess stepped into the hall, her feet sinking into the cushioned luxury of thick pile carpeting, a striking contrast to the décor of the main casino. Ivory woodwork framed pale green walls hung with excellent reproductions of Native American art, and soft lighting cast an aura of elegance over everything.

Elvora led the way to the end of the short hall, and opened the door to the Spirit Suite. Jess gazed around the large room. Attractive sofas and overstuffed chairs were positioned around a modern, glass-and-chrome coffee table. Ashtrays, boxes of cigars and cigarettes, bowls of matches, and dishes filled with hard candies and chocolates covered the gleaming surface. Directly to the side of the seating arrangement, a buffet table held steam trays, china, and silverware and, next to that, a fully-stocked bar. On the opposite side of the room, leather padded, straight-backed chairs encircled a large poker table.

Jess focused on the unmistakable figure of Sheikh Mohammed. Of medium height and heavy build, his movements were those of a man who seemed accustomed to power. He turned, revealing a craggy face behind a well-trimmed beard, deep-set dark eyes under bushy black eyebrows, and a thin mouth that bordered on a sneer. His dark business suit looked expensive, and he would have seemed like any other man, except for the red-and-white checkered scarf covering his head.

Elvora took Jess's elbow and steered her toward him.

"Sheikh Mohammed, may I present Miss Jessica Rayder?"

The man spoke flawless English. "Miss Elvora, you did not tell me how beautiful she is."

Jess didn't know what to do. *Bow? Nope, not on your life! Shake hands? Hell, why didn't Elvora prepare me?*

The sheikh solved the problem by offering his hand. Then, to her surprise, he raised her fingers to his lips.

"My extreme pleasure. May I call you Jessica?"

Despite her first impression of him, the sheikh seemed no different than Samir.

She smiled. "Yes, of course."

"Would you like a cocktail? We have anything you want."

"Mineral water, please. Thank you."

He gestured to someone at the bar, then smiled at Jess. "Miss Elvora informs me that you own horses. I *also* have horses. Racing Thoroughbreds."

Jess nodded while she listened. The racing industry was heavily populated with foreign owners, especially from the oil-rich countries where money was as plentiful as the black stuff that generated it. Commanding her attention with his intensity, Sheikh Mohammed expounded at length on his horse farm.

"My stables are the most modern design, with temperature control and automatic watering systems in each stall."

Jess smiled and nodded politely. *Big deal. We've had those conveniences for years.*

Mohammed's chest puffed noticeably. "I have two Belmont winners–I am hopeful for a Triple Crown someday. *Insha'Allaah.*"

Jess stole a furtive glance at her watch. *Almost eight. Let's get on with it.*

The door opened and a casino employee entered, carrying a cash box. One step behind, Samir Mahfood appeared.

Ж

## *Twenty-Two*

*What the hell is he doing here?*

Samir's smile faltered when he spotted her, but the reaction lasted for only a moment. He nodded briefly, then strode up to Sheikh Mohammed. The two men embraced, exchanging exuberant greetings.

The sheikh stepped back and gestured toward Jess. "Samir, this is Miss Jessica."

Samir's smile was cold as he gazed directly into her eyes. "Yes, we have met. The lady manages the barn where my Dania rides horses. Nice to see you again." He turned to the sheikh. "Your accommodations are comfortable?"

The two men moved away toward the bar, and Jess seethed under Samir's arrogant patronage.

Elvora appeared beside her. "Let me introduce you to the other players."

"Why is Samir Mahfood here?"

Elvora's solemn tone was almost reverent. "He's very important in the Muslim community. The sheikh specifically asked me to invite him."

As she'd suspected, Jess was the only woman in the group. Including the sheikh, her opponents consisted of five men. Politely shaking hands with each one, she formed instant impressions of the individuals with whom she'd spar. Two of the four looked to be of Middle Eastern extraction, probably part of Mohammed's entourage, but big, blonde Nate Jackson's Texas drawl confirmed him as all American. The fifth player was Asian–Jimmy Kee's face remained expressionless as he shook Jess's hand.

These men were a far cry from the college kids she'd trounced.

She threw one more furtive glance toward the sofa where Samir had settled. He was deep in conversation with another foreign-looking man. Irritation again crawled over her shoulders at the unexpected surprise of his presence, but she pushed it away and turned back to the table to mentally prepare herself for the game. Carefully stacking her chips into neat little towers, blocking out all extraneous thoughts, her focus centered and her pulse slowed. The background conversation in the room faded to a murmur.

Elvora stepped up to the table and rapped her knuckles on the edge.

"The game will be Texas Hold 'Em. This is a challenging game, filled with potential for big bluffs, big wins, and big losses." She scanned the players, then continued. "The two players to the left of the dealer will each put half the minimum bet into the pot before the first two cards are dealt. Players can call, raise, or fold when it's their turn to bet.

"The dealer will discard–or "burn"–the top card on the deck before dealing each of the five community cards. The flop is made up of three cards, the next deal is the turn card, and the fifth is the river. Players can use any combination of seven cards in traditional poker hands. Good luck."

She stepped back, and Jess glanced across the table at the Saudi sheikh as he started the deal. *I don't care who you are. . .I'm going to take your money tonight.*

The first two cards hit the table in front of her and Jess left them face down. She studied the other players' faces as they each peeked at their own first hand. Finally, she lifted the corners of her cards. The queen of diamonds and ten of spades.

Nate Jackson stared at his cards, then swore softly and laid them aside. "I fold."

The Arab man next to him also folded. Jess pushed two thousand-dollar chips into the pot–a small bet, but her limited cash forced the cautious move. Jimmy Kee raised the bet to five, and the next player folded. Sheikh Mohammed chuckled wickedly and matched the bet. Jess called it, mentally tabulating the chips in the center of the table. Fourteen thousand dollars. If she won only this hand, she'd be out of trouble with Frank.

Mohammed burned the top card, and laid down the three-card flop. Jack of spades, a pair of sixes. Jess raised the pot another three thousand. Kee and the sheikh matched it.

The sheikh again discarded the top card on the deck, and dealt the turn card. A six. Jess tossed another thousand into the pot, Kee folded, and Mohammed called her.

Despite the exciting possibility of winning a large amount on the first hand, Jess's breathing remained even, her pulse calm, her face expressionless as she waited for the river card. A second later, the queen of spades' benevolent smile radiated from the soft green baize.

Jess glanced across the table at Mohammed, searching for a possible hint of his position. She added a thousand dollars to the pile on the table. Mohammed stared at his cards for a moment, then smiled foolishly and pushed them into the center with the chips.

As the evening progressed, Jess relaxed into the game, her poker hands fluctuating between moderately good and fantastic. She placed prudent bets, won most of the deals, and gained a good impression of the other players and their competence. The sheikh was a rash bettor, drawing on chips from the endless stack at his elbow, but his skill didn't match his enthusiasm. The Texan did a lot of verbal swaggering and wasn't much of a bluffer.

Jess considered the group. With the exception of Mohammed and herself, the players were merely better than average butts-in-chairs to fill out the game. Briefly, she wondered if Elvora had purposely collected players who'd be no threat to the sheikh's ego.

The chips in front of her totaled about sixty-thousand dollars. The next deal went down, and she lifted the edges of her cards. A nine and the ace of hearts. Nothing spectacular, but the house cards could change that. Nate Jackson opened the betting with three thousand, and Jess decided to pass until she saw the flop.

The sheikh raised his eyebrows. "Being cautious?"

Jess smiled, but didn't respond. Familiarity and chat could be deadly. Mohammed pushed fifteen-thousand into the pile.

The flop cards hit the table, and Jess swallowed an almost automatic sigh of relief. Her instinct had prevailed again. A queen, a deuce, and a nine.

The sheikh smiled, his face flushed and features relaxed from the bottomless tumbler of Scotch he'd been nursing all evening.

"Just to make the pot interesting, I will throw in one of my best horses."

Jess grinned across the table. "What on earth would I do with a Thoroughbred?"

He roared with laughter at her cocky attitude, and the Texan snorted.

"She's right. Only horses worth a damn are Quarter Horses. Working horses."

Jess bristled, then brushed her irritation away. The idiot wasn't worth sacrificing her concentration.

Ten minutes later, Mohammed called for a break, and Jess counted her winnings. Ninety thousand dollars and a racehorse. Not bad for a girl.

Elvora appeared, a sparkle in her chocolate-colored eyes. "You're a worthy opponent for Mohammed. He's thoroughly enjoying himself."

Jess glanced at the sheikh as he headed for the bar.

"That's good, but I'm getting tired. Do you know how much longer he'll want to play?"

Elvora's laugh rumbled, deep and rich, "Until he wins, of course!"

Nate Jackson and the two Arabs did not return to the poker table after the break. Jess glanced surreptitiously at Jimmy Kee. His stack of chips had changed very little during the evening. A cautious player, and not much fun. She checked the sheikh's stake. He'd lost most of the hands, but his stack of chips had more than doubled. Obviously, he'd added to his playing funds. She looked at her own pile and relief swept through her tired body. *Mission accomplished.*

The sheikh dealt, and Jess folded. A four and a six held no promise, and fatigue slipped in, taking the edge off her concentration. She took a sip of water, wishing she could gracefully leave the game, but as long as she was winning, she'd have to stay in. She glanced at Samir, deep in conversation with the Arabs. He waved his hands around as he spoke rapidly in Arabic, his features animated. She wondered idly what they were talking about.

"Miss Jessica? It is your deal."

She jumped. "Sorry."

A minute later, she held the ten and five of hearts. She watched the sheikh ponder his cards, his indecision caused either by a poor hand, or the abundance of alcohol he'd consumed through the evening. *Tsk, tsk. Practice what you preach.* Finally, Mohammed tossed five thousand into the pot, and the play moved to Jimmy Kee. He stared at his cards for a moment, then slid them into the center of the table. Jess pushed her bet into the center, just to see where things were headed.

The flop consisted of a jack, a ten, and the four of hearts. Mohammed remained cautious with another bet of five thousand.

Jess matched him. *For a pair, I'll stay in.*

A five hit the table. *Two pair. Things are looking better.* Again, she matched the bet. The river card went down: a four. She glanced up at Mohammed and a blip skittered through her pulse. His shoulders straightened just the tiniest bit, but his features remained serene.

He pushed a small stack of chips into the center.

*Okay, that's it.* Jess laid her cards face-down on the table.

With a huge grin and a flourish, Mohammed laid a four on the table and scooped up thirty-five thousand dollars.

Rising from his chair, he nodded at her. "I will refresh my drink and then we will play one more hand, just you and I. Agreed?"

Weariness crawled over her shoulders, but she nodded. *I have over a hundred thousand dollars and a new horse. I can afford to be magnanimous. I'll let him win the next one, then I'm outta here.*

When the sheikh returned to the table, his movements were sluggish, his speech a little slurred. *He's so smashed, it might be hard to even give him this hand.* Jess averted her eyes and moved her chips around, neatly aligning them with the edge of the table.

The deal went out, and her charity disappeared. She held the king and ace of spades. She glanced up through her lashes at Mohammed, who moved his cards around on the table and fiddled with his chips. He finally pushed ten thousand into the center. Hesitating for only a moment, Jess matched the bet. The flop went down, and

Jess tried to conceal her disbelief. A ten, jack, and queen. *Sorry, Charlie, I'm not throwing this hand after all. You can save face another time.*

The sheikh gazed across the table and smiled, his white teeth glistening beneath his heavy black moustache. Jess nodded, but kept any expression from her eyes. Mohammed raised the bet, briefly disrupting her smug feeling. *He's just drunk. . .doesn't know what he's doing*. She matched the bet.

The turn card came into play. The ace of diamonds. Mohammed pushed another ten thousand into the center. Without hesitation, Jess matched it.

The river card–the nine of hearts. Jess struggled to keep from grinning. Mohammed's dark eyes burned across the table, sending shivers of both excitement and apprehension through her head. He'd be really pissed if she cleaned him out.

He smiled and nodded his head slowly. "Let us make it *very* exciting."

He pushed his entire stack of chips into the center of the table. "I'm all in."

For a brief second, Jess had the impression that his inebriation had passed and he was in complete control. *He's bluffing. There's no way he's going to beat a royal flush.* She struggled to maintain her calm facade. The pot contained enough money to keep her out of debt forever, but if she lost. . . Her heart hammered against her ribs, her composure shot.

The room grew very quiet, tension hanging in the air like tentacles. Slowly, she pushed all her chips into the center of the table. Anticipation simmered in the pit of her stomach as she closed in for the kill.

She smiled wickedly. "Your Sheikh-ness, I call you."

In slow motion, Mohammed's well-manicured fingers turned over two aces.

Ж

# *Twenty-Three*

"Wonderful game! You are, indeed, a formidable opponent." Sheikh Mohammed smiled eagerly. "Perhaps we can play again sometime?"

Jess stared at him. "You just lost a bundle and you're *happy* about it?"

He chuckled. "Of course–it's only money." He leaned close and murmured, "I understand you need it more than I do."

Anger churned through her chest, but before she could reply, he bowed deeply.

"Until we meet again, may Allaah keep you."

He moved away toward Samir's group.

Elvora appeared, holding a cashier's check. "May I call you again sometime?"

Jess managed a tired smile. "No, but thanks anyway."

With one last glance at the animated group of men, she slipped out the door into the quiet hall and headed for the elevator. Fatigue and anger clanged in her head, disturbing her thought patterns. Relief over her good fortune battled with the unsettling circumstances of Samir's presence in her private life. On the main floor of the building, she wandered down the wide marble concourse, looking at the darkened shop windows with unseeing eyes, her thoughts rambling. Samir had not spoken to her the entire evening. *Important Muslim, be damned. I want him out of my life*. She found a deserted cocktail lounge, and settled into a booth. A few minutes later, bourbon burned its way down her throat, reminding her how far she'd strayed from normalcy.

"May I join you?"

Samir's soft voice rekindled her anger, but she didn't look up from her drink. "Suit yourself."

Who did this bastard think he was? Telling Mohammed of her financial situation was the ultimate insult.

Samir slid into the booth. "You are angry with me?"

Her head snapped up and she pinned him with a nasty glare. "You're damned right I am! Why would you discuss my personal business with a stranger? Tell me that!"

Samir looked wounded. "Sheikh Mohammed is no stranger–we are cousins."

Jess scooted out of the booth. "Whatever."

When Jess returned to Easton later that morning, she noticed the empty parking spot next to the carriage house–an oddity, since Samir's nephews seldom left the farm. *What could they possibly find to interest them in the local area?* For one second, she felt tempted to go to their room and have a look around, then groaned and shook her head. *I'm starting to think like Faith.*

She entered the barn, and a joyful nicker drifted from Casey's stall. Jess slipped into the cozy cubicle, and laid her cheek against the mare's warm neck, closing her eyes and feeling the weeks of tension fade.

"You always love me, no matter what."

Five minutes later, she haltered the horse and led her into the aisle. As she moved through the familiar rote of grooming, she organized her thoughts. She'd get over to the bank first thing in the morning, to Frank's after lunch, then finish up at Naomi's. Once the money thing was handled, she could devote her energy and time to helping Faith crawl out of the pit.

She saddled Casey and swung up onto her back, then headed out the back door of the barn. Moving away from the practice ring, she guided the mare toward the woods, feeling strength and resilience flow back into her mind and body. All her troubles were over.

A twig snapped and Casey shied sideways, nearly unseating Jess. She pulled back on the reins gently, and patted the mare's neck. Suddenly, she was looking at a man wearing Carhartt overalls and a brown camo hunting cap. She urged Casey forward.

"What are you doing here? This is private property."

An easy smile brightened his face. "Sorry. My dog wandered away from my camp in the state forest. Guess I didn't realize I'd gone so far." He looked around, then squinted up at her. "You didn't happen to see a black and tan German Shepherd, did you?"

Jess relaxed back in the saddle. "No, but I could call you if I see him."

The man pulled off his cap, and smoothed his hair back. "Nah, he'll come back. He's probably out gettin' laid." He yanked the cap down over his forehead and turned away. "Sorry to have bothered ya."

Jess watched him for a minute, then headed down the trail, her thoughts moving on to the fresh new future ahead.

When Jess returned from her ride, Hafez's faded green van was parked by the barn door. The nephews climbed out and opened the vehicle doors just as Jess trotted Casey up to the barn.

"Been to town?"

Mustafa smiled politely, bobbing his head. Hafez gestured toward the vehicle.

"Yes, Miss Faith wanted some special grain. We had to travel to Stamford to collect it."

Jess dismounted. "What special grain?" She walked to the back of the van and looked inside at four burlap sacks. "When did Faith give you this order?"

Hafez's dark eyes didn't blink. "Yesterday morning. You were not here."

He pulled a rumpled slip of paper from his pocket and held it out. Faith's scrawl rambled across the lined notebook paper–a make-shift purchase order that could have waited until the next day.

"Okay, go ahead and unload it."

Irritation prickled her neck. Why was Faith in such a damned big hurry for that feed? After putting Casey back into her stall, Jess went to the office and pulled out the inventory sheets. She ran her finger down the list to the grain line. There should be four bags in the feed room–more than enough to get through the week. She made a mental note to ask Faith about it later.

"Hey, how was your sleep-over with Howard?"

Jess jerked at the slurred speech.

Faith's eyes shone, her cheeks were pink, and dimples winked around her insinuating smile. "I didn't expect to see you until tomorrow."

Jess strode forward, causing Faith to step backward. The odor of alcohol swirled between them.

"*Obviously.* Do you think just because I'm not around, it's okay to drink? If nobody knows, it doesn't exist?"

A ruddy flush crept across Faith's cheeks. "Oh, here we go again–Miss holier-than-thou! Can't you just leave me alone?"

She turned away, but Jess grabbed her arm.

"No, I can't! You're jeopardizing everything I've worked so hard to acquire. I won't let it happen!"

Faith's delicate features mutated into an ugly sneer, and she snatched her arm away. "*You've* worked? At what? *I'm* the one who keeps this place going–or have you forgotten?"

Jess closed her eyes briefly. *Why am I doing this? She's sick.*

"No, honey. . .I haven't forgotten." She touched Faith's shoulder. "I'm sorry, I'm really tired. . .Want to talk about it?"

Faith's features relaxed and her eyes brimmed, but she shook her head. Jess took her hand and led her to a chair.

"Did something happen with Bill?"

Faith took a deep, shuddery breath and nodded her head. "I spent yesterday trying to drum up some money, but I couldn't come up with enough to do us any good." She looked away. "I've felt so great the past few days, I thought I could face him. Thought he might be willing to give me a loan, just for old time's sake. . .maybe even reconsider our relationship."

A deep sob convulsed her narrow shoulders, and Jess's chest tightened. She could only imagine what had happened.

Faith took a deep breath. "I went to his new apartment, and there was–" Tears streamed down her cheeks and her voice cracked. "Oh, God, Jessie, a woman in a flimsy robe answered the door–he's already found someone else!"

She leaned forward in the chair and buried her face in her hands, her shoulders heaving with gut-wrenching sobs. Jess didn't know what to do–she couldn't say everything would turn out okay–it wouldn't. Should she have told Faith about the encounter with Bill at the casino? Would it have caused any less misery? Guilt and pity welled up in her throat as she watched her friend spiral into the depths of pain. It was no wonder the poor girl had turned to alcohol–her life had been a succession of losses, more than enough to turn the tide for someone with such a gentle nature.

Faith's emotion subsided, and she lifted her glistening face. "Jessie, I'm so sorry. I need your help with this–I can't do it alone."

Jess reached out and stroked her arm. "I'm here. We'll lick this together."

Faith swiped at her tears, managing a tremulous smile.

Grinning, Jess dipped into her pocket. "Guess what? I have the money for Frank."

Faith gasped and her eyes widened at the figures on the cashier's check. "How? I mean–"

"Poker. I cleaned out a visiting dignitary last night."

ꭗ

## *Twenty-Four*

Faith's voice was thick with panic. "Jess, I need to talk to you, I'm on my way over."

Jess glanced at the clock–she'd overslept.

"What's the matter?"

"I don't want to talk about it on the phone."

Jess hung up and headed for the kitchen. Five minutes later, a wave of concern surged through her head.

Faith's eyes glinted with fear. "Those men, the Arabs. . ." She took a deep breath and shuddered. "Jessie, they really scare me. Something's not right about them."

"Like what?"

Faith moved restlessly around the room while she talked. "They seem. . .sneaky, I don't know. . .sinister. I haven't been able to put my finger on it, but I feel really nervous around them."

Jess relaxed. Faith's attitude about foreigners apparently disturbed her more than she admitted.

Faith stopped pacing. "I was in the hayloft setting mousetraps this morning, and I heard Mustafa gabbling in that monkey talk of his, really excited and intense–you know, all stirred up. I peeked through a crack between the boards. He was out by the edge of the woods talking on a cellphone and waving his arms around. A minute later–so help me God–he threw the phone way out into the woods! Why would he do that?"

Jess shrugged. "Anger, maybe?"

"He didn't sound angry. More agitated, like he was talking about something important. I don't know. . .I got really scared. I don't like them here, Jessie. *Please*, can we get rid of them?"

"I don't see how. The Mahfoods are good customers. It would offend Samir to even broach the subject."

*And why am I worried about offending Samir?*

Faith chewed on her thumbnail, then looked up. "What if they're part of some deadly plot?"

Jess laughed out loud. "You have one hell of an imagination!"

Faith stood up and frowned. "Well, I intend to keep an eye on them, anyway. We sure don't need any more problems."

"Speaking of that, what time is the AA meeting today?"

Faith blinked. "Oh, uh, seven, I think. You don't have to–"

Jess jumped off the kitchen stool. "Yes, I do. We talked about this yesterday."

"I know, but I don't need you to hold my hand."

Jess bit back a nasty retort, then took a deep breath and handed Faith the information she'd printed out about Black Rock Rehabilitation Center. "Either you take some time to dry out, or we're finished."

Two minutes later, she watched from the porch as Faith marched angrily across the field toward the barn.

The sky had cleared, and the scent of recent rain hung on the fresh air. Pockets of morning mist hovered over the grass, giving the scene an eerie appearance. Near the barn, Mustafa pushed a cart toward the manure pile at the back of the property. Mona led two horses out to the pasture. Life moved on like clockwork, oblivious to the fine line Faith had drawn between survival and disaster.

Frank's wrinkled face broke into a grin.

"Good for you!" He gazed at the cash Jess had just handed over, then looked up and winked. "I really didn't wanna sell the place–especially to some furiner."

She tilted her head. "You really had a buyer? It wasn't a bluff?"

He chuckled. "No bluff, Missy. A real, honest-to-goodness A-Rab." His smile changed to a frown. "Don't trust 'em, though. Don't care how much money they got."

For one second, Jess wanted to pursue the conversation, get the details, find out who had almost taken her farm.

Frank cleared his throat. "I'll get you a receipt for all this money."

He shuffled over to an old roll-top desk piled with papers and magazines, then returned with a small slip of paper. He gave her a serious look as he handed it over.

"Next time, don't wait so long to ask for help."

She grinned sheepishly, feeling like a chastised child. "There won't be a next time. I'd like to talk to you about buying the place."

His sparse eyebrows came together. "Oh, I don't think–"

"Frank, you were willing to sell the property to someone else–why not us? Just think about it, okay?"

He pursed his lips. "Gimme some time. I'll get back to ya."

Jess climbed into her car, amazed that she'd taken such a bold step, considering the situation with Faith.

During the half-hour drive to Naomi's, Jess thought again about Faith's story. Why *would* Hafez throw away his phone? An uneasy stir moved through her chest. Was she being too casual about the recent events involving the nephews? She pulled into the Morton farm, and parked. Perhaps it was time to start paying a little closer attention to everything around her.

ꭗ

## *Twenty-Five*

Samir beamed, listening to his precious daughter's delight.

"Papa, I will be able to ride my new horse on Thursday!"

He stroked her shiny black hair, and love surged through his chest.

*"Quy-eesa, Habibi. Insha'Allaah."*

Dania planted a moist kiss on his cheek, then disappeared into the next room, leaving him to his thoughts.

Jessica Rayder's presence at the poker game had been a strange and unsettling coincidence–and her phenomenal good luck certainly changed his own ability to manipulate the landowner. *Allaah works in mysterious ways.*

He rose from his easy chair, and peeked into the kitchen. Zada hummed as she prepared the midday meal, her fingers nimble and skilled as she filled tiny eggplants and peppers with savory rice. A twinge of sorrow, then another deeper emotion surged through Samir's heart. *When this is over, I will take her home where she belongs.*

Jess felt as though a great weight had lifted from her shoulders. Naomi had been gracious about the delay in the payment, even promising to visit Easton to watch Dania ride Buster. Turning off the ignition, Jess sat for a moment, relishing the sensation of release. From the corner of her eye, she saw Mona standing by the carriage house. *What's she doing way over there?* Jess frowned. She'd allowed a stranger into her business without so much as a simple background check. She closed her eyes. *For that matter, I don't know squat about Samir's nephews, either.* Desperate circumstances had distracted her, and now she felt unsettled by the results.

She entered the barn, looking up and down the aisle, then called out, "Mona?"

The woman appeared at the back door, and Jess headed in that direction, not sure what she planned to say.

"I saw you over by the carriage house. Is there a problem?"

"Nah, I thought I saw a red fox standing by the edge of the woods. I was just tryin' to get a better look. Did you know the red fox is declining in Connecticut? They're on the protected list. I'm gonna report this sighting to the Friends of Wildlife."

"Oh. Interesting. I couldn't imagine what you were doing."

Mona grinned and opened a stall door. "I'm big into nature and animal protection."

Jess walked back toward the office, feeling a little foolish. Just then, one of the men stepped out of the feed room, and took a long drag on a cigarette.

"Hafez! Put that damned thing out!"

She marched up to him, anger surging through her chest and constricting her breath. He flicked the butt onto the concrete floor and ground it out with his boot, his eyes never leaving her face.

Her voice cracked. "Don't you *ever* smoke in here again! Do you understand me?"

Up close, his eyes formed black holes in his muddy brown skin, and the acrid odor of cigarette smoke curled between them. His tone belied any remorse. "Sorry."

The phone rang, and she hurried into the office, feeling his stare drill through her back. A chill swept over her, and she shuddered with a sudden, unnamed fear.

A second later, a familiar voice warmed her.

"Howard! I was thinking about you a little while ago. In fact, I planned to call you this weekend."

"Really? Must be ESP. I've been thinking about *you* all week. How are you?"

For one instant, she almost felt she could tell him about her poker adventure, but her usual reserve prevailed.

"I'm good. We're gearing up for another show next weekend. What have you been up to?"

"Same stuff, different month. . .Hey, I was wondering if you might be able to get away for awhile, come out and see me."

Jess grinned–they were definitely on the same wavelength. "I've been considering it, but I'll have to wait until after the Brandford Classic. Faith needs my help."

"When is that?"

Third week in September, then I'll be free."

He sounded disappointed. "I was hoping to see you sooner."

She smiled, delighted by his interest, and energized by her feelings of optimism about the future.

"Well, maybe. I'll see how it goes."

After hanging up, she gazed out the window at Faith in the arena and her enthusiasm faded. Her partner could be the biggest stumbling block to success.

Jess switched off the light in the office and walked slowly through the quiet barn, thinking about all the directions her life had taken lately. She stepped into Casey's stall, and the mare chuckled softly, eagerly nuzzling Jess's shirt, searching for treats.

Jess offered a handful of carrot pieces. "Here you go, Sweetie. Did you miss me?"

Casey bobbed her head, then checked the pockets again. Love filled every nook and cranny in Jess's heart, and she stroked the mare's neck, finger-combing the long mane as she murmured to her old friend.

"We're gonna be fine, baby. Mama fixed it. You'll never have to leave this place, I promise."

Casey's muscles tensed and her ears pricked forward, intent on some small sound Jess couldn't hear. Suddenly, the mare moved away and swung her body around so she faced the stall door. Jess followed her gaze, but saw nothing.

A second later, Mustafa peeked into the stall, his dark eyes intense with concentration.

"What is it, Mustafa?"

His brown face remained expressionless. "Nothing. I am returning a halter to the hook."

He turned and walked away.

A cold, sinking sensation flooded the pit of her stomach. *How long had he been standing there?* The men in her barn were too damned quiet, almost invisible, and their presence was beginning to unnerve her.

She latched the stall door and called out. “Faith? Where are you?”

Overhead, she heard the thump of boots and Faith’s muffled reply. Her partner stepped off the ladder as Jess entered the feed room.

“When you’re finished, come on over to the house. I’ll make us some lunch.”

Faith tilted her head and narrowed her eyes. “Is this a come-to-Jesus meeting?”

Jess nodded and Faith’s shoulders slumped.

In the spacious kitchen, Jess concentrated on opening a can of tuna, trying to will away her nagging anxiety. Her world was back on track, but she still felt vulnerable. The postcard from Howard caught her eye and she picked it up. The lodge looked so serene, so inviting. *God, I wish I were there right now.*

Faith arrived, and her subdued demeanor gave Jess some hope that the conversation would be civil. Lately, it didn’t take much to set her friend off.

Faith took a long drink of iced tea, put the glass down on the counter, and looked up. “What’s the plan?”

Jess set down the plate of sandwiches, and settled onto a stool. “Since we’re fully into show season, it doesn’t make sense for you to take six weeks off, so I’d like you to move in here with me until after Brandford. Then we’ll close up shop while you’re on leave. We can start the winter season fresh. Okay?”

Faith’s eyebrows came together, and Jess braced herself for an argument.

Faith’s features relaxed. “You’re right. I have a harder time being good when I’m alone.” Her lower lip quivered, and her voice dropped to a whisper. “Thank you, Jessie.”

Jess slipped off the stool and wrapped her arms around Faith’s shoulders. Hugging her tightly, Jess blinked back her own tears.

“Forever friends, remember?”

A sharp rap on the back door interrupted the emotional moment.

Jess started toward the door and spotted Mona through the

window. “Now what the hell does *she* want?”

Mona’s face reflected uneasiness. “Hi, Jess. Sorry to bother you, but I was wondering–”

The front doorbell rang, and Jess turned. “Faith, see who that is. . .Sorry, Mona, you were saying?”

“May I come in?”

Jess hesitated, then stepped back. “Sure, what’s the problem?”

Behind her, Faith’s voice quavered with alarm.

“Jessie, it’s the FBI.”

Ж

# *Twenty-Six*

Jess stared at the two men standing in the living room. They weren't wearing the stereotypical black suit she'd have expected. In their blue jeans, plaid shirts, and work boots, they looked more like construction workers.

The taller of the two stepped forward, offering his identification. "Miss Rayder, I'm Agent Peterson, and this is Agent Kerr."

A discrete cough reminded her about Mona, and she turned back to the stall cleaner.

"Can we talk later? I need to–"

Mona pulled out a small black wallet, then flashed a shiny badge and an apologetic smile. "Sorry."

"What's going on?"

Agent Kerr answered. "We have some questions about the two foreign employees who work here."

*Oh God, now what?* She glanced at Faith's frightened expression. "Yes, what about them?"

"Agent Johnson has been monitoring their activities since they arrived. Would you tell us how you came to hire these men?"

"They're relatives of one of Faith's students. They needed work, we needed help."

"Had you ever met Hafez al-Nabi or Mustafa al-Ani before they came to work here?"

Jess shook her head.

"Do you know Samir Mahfood?"

Jess's breath came in short, thin gasps, making it difficult to control the timbre of her voice. "His daughter is a student here. You know, I think we have a right to know why you're asking all these questions."

Agent Peterson gestured toward the living room. "Could we sit down? This might take a while."

Jess sat next to Faith on the couch, the men chose armchairs, and Mona remained standing. Agent Peterson leaned forward, a friendly smile crinkling the skin around his brown eyes.

"Ladies, we don't mean to worry you, but we'd really appreciate any help you can give us in this investigation."

Jess studied him for a moment. He had the look of a man who'd seen too much mayhem in his life. A quick glance at Kerr gave her the same impression, but the burly agent's face sported the scowl of a cynic.

She nodded. "We'll do whatever we can. Now, what's this about?"

Mona cleared her throat. "Hafez and Mustafa are possible suspects in a terrorist execution cell we think is developing here in New England–"

Faith gasped. "I knew it!"

Mona nodded. "The Bureau's been watching Samir Mahfood since 9/11. It appears he might be the organizer for the cell."

Ice moved through Jess's chest. Of all the things she'd considered about Samir, being a terrorist hadn't been one of them.

"How *could* he be? He's lived here for at least twenty years!"

Kerr smirked at her apparent naiveté. "Radicals in the Middle East are well-known for recruiting ardent young men to serve the cause. They spend years grooming them to infiltrate western society. We think Mahfood is the central figure in a sleeper cell that could be called upon at any time."

The idea that she'd been close to him–even friendly–frightened Jess half out of her wits. Her thoughts raced as answers appeared to past questions. Like, where did all his money come from? Carpets? Not likely. Paying cash for everything, buying expensive horses without batting an eyelid.

Mona's words crackled through the air. "There's something else–I found evidence of weapons in your hayloft."

Faith began to weep, and Jess simply gaped while Mona continued.

"I used an electronic sniffer up there one afternoon, and it registered quite high, but Hafez surprised me before I could locate the source of the reading."

Jess's fright grew, and her own voice sounded hollow in her head. "Did you go back later?"

"No, I need your help for that. We don't want the suspects to know we're watching them."

The three agents discussed how best to search the hayloft, then Mona turned back to Jess.

"You'll need to send both of them into town for something, an errand that will take them away for at least an hour."

"When do you want this to happen?"

"Today. Peterson and Kerr will return to Hartford, and I'll carry on as usual."

Agent Peterson cleared his throat. "We've devised a cover story that will allow us to come and go freely." His expression grew serious. "I noticed the tarp on one of your buildings. Leaky roof?"

Jess nodded. "Storm damage. The landlord was going to fix it as soon as the weather dried out." *At least he was, until we got behind with the rent.*

Peterson nodded. "Okay, anything else you might plan to build?"

Faith finally regained her composure. "We've talked about putting a roof over the outdoor arena. It gets awfully hot out there in July."

Peterson made a note, then looked up. "Good, that works. We'll come in as contractors who are evaluating the project. That should give us a lot of flexibility. From now on, unless the suspects are off the premises, we'll all meet outdoors somewhere."

Jess cocked her head. "What's wrong with right here in my house?"

Kerr snorted. "Those guys are watching us as closely as we're watching them. Unless you're in the habit of entertaining bunches of people in the middle of a workday, we need to make our presence here seem as normal as possible."

Peterson nodded. "And you'll need to play the part. Be excited. You're finally getting some additions to the place, and so on. Remember, they see everything you do."

The memory of Mustafa's dark face peeking over the stall door sent a shiver racing over Jess's shoulders. She nodded, then looked directly at Mona.

"Why did you start watching *us*?"

"Samir's movements changed. He deviated from his normal routine, started coming out here–ostensibly to watch his daughter ride."

Faith's tone was sharp. "She *does* ride–and she's very good, too!"

Jess heard the disappointment behind the words. They both knew Dania would probably never ride again.

Peterson spoke up. "Okay, but at about the same time, we intercepted a telephone conversation between Samir and one of the suspects. Something was happening, and we couldn't let Samir out of our sight for even a minute."

Mona turned to Jess. "I'll go out and start bringing in horses. When you've gotten rid of them, come get me."

Samir rolled the prayer beads through his fingers, his mind far from prayer as he stared through the windshield at nothing. Mustafa didn't like the tense atmosphere at the farm. Both he and Hafez had the feeling Faith Angelo wanted them to leave, but Samir had assured them the situation was under control, and had firmly reinforced his instructions to maintain a low profile.

His friends at the café were obsessed by the massive increase in security, and widespread public paranoia, as the anniversary of September Eleventh approached. The Americans feared some sort of retribution for the war in Iraq. What did they expect? America–the most powerful nation in the world–dropping bombs on starving Afghans, razing Iraqi villages without thought to innocent women and children. The United States would reap the harvest she'd sown.

Samir thought about his recent trip to New York, where he'd personally seen and felt the antagonistic attitude of the citizens of that broken city. In Hartford, his situation was good. Respected and well-liked, his participation in the community and his generosity to charities gave him stature. He felt comfortable and secure. Manhattan had been quite another matter.

During the two-day visit, he'd felt suspicious eyes following him wherever he'd gone. A chilly distance had separated him from shopkeepers and pedestrians. Even his meeting with Shafik Diab, an Egyptian oriental carpet importer, had been tense–the man acted nervous, as though he feared surveillance of his meetings with other Middle Easterners.

*No matter. None of them are important. The Truth will be visited upon all of them. Allaahu akbar.*

He thought about Easton Ridge again and smiled. Soon, he would have the final piece of the plan.

# *Twenty-Seven*

Faith's color had returned, and her eyes snapped with indignation. "I can't believe this! I *knew* there was something about those two!"

Jess shook her head. "*Them!* I can't believe *Samir's* involved in this."

"Jessie, what are we gonna do?"

"I don't know yet, but one thing's for sure–this is really nasty stuff. I think it's time to get some legal advice."

Faith left the room, and Jess battled with her emotions as she stared at the phone with unseeing eyes. Disappointment grew in her heart. Howard was the glimmer of excitement in her life, the promise of a bright future. Asking him to haul her out of shark-infested waters would destroy the sense of mystery between them. Her eyes burned. *Not exactly what I intended.*

She heard the toilet flush, then footsteps on the hardwood floor in the hall. Faith entered the kitchen, and Jess tried for an optimistic smile.

"You feel okay? Can I get you anything?"

"Yeah, vodka tonic, maybe a gun."

Jess's control snapped. "You can't act like this! I need your help."

"I know, I'm sorry. . .Did you call Howard?"

"No, I want to go over the situation with you again before I talk to anyone." She leaned her elbows on the breakfast bar and cradled her head in her hands. "I can't fucking believe this."

"Wow, two phone conversations in the same day! You must

be missin' me."

Howard's voice bounded through the phone, filling Jess with both joy and dread. She wondered if his happy greeting would be the last personal exchange she'd ever have with him.

"Howard, something very serious is going on here. We're really scared."

Concern replaced the jovial tone. "Tell me."

She sketched out the tale, describing her financial problems, Samir's involvement, and the poker game, but leaving out the source of her stake. He listened quietly, only interrupting once to ask for clarification on something. When she'd reached the end of the horror story, he cleared his throat, and she prepared herself for referral to a local attorney.

"Jess, don't discuss this with anyone again. I'll fly out early in the morning. Go ahead with the FBI plan to send the suspects on an errand, but do *not* talk to the agents again–just say you've consulted an attorney. Understand?"

Her throat felt so tight she could barely swallow, and her voice came out almost a whimper. "Yes. Howard…?"

"It'll be okay, hon. Stay calm. I'll see you in the morning."

Jess hung up the phone and turned to Faith. "You go on home. Howard will be here tomorrow."

Faith's voice rose. "But, Jess, I want–"

"Faith! It's your afternoon off. We're supposed to carry on as usual. Go home, I'll call you. And stay–"

"Don't even start, Jessie! You think I'm stupid?"

"No, I don't think you're stupid, but we can't afford even a tiny mistake right now."

Faith spun on her heel and marched out the kitchen door, slamming it behind her.

Jess couldn't erase the thoughts that her home and life had been invaded, her privacy penetrated by the very people who'd devastated America less than four years previous. Walking woodenly toward the barn, she wondered how she'd be able to speak normally to Hafez or Mustafa, when all she really wanted to do was kill them. *If I ever needed a poker face, it's now.*

Casey called out as Jess moved down the aisle, the shrill whinny a reminder of how much was at stake. Jess slid the stall door aside and wrapped her arms around Casey's warm neck, inhaling her unique scent, and sinking into fear.

A few minutes later, Jess checked the inventory log, searching for something that would require a lengthy trip. Saddle blankets. She'd been meaning to order new ones. She placed the order with a large tack store in Enfield, then left the office in search of the nephews.

At the far end of the aisle, Mona led a bay gelding into a stall, but Jess heard no other sounds of activity. *That's strange, the guys are usually busy with the evening feed by now.* An uneasy feeling crawled into her chest. Continuing down the aisle, she approached the north doors that faced the carriage house. Maybe they were on a prayer break. As she passed the feed room, she heard muffled voices. She stepped inside the empty room to locate the source. Hafez and Mustafa were up in the hayloft and, given the intensity and emotion in their voices, it sounded as though they were having an argument.

Jess pictured them organizing their weaponry, donning fatigues, taking her hostage. She took a deep breath to dispel the disturbing images, then moved to the base of the ladder.

"Hafez?"

The conversation stopped abruptly, then a brown face appeared in the hole directly above her.

"Yes?"

"I need you guys to run an errand for me."

He nodded and disappeared, and Jess stepped away from the ladder. The voices overhead now murmured softly and indistinctly, the tone much subdued. A minute later, both men climbed down the ladder, and fear oozed into Jess's chest.

She stood two feet from the enemy.

"I have a large order to be picked up at Ranchero Tack in Enfield." She willed her fingers to stop trembling as she handed the purchase order to Hafez. "Do you know where that is?"

He nodded. "We have a map."

"Good. It'll take you a couple of hours, so you'd better leave now. Mona and I will finish feeding."

The men nodded and left the room, not speaking to each other on their way out. Something in their manner told Jess she'd surprised them in the middle of an important conversation, and a chill shuddered across her shoulders. She stepped into the tack room and moved to the window that faced the front of the building. Five minutes later, the van pulled slowly around the corner and headed down the driveway. Jess watched until the vehicle turned onto the highway and disappeared.

"Are they gone?"

Jess jumped, smacking her elbow on the windowsill. "Dammit, Mona! Quit sneaking up on me!"

Mona's crooked grin broke the tension. "Goes with the territory. How long will they be gone?"

A deep breath quelled the nausea rising in Jess's throat. "At least three hours."

She started for the door, but Mona reached out and touched her arm.

"Jess, this probably sounds corny, but I want you to know how much I've enjoyed being here, even though it was under false pretenses."

Jess scowled. "I should have suspected something earlier. I watched you ride one afternoon. . .you're too good for a beginner."

Mona looked embarrassed. "Yeah. Before I joined the Bureau, I rode with the NYPD mounted patrol in Central Park." Her face darkened. "After the Trade Towers, I decided to dedicate my life to wiping out these bastards!"

Mona's vehemence touched Jess. She hadn't fully considered the effects of the terrorist attacks on others and, for a moment, she sympathized with the woman who'd become so involved in the future of Easton Ridge.

Mona turned away. "I need to get upstairs. Keep a lookout, and let me know when they come back."

ꭗ

## *Twenty-Eight*

The hands on the clock slowed to a crawl, and a dull headache thumped at the base of Jess's skull. Alone in the office, she thought about the events of the past week, and a hollow feeling gathered in her chest. Could she have prevented this mess if she'd been paying closer attention? Her brain whirled with the finances, her precarious health, Faith's drinking problem–distractions that had required inordinate amounts of mental energy.

She shook her head and exhaled. How could she have been so stupid to take those men in without checking them out? She'd sidestepped a basic business practice, and now she and Faith were paying for it. Moving to the window, she scanned the road, her thoughts scrambling to justify her actions. A whole new world lay out there, and though she'd always trusted her instincts, and believed in everyone's equality, that was clearly not enough. America had never been attacked on home soil, and the experience had spawned an unfamiliar set of emotions and attitudes.

Samir and the nephews had slipped into her life, and she'd politely held the door open for them.

She folded back a clean sheet on a yellow legal pad, and began making notes in chronological order, intent on remembering every detail. A muffled sound outside the door caught her attention, and she quickly slipped the legal pad under a stack of papers on the desk as Mona stepped into the office.

"Damn, it's hot up there." She swiped her forehead with her sleeve, and exhaled sharply.

Jess disregarded Howard's warning, her curiosity too strong to remain silent. "Did you find anything?"

"Yeah, two bags of grain with parts for a hand-held rocket launcher."

The words ricocheted through Jess's head, and she struggled to breathe through paralyzed lungs. The mysterious grain order–right under her nose.

Mona's eyes narrowed. "What is it?"

"Nothing. . .I just remembered seeing some spilled grain in the loft a couple of days ago. I thought it was mice."

Mona pulled out a small notebook. "What day was that? What were you doing up there?"

Jess's words snapped with irritation. "I *do* work here!"

Mona's jaw hardened, and Jess realized she'd overreacted.

"Mona, I've called an attorney. I don't want to discuss this any further until he gets here."

Mona cocked her head, her eyes reflecting surprise. "Oh? Why do you think you need one?"

"I just. . .Jeez, this terrorism thing is more than I can handle alone."

"Yeah, it's scary. . .Do you mind if I check out the carriage house?"

"No, of course not. Do whatever you have to."

Thirty minutes later, Mona reappeared. "The room's cleaner than a monk's cell. Now, I just need to figure out a way to get inside their vehicle." She thought for a moment. "When will your lawyer be here?"

"In the morning."

Mona glanced at the window and her features tensed. "Here come the boys. It's business as usual. Call me on my cell when your attorney arrives."

She left the room, and Jess's stomach knotted. The wheels were in motion and she wished to God she knew where they were headed.

She gazed at Naomi Morton's receipt on the desk, and feelings of dread seeped into her thoughts. Before this ended, she might have to admit what she'd done.

She folded her page of notes four times, and stuffed the wad into the pocket of her jeans. Heading toward the tack room, she found it hard to act nonchalant. Every step echoed loudly, her face felt wooden, her movements robotic.

Mustafa and Hafez were unloading the saddle blankets.

She cleared her throat to announce her presence. "Just pile them on one of those tack trunks. I'll put them away later."

Hafez nodded. "Is there anything else you want us to do?"

Jess shook her head, wanting nothing except to run them out of her barn.

He bobbed his head. *"Ma'assalama."*

After the men crossed the yard to their quarters, Jess slid the heavy barn door closed, and headed back to the house.

Howard phoned at nine the next morning.

"Hi, it's me. I'm at the airport in Hartford. I'll rent a car and see you in about an hour. Meet me at your house, not the barn. Oh, and Faith needs to be there, too."

Jess set the phone slowly back on the hook. Howard's usual mischievous lilt had disappeared, replaced by an edgy tone that conjured up images of high-visibility court cases, power plays, and posturing before a jury. Suddenly, she felt invaded and vulnerable. *Bugs. The place is probably peppered with them.* Her indignation surfaced. *Mona's been here for weeks, with freedom to be anywhere in the barn. Dammit! That stuff is supposed to be illegal...* A quick memory of something stirred in her head, an article she'd read about changes in surveillance techniques and capabilities since 9/11. She exhaled sharply. *No point in worrying about it now. I have bigger problems to solve.*

ꭗ

# *Twenty-Nine*

Howard stepped through the door, and Jess took a quick breath. Dressed in an expensive, dark blue three-piece suit and crisp white shirt, he appeared to be all business. Except for his warm smile.

"Hello, Jess." He kissed her on the cheek, then turned and tossed a brown leather briefcase onto the couch.

She closed the door, savoring the light tingle where his lips had brushed her skin.

"How was your flight?"

*Good grief, is that the best you can manage?*

"Fairly good, a little bumpy over Kansas. When will Faith be here?"

A small twinge of disappointment sang through Jess's head. He'd obviously already focused on the challenge of her circumstances.

"I'll call her in a little bit. . .how are things out West?"

He turned, uneasiness flickering through his eyes. He stepped up close and took hold of her shoulders.

"Jessie, we have to stay focused." He brushed a strand of hair off her forehead. "This is a deadly situation–we can talk about personal things later."

She nodded, wanting to freeze the moment so she could enjoy it a little longer.

He released her shoulders. "Are you okay?"

Her voice caught. "I'm fine."

"Okay, let's get organized." He picked up the briefcase and moved toward the breakfast bar.

Tension tightened her throat. "The FBI agent wanted me to call when you got here."

"I'll call them after I've heard your story and figured out where we are. From now on, I'll do the talking–you have to trust me."

The doorbell rang and he looked out the window. "It's your partner."

In moments, Jess's confidence plummeted. Faith's eyes were bright–too bright–her smile too sassy for the circumstances. An alarm went off in Jess's head, and a quick look at Howard's face revealed that he recognized the signs, too.

Faith sauntered to the couch and dropped into the deep cushions. "I'm ready to catch terrorists!"

Howard sounded disgusted. "Jess, why don't you make some coffee–we have a long morning ahead of us."

Ten minutes later, Jess's story began with the blizzard that had set the financial downslide in motion.

She shook her head. "We simply could never catch up. The cost of running this business and maintaining twenty-two horses is astronomical."

Howard scribbled something, then looked up. "I can imagine. I'll need a complete breakdown of the expenses, loans, income."

"What for?"

He frowned a little. "I need to know *everything*, all the details."

She took a deep breath, then hurtled into the saga of how Easton Ridge had met the enemy.

"Samir seemed nice in the beginning. I certainly had no reason to distrust him."

Faith snorted. "I didn't like him *or* his wife from the day I met them." She paused and her voice softened. "Dania's a nice little kid, though–damned good rider." She drained her coffee mug, then stood up, flashing a crooked smile. "Back in a minute."

As soon as she'd closed the bathroom door, Howard exhaled sharply. "This is not good, Jess. When did she start drinking again?"

"I honestly don't know. . .I've been so wrapped up in my own problems. I feel terrible–"

"No, don't beat yourself up. You're not her keeper." His voice dropped, thick with concern. "You both need your wits about you this afternoon. I'm concerned that if the feds think you won't help them, they'll try to implicate you both as conspirators. They can frighten you enough to get you to cooperate fully. They play this game to win." He winked. "You of all people should understand gamesmanship."

His attempt at humor thudded through Jess's chest. In minutes, she would humiliate herself in front of the two most important people in her life.

Faith returned, her step less jaunty, her face pale. She settled on the couch, avoiding eye contact.

Howard rose and stretched. "My turn." He headed toward the hall.

Faith's voice was barely audible. "I'm really sorry."

Jess patted her knee. "I know. Let's see if we can get through the afternoon, then I'll make up the guestroom." She met Faith's sad gaze. "I don't want to be alone, either."

Howard picked up his legal pad. "Okay, I want all the details of every day since Mrs. Mahfood came to the stable."

Faith remained silent while Jess related Samir's apparent empathy, and his offer to help with the chores.

Howard sounded skeptical. "Didn't you think that was unusual? A middle-aged businessman interested in barn work?"

"Sort of." Her irritation flared. "But, hell, I'm not in the habit of second-guessing people's motives." She sighed. "Besides, we *really* needed the help."

"Okay, you mentioned an expensive horse for the little girl. How much did they pay?"

*Dear God, here it comes.* Jess cast a sidelong look at her partner. Faith's eyelids drooped as she fought the sedative effects of alcohol.

"Eighty thousand."

Howard whistled. "For a *horse?*"

Faith snapped to attention, her tone indignant. "For a *very good* horse! Equestrian athletes don't ride thousand-dollar nags."

Jess grinned. "Get Faith on her soapbox and she's a terror."

Howard chuckled. "Okay, I believe you. Did they pay cash for the animal?"

Jess swallowed hard. "Just the down-payment. Ten percent."

Howard shook his head while he wrote. "Eight grand, just like that. I'm in the wrong business." He looked up. "I guess I'll need to talk to the woman they bought the horse from. She'll be part of this investigation, too."

Panic roared into Jess's chest and she fought for the next breath.

"No, she's not involved. In a horse sale like this, the trainer acts as agent for the client. When the buyer is ready, the down-payment goes to the trainer, who then deals with the seller." She glanced at Faith, who nodded. "For that service, the trainer gets a commission on the sale price."

"How much?"

"Usually fifteen-percent."

Howard's eyebrows came together. "That's a hefty amount–enough to get you out of trouble."

Faith jumped in. "Oh, we don't get the commission until the contract is fully paid."

Howard's eyes narrowed, and Jess could see the wheels turning. She braced herself for his next question.

"When did you give the down-payment to the seller?"

She looked away. "Yesterday."

Faith sounded disgusted. "Can you believe the post office lost the check? Poor Jessie had to make a special trip to Waterbury to give Naomi the money."

Jess exhaled silently. She'd forgotten about the post-office cover-up story.

Howard scribbled something, then looked up. "When did Samir approach you about hiring his nephews?"

"The weekend of the Springfield show. . .actually, the day before I met you for dinner at Seven Rivers."

A brief shadow flickered through Howard's expression, then he nodded. "Did he say why he was being so magnanimous?"

"He told me he knew we were having money problems." She shook her head. "I think I might have been indiscreet at some point during a conversation. He also knew we do all the chores by ourselves. He needed something to occupy his nephews for the summer. Anyway, I thought he was just being helpful."

Howard looked at his watch. "Okay, let's talk about the poker game, then I'll call the agent." He consulted his notes. "You said Samir showed up at the game. Did he appear to know you'd be there?"

"No, I think he was as startled as I was. . .but I could be wrong. I was entirely focused on winning a pile of money."

"How did he act?"

Jess rankled at the memory. "He was patronizing, treated me like the hired help. . .macho men-stuff in front of the sheikh. We didn't speak the rest of the evening."

Howard set the legal pad aside, and crossed his legs. The shift in body language sent a warning through Jess's head that she wouldn't like whatever was coming next.

"In your current financial circumstances, how could you afford to get into a private game with high-rollers?"

Jess met his gaze. *Please, please, don't go there.*

Faith sat up straight. "That's right! I never even thought about that. How *did* you get the money for a poker game?"

Jess stared at a small stain on the carpet. "The down-payment on Dania's horse."

No one made a sound, then Faith jumped up and leaped away from the couch, as though she might become tainted. Jess closed her eyes at the outrage in her partner's voice.

"Are you kidding me? You used *client* money? You let everybody think the check was *lost in the mail*?" Her voice rose. "You're a damned liar and a hypocrite!"

Jess's chest tightened with remorse, and she could barely breathe. "We were out of time. I couldn't think of any other way to save us."

Faith's cheeks flushed, blotchy and ugly. Her voice snarled. "Did you ever once consider that you might have *lost*? *Really* flushed us down the toilet?" She jammed her hands on her hips. "I hate you!"

Howard lurched out of the chair. "Hey, calm down! You girls have more serious things to worry about than this."

The phone rang, and he leveled his tone. "Faith, you keep your personal problems out of this meeting, you understand? Don't offer anything. Answer the questions without embellishments or opinions."

Her shoulders slumped, and she looked like she might cry. She threw one last venomous glance at Jess, then nodded silently.

Jess picked up the phone in the kitchen.

Mona's tone was crisp. "Jess, are you about ready? We need to talk again, but not at your place. Meet the guys in the open arena."

)(

# *Thirty*

Jess threw a nervous glance toward the barn on the walk across the driveway. In the arena, Peterson appeared to be taking measurements with some sort of electronic device. A black pickup truck loaded with shovels, wheelbarrows, and other tools was parked next to the fence. A sign on the side of the cab read, "Crawford Construction." She looked toward the carriage house where the nephews knelt on their prayer rugs. *Fanatics.*

Howard's voice intruded, low and urgent. "Quit looking around for them. You'll raise a red flag."

Agent Peterson smiled. "Morning, great day, huh?" He shook Howard's hand. "John Crawford." He stepped back. "Our field teams have swept your property for listening devices, and I confirmed the immediate area when I drove in."

Jess gasped, and the agent threw her a warning look. "However, we must all be very careful to maintain the image, at all times, that we are discussing the construction project."

He gestured toward the covered arena. "This is a dicey situation, and the charade must be believable, or we'll lose these guys." He picked up a large roll of paper and handed it to Howard. "Since you're playing the architect, I'll let you wave this around."

Another truck pulled up, and Agent Kerr climbed out. A minute later, he pushed back his ball-cap and stuck out his hand, his voice low and condescending.

"Well, well, if it isn't Mr. London, protector of the masses. I thought you gave up and crawled off to Timbuktu."

Howard's expression revealed nothing as he extended his hand. "Hello, Kerr. It's a real pleasure to see you again, too."

The stocky agent shook Howard's hand, then moved to the end of the enclosure. Peterson followed him, and they started measuring the length of the arena.

The veiled hostility did nothing to bolster Jess's confidence. "What was *that* about?"

Howard shook his head. "Long story. I'll tell you later."

After a couple of minutes, the agents returned to the group, and Howard unrolled the large sheet of sketches.

Peterson turned his back to the barn. "We'll look at this for a minute or so, then we can talk."

Howard's tone was firm. "My clients would like to help you, if they can, but first I need to know the details of your interest in them."

Kerr muttered, "Always the hero."

Peterson nodded. "Mr. London, your clients aren't under suspicion and, yes, we definitely want their cooperation in routing out this group." He pointed at something on the drawings, then picked up a clipboard. "Just to be safe, keep your backs to the building, in case they're watching through binoculars."

Jess felt horribly invaded.

Peterson continued. "In relation to Samir Mahfood's first visit to the stable, how long afterward did Hafez and Mustafa arrive?"

"About two weeks.

"Did you ever overhear them talking about anything other than their work?"

"I wouldn't know. They always spoke Arabic to each other."

Faith chimed in. "I heard Mustafa talking on a cellphone out behind the barn. I didn't understand him, but his tone of voice scared me."

"What do you mean?"

"He was real excited, almost like he was high. It made my skin crawl."

Peterson wrote something, then pointed toward the bleachers. "After Samir's first visit here, when did you see him again?"

Jess's gaze automatically followed his gesture, but she felt awkward with the charade. "Two days later. He came to my office, said he wanted to spend more time here."

A quick look passed between Kerr and Peterson. "Did he give

a reason?"

"Something about enjoying the freedom of living in America."

Kerr's jaw tightened. "Bastard," he muttered.

Peterson consulted his notes. "When did you see him next?"

Faith snorted. "He showed up the following afternoon, dressed like a Hollywood cowboy."

Jess suppressed a grin at the memory. "He came to help us clean stalls. I thought it was a generous offer."

"Didn't you think that was a bit odd?"

"Yeah, but he knew we didn't have any barn help, and like I said–"

Howard coughed. "Jess's opinions aren't relevant." He pointed toward the side of the arena. "I'd like a short break to confer with my clients."

Peterson set aside the clipboard, and Kerr pulled a pack of cigarettes from his pocket.

Howard led the girls to the fence. "Okay, I think the questioning is about to get tougher. Do either of you remember anything that might be vital to their case?"

Faith nodded. "When he was asking about conversations, I almost said something about Mustafa throwing the phone away, but I remembered what you said."

Howard cocked his head. "What do you mean?"

"You said not to add anything. Just answer the questions."

He pursed his lips and thought for a moment. "I see. Okay, we'll give them that tidbit when we go back over there." He turned to Jess. "Do you have anything further to add?"

"No, I'm afraid I basically ignored the nephews. I had other things on my mind."

She glanced at Faith and saw the loathing in her eyes. *God, will I ever be able to heal this wound?*

The agents had unrolled the drawings and appeared to be examining them in great detail.

Howard opened the conversation.

"John, through a misunderstanding of my counsel, Faith left something out of her story."

Faith's voice shook while she related the strange incident

behind the barn. Peterson scribbled furiously in his notebook, then looked up.

"We need to see exactly where this took place. Jess, can you get the suspects away from the farm again for a couple of hours?"

"I'll try."

Kerr pulled out a cellphone and stepped away from the group. Jess glanced at her watch. The interview had already consumed about twenty minutes.

Peterson resumed the questioning. "Okay, after Samir showed up to clean stalls, when did you see him again?"

"At a horse show in Springfield the following Thursday. He and his wife came to watch their daughter ride."

"Did he talk to you about anything other than his daughter's lessons?"

"No, but he came to the farm the next afternoon. He seemed to know about our financial problems. That's when he offered his nephews to–"

"Did you *tell* him about your finances?"

"No, but he did have some details. . ." Without thinking, she cast a worried look at Howard.

Peterson's tone held a warning. "Watch your facial expressions. You're happy about building a new arena, remember?"

She struggled with the masquerade. "How would Samir find out about those things?"

"A private eye could tell him anything he wanted to know."

She didn't respond, horrified by the thought of someone nosing through her personal agonies. Rage filled every pore and, for a moment, she wanted nothing more than to see Samir burn in hell.

Peterson's voice derailed the thought. "Did Hafez or Mustafa ever do anything else unusual, that you can remember?"

"No, they stayed to themselves, didn't speak unless spoken to, kept regular hours, prayed all the time."

Kerr stepped back into the conversation circle. "Tell us how you got involved in a private poker game with Sheikh Mohammed."

A sick feeling churned through Jess's gut. "Is he part of this, too?"

"There's a possible connection, but we can't prove it yet."

She fought the rising nausea. She'd spent hours in the midst of those men, handled all that tainted money, carried it home to salve her wounds–money that had circulated amongst God-only-knows what criminals and thugs. She'd been gambling with the enemy.

"Jess? You were going to explain how you came to be included in the poker game?"

She blinked, dragging herself back from the edge. "The casino manager approached me. She wanted another person to round out the game. She'd seen me play."

Faith snorted and muttered, "A nice little secret life."

Peterson continued. "Did you know Samir Mahfood would be there?"

Jess shook her head. In retrospect, she'd unwittingly allowed herself to become a pawn in a terrifying game of skill.

Feeling she had nothing to lose, she arrowed a question at Peterson.

"Which one of the players was *your* guy?"

The agent grinned. "Jimmy Kee."

"Figures. He wasn't much of a poker player."

Howard cleared his throat loudly, but Jess ignored him.

"You already have an eye-witness account of the game. Why are you asking *me?*"

"*Jess!*"

Peterson shook his head. "It's okay, London. She's right." He smiled. "I'm just interested in your observations of the evening. Did the other two Middle Eastern players do anything that seemed odd?"

Jess hesitated. The Asian undercover agent would have been more aware of behaviors and nuances than she, and would surely have submitted a full report. Caution slipped into her thoughts and she threw Howard a quick look before answering.

"I just concentrated on the game."

Peterson seemed to accept the dodge. Pocketing his pen, he gazed around the property. "What does it cost to run a place like this?"

"What does that have to do with the investigation?"

Peterson smiled. "Nothing. Just curious."

Howard pressed. "I'm asking again–are my clients under suspicion?"

"Mr. London, a recreational gambler–especially a woman–would have a hard time getting into a private game like that, without some inside help. Pretty amazing coincidence, don't you think?"

"If you want their help, you'd better take another tack."

Peterson nodded, then turned to Jess. "You coordinate with Mona to get the suspects off the property. A search team is standing by."

After the agents drove away, the tension in the air began to fade.

Jess's voice cracked. "That's the hardest thing I've ever done. Where do you think this is headed?"

Howard gazed at her for a minute, then shook his head and crossed his arms. "I'm not going to kid you–it'll get worse before it gets better. These guys are bulldogs–they've obviously been gathering information on this group for a long time. Unfortunately, you've become part of the process. Right now, they're verifying each piece of data, connecting it to other pieces, trying to find a pattern, a loop-hole–anything that will strengthen their position."

Faith exhaled sharply. "Do you really think they'll try to implicate us?"

"No, I don't. But for sure, the more cooperative you are, the better you look."

He straightened his tie. "I have some things to do in Hartford, but I'll be back later. Good luck this afternoon, and be careful–both of you."

Faith headed for the gate. "I'm going to the barn."

Jess started to follow. "Faith, wait–we need to talk. I want–"

Faith whirled on her heel. "This is no longer about what *you* want, Jess. You've hidden things from me, lied to me, run the show *your* way. I've had enough. I have plenty of my own problems without being caught up in yours." She slid the gate latch open. "And don't bother with the guestroom–I'm going home."

Her boots crunched across the gravel, and a numbing weariness seeped into Jess's body.

Howard touched her shoulder. "Once you get this phone-in-the-woods thing sorted out, you *have* to sit down with her and draw up a truce. She'll never cooperate in her current frame of mind."

Jess turned and searched his face. “Do you think what I did was so terrible?”

He smiled wryly. “Not really, but you took a helluva risk.”

# *Thirty-One*

Jess found Mustafa working on one of the pasture fences.

"When you're finished there, I need some supplies picked up for the horse show this weekend."

He answered without looking up. "Yes, Miss."

Fifteen minutes later, Jess looked over the new purchase orders. Fourteen bales of straw, twelve 8-foot poles, jump cups, eight potted trees, and twenty-five small shrubs. If she didn't place the order ahead of time, it would take the suppliers a while to get the items together.

Mona stepped into the office. "How soon can you get rid of those two?"

"Shortly. I'm sending them to Enfield to pick up some stuff for the show. Between the stable supply store and the landscaping outfit, plus an hour's drive each direction, they'll be tied up for at least four hours."

"Good. I'll be in the tack room."

While she waited, Jess tried to concentrate on what needed to be done for the show, but her brain wouldn't function. Her foremost thoughts centered on the unfolding intrigue, but she could not imagine how the situation would evolve.

Mustafa appeared in the doorway. "I am finished."

She handed him the keys to her old pickup, a relic from the first years at Easton Ridge. "Take the farm truck. The poles won't fit in your van."

From somewhere outside, she heard Hafez's excited voice. Mustafa left the office, and Jess quickly stepped to the window. Hafez stood beside the van, talking on the phone, his face intense with excitement, or some deeper emotion. Anxiety stirred through Jess's head. *Maybe he's using this trip to set up a meeting with Samir, or someone else in the network.* The gravity of the situation assaulted her again. Seeing parts of the big picture moving doggedly toward the construction of terror, she finally accepted the importance of her role–one that would test her instincts to the limit.

Mona's voice interrupted the solemn introspection.

"Are they gone?"

"Yeah, they just turned onto the highway."

Mona whipped out her cellphone and punched auto-dial.

"Pete? They just left. Do you have them on the monitor?" She frowned, her voice rising. "What do you mean? How could you miss them?"

Jess gasped. "Mona, wait–they took the farm truck, not the van."

"Oh, shit! Pete? See if one of the guys can catch up with a blue eighty-nine Ford pickup."

She pocketed the phone and scowled at Jess. "I wish you'd told me you were going to send them in the truck. You really screwed this up."

"Wait just a damned minute! I'm doing everything I can to help you, but I can't read your mind. If you had a plan to follow them, you should have told me."

Hostility crackled through the air, then Mona nodded. "You're right." She glanced at her watch. "Get Faith over here. Peterson's sending a search unit. We *have* to find that cellphone."

Faith's voice cut through the tension as she moved into the office. "I'm right here." She didn't look at Jess.

Mona made a quick call, then pocketed the phone again. "They'll be here in five minutes."

Jess cocked her head and raised an eyebrow. "Five *minutes?*"

"We have a staging house just around the bend."

Jess gazed at the agent for moment, putting all the pieces together. Mona's availability, living close-by. The whole operation had been set up for weeks.

"I see. . .by the way, while I was giving Mustafa instructions, Hafez was outside on the phone, talking a mile-a-minute in Arabic and looking at a map. I got the impression he was planning to meet someone."

Mona's face broke into a wicked grin. "Excellent. The more we have on these bastards, the better."

Twenty minutes later, Jess scooped up a handful of carrots and headed for Casey's stall. She needed to be alone and sort out her thoughts. While Casey munched, Jess moved to the window facing the woods behind the barn. From that vantage point, she watched Faith talk to four men and Mona. Then, they all moved to the spot from where Hafez had thrown the phone. After a little more discussion, the search team fanned out and entered the woods.

Though it was daylight, Jess could see high-powered flashlights sweeping back and forth through the dark forest. How long would it take them to find the phone? *Would* they find it? The underbrush grew thick that time of year–the search would be like looking for the proverbial needle in a haystack.

Hay reminded her of the weaponry in the loft, and cold fingers of fear clawed at her chest. Horrifying images of the Trade Towers played through her head, crumbling in slow motion as though it had happened yesterday. Terror had come home to roost.

Casey's gentle nudge brought her back with a start, then determination replaced fear. With a final glance at the team working methodically through the woods, she left the stall and headed for the office. She had no idea what the next few days would bring, but she had a business to run and a horse show to organize. *And* she had to figure out how to deal with Faith.

The final Easton Ridge schooling show of the season was a big event. Jess always pulled out all the stops, catering a lunch, offering a full bar, and purchasing classy trophies for the students who'd worked so hard all year. Unfortunately, this year she'd left everything until the last minute, and would be hard pressed to get her act together. *Well, it's not as if I was lying around doing nothing*. Unplanned circumstances notwithstanding, she needed to concentrate all her efforts on making the show a success.

She gazed at the circled show date on the calendar. September Eleventh. *Maybe it's an omen. A good one, I hope*.

An hour later, still alone in the barn, she checked off the last item on the list, then rose to stretch. Focusing on the show details had calmed her brain and given her anxiety some respite. As she gazed out the window, a late model Cadillac turned into the driveway and pulled up in front of her house. Howard climbed out of the car and her stomach churned, the earlier calm vaporizing. Too many things were going on in her life, none of which she seemed able to control. She closed her eyes and wished there were some way to make all the problems disappear.

# *Thirty-Two*

Howard's voice boomed through the telephone.

"Jess, could you and Faith come over here for a little while?"

"Be there shortly."

She walked briskly down the aisle and out the side door. Faith stood at the edge of the woods, arms crossed, her face pinched with anxiety. Jess felt a stab of sorrow at the terrible turn their friendship had taken.

"Faith? You okay?"

"Yeah, I'll be glad when all this is over."

Jess nodded. "Whenever *that* might be."

Loud voices echoed from the depths of the woods, and Faith took a couple of steps closer to the trees.

"Sounds like they found it!"

Jess's pulse quickened. "Boy, I hope so! I don't know how much more of this play-acting I can handle."

The search unit emerged from the underbrush, every face bright with victory. Mona gave a thumbs-up signal, and one of the men lofted a plastic bag containing a tiny muddy phone.

The group headed toward their vehicles, and Jess turned to Faith.

"Howard's waiting for us at the house."

Faith brushed past her and struck off across the grass. Jess hurried to catch up, wondering how long it would take to get Faith to talk to her.

Howard sat in the porch swing, a yellow legal pad balanced on his knees. He looked up and smiled. "I was beginning to think you'd forgotten me."

Jess leaned against the porch rail. "Almost. The search team found the phone. . .they seem confident they'll discover what Samir and his group are up to." She glanced at Faith. "Sure wish we knew what's going to happen, and when."

Faith hiked one foot onto the bottom step of the porch. "Do you need me, Howard? 'Cause if you don't, I could sure use a shower and an early night. Dania's coming for an extra lesson tomorrow morning."

"I'd like you to stay for a little while. I have some interesting background information to share."

Jess pushed away from the rail. "Let's go inside. I'm parched."

A few minutes later, Howard took a long swallow of iced tea and looked across the breakfast bar at the two women.

"I spent some time in Hartford at the state library. If we're going to be of any help in the war against terrorism, we need to know the enemy."

Jess's stomach lurched. She could *not* get used to the idea that she'd blundered into such deep water.

Howard consulted his notes and cleared his throat.

"Let me start by telling you there are six million Muslims in America, and they are not all terrorists. They are law-abiding citizens, enjoying the fruits of American independence and opportunity. Now, I don't know if you ladies have followed the news, but the FBI has stepped up its concentration since arresting that truck driver in Ohio. He was an American citizen, but he quickly named names. His contact in Pakistan had ordered him to start organizing a plan to destroy the Brooklyn Bridge."

Faith gasped. "Oh, my God! You mean these people are still trying to attack us?"

Jess flinched inwardly. Faith had never shown much interest in world news and, for both of them, time had eased the fervent daily quest for any tidbit about terrorism. And since leaving her city life behind, Jess had focused her attention on the stable, and those things that directly involved her.

Howard nodded solemnly. "Yes. According to one article, even the destruction of their headquarters in Afghanistan didn't slow them down. It merely heightened their motivation to retaliate. The only question is where and when."

Jess snorted. "I can't believe a bunch of rag-heads–" She stopped abruptly, startled by Howard's offended expression. "Uh, sorry. I'm just amazed how a third world country that can barely feed its own population, can find the resources to wage war on other nations."

"Fervor is the force behind the thinking, Jess. Islamic radicals believe Jihad is the supreme religious duty, and they put it before everything else, including their own well-being. This is the context of the network that has declared war on the western world. To these believers, it is an honor to die for the cause."

Faith's disgust curled around her words. "If they're so religious, why do they think it's okay to murder thousands of people?"

"There's a misconception–even amongst Muslims themselves–that Islamic radicalism and Islam are the same thing. The Islamic religion itself isn't any more violent than other religions. But for the radical sector, any area not yet under Islamic control is considered the enemy, whether it's here, or the Middle East, or North Africa."

Jess shivered at the enormity of the description. The wicked fingers of evil had reached across oceans and continents, feeling their way, searching for an opening, slipping into Easton Ridge unhindered.

Both repulsed and intrigued, she wanted to know more. "What exactly is a terrorist cell? I hear the term all the time, but have no clue what it really means."

"Ahh. . .I'm glad you asked. That's really what prompted me to do some research. Cell organization goes clear back to Napoleonic times." He nodded at her surprise. "That's right, the concept is not new. The basic principle is, that by dividing a large organization into many smaller parts, the amount of information needed by each division is specific only to that group's mission. Therefore, the parent organization is more likely to survive if one of the components is compromised."

Jess's analytical mind warmed to the subject. "Each cell operates individually, without relying on the others, right?"

"Basically, and the functions of the cells can change from one operation to the next. Multi-tasking, as it were." He looked at his notes. "There are several different kinds of cells: planning or support, sleeper or submarine, and execution. An operations commander sometimes comes in at the last minute to give final instructions, then leaves before the attack."

Faith shook her head. "I almost wish I didn't know all this stuff."

"For most of the population, that would be okay, but you *both* need to be aware of the gravity of your situation. Samir and his boys didn't stumble into your lives without thought. He located a chink in the wall, found a way to nudge it until he could get through. He has a purpose, and it isn't to learn more about riding. He's driven by the very same passions I described earlier."

Tension burned across Jess's shoulders. "Mona said Samir was part of a sleeper cell. Why is it called that?"

"A group of people live here in the States for years, become citizens and acquire a solid, believable background. They blend into our society, keeping low profiles until they are needed."

"So how does the FBI find them if they're so invisible?"

"Long, exhausting work. One article stated that over a thousand al Qaeda suspects in the U.S. are being tailed, or are under electronic surveillance. Apparently, many of their names turned up on records found at the training camps in the caves of Afghanistan."

Faith sounded incredulous. "Why don't the agents just arrest Samir and the A-Rabs, instead of sneaking around?"

"With a sophisticated network like this, where each group is more or less independent from the others, it would be like stepping on three ants from a subterranean anthill. The only way to catch all the ants is to get to the center of the colony."

Howard set his notes aside and looked at both women for a minute. "Hard as it will be, you have to carry on your normal routine. If you can do that, you might be key players in averting another 9/11."

Jess stared out the living room window, feeling totally isolated, imprisoned in a life that had changed without her cognizance. Faith had left without saying goodbye, and Howard's car had just disappeared down the highway. His words echoed through her head, at once filling her with resolve, then immediately crushing her with their weight. Would she and Faith be able to play-act for the length of time needed to catch the bad guys?

Suddenly, those same bad guys were driving her truck toward the barn. She glanced at her watch–they'd been gone for over five hours. What hateful things had they planned during their absence?

Hafez was unloading the jump poles when Jess arrived, slightly breathless from the brisk walk to the barn.

"Just put them in the center of the outdoor arena. Tomorrow, I'll show you both how to set up the jumps and take them down. That will be your responsibility at the show on Saturday."

She caught a brief glance between the two men, then Mustafa bowed slightly.

"Yes, Miss."

Jess left the workers, and entered the barn. A minute later, Mona knocked on the doorjamb, then stepped into the room. "Working late?"

"I lost a lot of time this past weekend, and we have a horse show on Saturday, as I'm sure you know."

The agent nodded thoughtfully. "Yeah, but I almost forgot." She grinned. "Well, see you in the morning."

She disappeared into the depths of the barn, and Jess put her head in her hands and closed her eyes. *I have to get my act together, put all the pieces where they belong, or I'll never be able to pull this off.*

The silence in the house felt oppressive. Any other time, Jess would have relished the quiet, snuggling into the privacy of aloneness, but now the atmosphere held ghosts of the day's visitors. Unable to shake them off, she went out to the front porch and settled into the swing. The soft evening air felt good against her face, and the fading daylight cast a Kinkadian glow over the landscape.

Her tension began to fade, and she stretched out on the thick cushions, enjoying the gentle motion of the swing. Against the darkening sky, stars twinkled in contrast to the moving lights of airplanes circling on the approach to the airport. Exhaustion pressed in on her, weighting her eyelids, and diffusing her worries.

The telephone shrilled from somewhere, and she struggled with the sound, deep in the recesses of her subconscious, then awakened with a start. Confused, she sat up and looked around. The sky had gone pitch black, and the chill in the air felt uncomfortable. The phone rang again and she leaped up. As she reached the door, tires crunched on the gravel driveway, and panic seized her by the throat. Torn between answering the phone, or waiting to see who was out there, she hesitated. The ringing stopped.

She quickly slipped inside the house, and moved to the window, her heart banging against her ribs. A moment later, Howard stepped up onto the porch, and her adrenaline dropped like a skydiver.

She opened the screen door with shaky hands, and Howard's eyes widened.

"Jess, what's the matter? You look like you've seen a ghost!"

"You scared the hell out of me. I thought you were the FBI coming back to drag me away in shackles."

"I've been calling all the way over here. Where were you?"

"Asleep on the swing."

She took a deep breath and focused. Tight-fitting blue jeans and a dark plaid sport shirt had replaced Howard's solemn lawyer attire. *He looks even better out of a suit than in one*. She chuckled at the Freudian thought.

"A joke to share?"

"No joke, I'm just exhausted. Inappropriate responses to most things." She smiled. "Okay, I'm ready. What's next?"

His moustache curled around his grin. "Nothing. Time to relax."

ᕽᕼ

# *Thirty-Three*

Howard's blue eyes sparkled with mischief, sending a flutter through Jess's insides. *Damn, he looks good!* Years of ignoring her own needs faded, and she faced the fact that she wanted him, wanted something more than the safe, solitary life she'd embraced for so long. Had he been thinking about her in the same way?

His smile kindled a spark of hope. "I could use that glass of wine, now."

She watched the rich color of Merlot swirl around the bottom of the glass, then rush toward the rim. A deep breath did nothing to calm the jittery sensation in the pit of her stomach.

A minute later, he touched his glass to hers, and took a sip before relaxing back on the couch. The circumstances surrounding his visit never came up–instead, he talked about the hunting lodge, the press of business during the imminent elk hunting season, and his involvement in a community charity auction planned for late November. Jess sat close to him, listening to every word, hearing the pride in his voice, seeing the confident bearing of a man who'd planned and done the things he'd always wanted. What was the difference between them? She'd *also* worked hard to attain her own dreams–had her goals been important enough? Or had she just skimmed along on inertia and luck? The events of the last few weeks were proof that she'd simply assumed she would prevail in anything she tried.

And what about the future? Did she have a plan? Had she learned *anything* from this nightmare?

Howard sat quietly, gazing into his glass. Before she could lose courage, Jess set her own glass down, and reached for his hand. The warmth of his skin sent a shiver of surprise through her thoughts. His fingers twined through hers and squeezed gently. Their eyes met, and for an instant, Jess saw answers to all her questions. Good answers. The answers she wanted to see.

She leaned into the circle of his arms. At first tentative, then bolder, Howard's lips caressed hers, jolting her emotions into full throttle. Joy and longing filled her and she kissed him back with every whisper of desire in her body.

A moment later, he slowly pulled back and stroked her hair. "Ahh, Jessie, what a mess."

She searched his face. "What do you mean?"

He grinned sheepishly. "I've broken one of my own rules. Never get involved with a client."

"I *wasn't* your client!"

A deep chuckle rumbled through his chest. "I know–I got it bass-ackwards." He stroked her shoulder. "We'll get through this, I promise."

There was her answer–now, what could she do about it? Geography would definitely be a problem. She smiled. *Getting a little ahead of myself.*

"Another joke you don't want to share?"

She slipped a hand into his, feeling comfortable and normal for the first time in a long while.

"Maybe later. . ." She tilted her head and met his ever-startling blue gaze. "I know almost nothing about you. You're such a master at focusing all conversations on me."

A chuckle. "Lawyer ploys. Tricks of the trade."

"Okay, so now *I'm* cross-examining. When did you retire? Why so early?"

"Whoa! You sound like one of the feebs."

She affected a serious scowl. "Just stick to the facts, Mr. London."

"I left the practice exactly four years ago this November." He shook his head and his voice softened. "Someone was looking out for me. Our offices were next to the Trade Towers."

"Oh, my God! Did you have partners? I mean–?"

He nodded. "Two. They were both at a convention in Miami when the attack came. But a paralegal and the secretary were there."

Jess's heart hammered so heavily against her ribs she couldn't ask the question hovering on her lips.

Howard exhaled softly. "They were both badly injured."

"I'm so sorry. . .I shouldn't have asked."

"No, it's one of those things every New Yorker carries with him in every fiber. The memory will never go away, but time takes the edge off the pain." He slipped his hand out of hers, rose, and began to pace. "Every time I visit The City, I feel so out of place. Every cab driver, newsboy, hotdog vendor seems to be a dark foreigner. Are they friend or foe? I watch the throngs of people flowing up and down the sidewalks, inhabitants of a city deeply scarred with pain, citizens who've resumed their former lives, but with broken hearts." He stopped and looked down at her. "I can't even look at the skyline, knowing what I won't see."

Viewing his open wound, Jess felt the tears gathering. "Being in the middle of *this* mess must be very hard for you."

"No, not at all. I'll do anything I can to help bring America's nightmare to an end."

Ӿ

# *Thirty-Four*

Jess's eyes burned with lack of sleep. She'd lain awake most of the night, listening to the ticking clock and the quiet sounds of the house, the day's script playing over and over in her head. The revelation of Howard's personal pain marred the brief joy of knowing his feelings for her.

She rose to face a day that promised who-knew-what. She planned to spend the morning finalizing arrangements with the suppliers for the show, maybe go riding in the afternoon. While the coffee brewed, she gazed out the window at the faint pink glow silhouetting the trees on the eastern horizon. Her thoughts again turned to Howard. Long ago, she'd stowed her romantic dreams where they couldn't cause her any pain. He'd set them free with his touch, and she felt young and eager again. When the nightmare was over, she vowed to open herself to those feelings.

Mona phoned a few minutes later. "Hafez is looking for you."

"Tell him I'll be over in a minute."

A cold sensation oozed into her gut. What was so important it couldn't wait another hour? She grabbed a mug of coffee, and set off toward the barn.

Hafez met her at the door. "Ah, good morning, Miss. Is a beautiful day, no?"

She struggled not to react negatively to the sudden familiarity from a man who seldom acknowledged her existence. "Yes–Mona said you needed something?"

Dark eyes flashed. "Please, we need to travel to New Jersey today. Our college records are complete, and we must pick them up."

Jess frowned. "Can't the college mail them?"

An embarrassed smile softened the man's sharp features. "Ah, yes, but we owe some money first."

Jess thought for a minute. *Sounds like bull to me.*

"How long will you be gone?"

"Only until tomorrow morning. *Insha'Allaah.*"

"Let me check with Mona and see if she's willing to cover stalls for you."

Hafez bowed. "*Shukran.*"

Jess walked down the aisle, her head spinning with possibilities. What if they were planning to simply disappear? If they got away, the specter of another attack would shadow her forever.

Mona stood just inside the office door. "What'd he want?"

As Jess related the request, a wicked smile spread over Mona's features, and her voice dropped to a whisper.

"Sure, I'll cover for 'em."

Jess lowered her own voice, glancing at the open office door. "Aren't you worried they're going to do something bad?"

"Jess, these guys are all bugs under a microscope. They can't even take a whiz without us knowing it."

Mona headed into the aisle, and Jess watched her confident stride, slightly annoyed at the cocky attitude.

*I sure as hell hope so.*

Within half an hour, Jess watched from her living room window as the van turned onto the highway. She felt something akin to relief, but wasn't sure why.

Howard arrived shortly after nine, looking rested and optimistic. He tossed a white paper bag onto the breakfast bar and pulled out a stool.

"Bagels and cream cheese, my passion." He grinned. "Just try finding *that* in the backwoods of Idaho."

She loved the way he looked, sitting there in her kitchen. She set a mug of coffee in front of him, then leaned on the counter.

"What's the plan, Counselor?"

"We're going to be as friendly and cooperative as can be. Help them follow the trail of breadcrumbs and make their case."

She hesitated. "Being friendly to Agent Kerr might be a bit of a stretch."

Howard glanced up, a frown knitting his eyebrows. "He has the memory of an elephant, and an ego to match."

"What happened between you two?"

"About ten years ago, an FBI team botched a stakeout, and my client was killed. She was supposed to be fully protected."

He fell silent. The memory obviously still disturbed him. "I raised a stink and took it all the way to the agency director. Kerr was the team leader, and he caught all the bad press."

Jess thought about the current scenario and wondered if the conflict would cause problems.

Howard gave her a serious look. "I want you to put everything out of your mind, except things that pertain to the Arabs. Think back, try to remember everything that happened, whether you think it's important or not."

Just then, Faith came through the back door, her features relaxed, her eyes alert. "Did I miss anything?"

Howard brought her up to speed on the plan, and Jess slipped down the hall to her room to put on some shoes. Five minutes later, she heard the doorbell and, when she returned to the living room, Kerr and Peterson were sipping coffee from insulated cups.

Peterson smiled. "Morning. Were you able to get some rest?"

"A little." She glanced around. "Where's Mona?"

"Cleaning stalls–doesn't want to get fired."

His relaxed, friendly manner put Jess at ease, and she chuckled. She glanced at Howard and saw the warning in his eyes. *Right. Don't stumble into stupidity.*

Kerr took out his notebook and wrote something across the top. Howard cleared his throat and opened the conversation.

"Are we all on the same side this morning?"

Peterson nodded. "Yes, of course." He looked down at his own notes. "We were discussing Jessica's gambling."

Howard broke in. "Hold on. You were also implying that my client has something to hide. Let's clarify the situation before we go any further."

Kerr broke in. "Give it a rest, London. We're after the terrorists, not the lady in distress."

Peterson looked first at Jess, then Faith. "I repeat–neither of you are suspects in this case. Understand?"

Howard cleared his throat. "Thank you. Now, do you have any idea why Mahfood chose this place?"

"We know he was shopping for a rural property. He visited a couple of farms up in the Bristol area, but he concentrated on run-down places–nothing as fancy as this." Peterson looked directly at Jess. "We also know he tried to buy off your landlord."

Jess was stunned. *No wonder Frank suddenly got pushy.*

"We think Mahfood was trying to set up a safe house at that point. Jess stumbled right into his plans, and he used her."

Before Peterson could continue, Howard asked for a minute to confer with his clients. Kerr pulled out his cigarettes and headed for the porch, and Howard motioned the girls toward the bedroom.

He closed the door and faced them. "Okay, I think we're on solid ground now, but don't let your guard down. Even though they appear to be focused on the gang, they're still observing you."

Faith spoke for the first time. "What if the A-Rabs do something terrible to us before the FBI catches them?"

"I don't think that'll happen. They're obviously being watched every minute."

Until that moment, Jess hadn't considered the physical danger that might accompany their involvement with Samir. All her courage evaporated. Not only had she screwed up the life she and Faith had built, she'd put them both in harm's way, as well.

Mona had joined the group and, from the dark scowl on her face, didn't like what Kerr was saying to her. When Jess appeared, the two agents abruptly stopped talking.

Peterson consulted his notes. "Did either of you ever see Hafez or Mustafa with a computer?"

Jess frowned. "Once I caught Mustafa fooling with the one in my office, and gave him hell. He said he was getting some information from the college they attended."

She immediately noticed Howard's frown, and realized she'd forgotten to mention the incident. It hadn't seemed important at the time, other than being an irritation.

Howard cleared his throat. "Agent Peterson, are these men college students?"

The agent snorted. "On paper. Like so many of the terrorist suspects, they registered at a college, but never attended any classes. Foreign nationals used to be able to easily enter the U.S. on a temporary student visa. Then, they'd just disappear. Thousands of foreign students entered the country before 9/11. We've been sifting through them for years."

Jess's confusion grew. "But the nephews just left this morning to pick up their college records in New Jersey." She shook her head. "Neither one of them appear to me to be college material."

Kerr barked a derisive laugh. "You think all these guys are just peasants sitting around reading the Kor-an? Think again. Some of them have advanced training in computer science, and are right up there with the best of our intelligence officers."

Jess's brain began to numb with the overload of frightening information being forced through it. How could these vicious people have infiltrated her life so easily? Why hadn't she seen it happening? The answers to those questions filled her with despair.

Peterson stood up. "Jess, we need to take a look at your computer. The hard drive will disclose al-Ani's search history. We'll get a tech over here right away."

Mona spoke for the first time since she'd arrived.

"The boys seem a little subdued this morning. I'm worried they might be getting ready to slip away. The weapons are still in the loft, but the money's gone."

Howard's tone tensed. "Could you elaborate?"

Mona hesitated, glancing quickly at the other two agents before answering. "I found a large amount of cash buried behind the hay the first time I went up there to look around." She shook her head, her tone disgusted. "But it looks like they've already channeled the money to wherever it was headed."

Mona's features tightened as she related the details. Obviously, she was distressed by her failure to secure such critical evidence. Jess recalled the fervor with which Mona had defended her goal of tracking down terrorists, and a small wave of sympathy pervaded her own thoughts.

"Maybe that's where they're headed right now. If your guys are following them–"

Kerr interrupted. "The situation is under control. Now, everyone needs to get back to work, business as usual. Mona, you coordinate with the computer lab when they arrive." He turned to Faith. "You go ahead with your lessons, and whatever else you do."

Jess interrupted. "What're you going to do with my computer? The entire business is on that machine."

"The tech will clone the system onto another hard drive. Your data won't be harmed."

Howard closed his notebook. "I'd like to stay involved in the plans, Agent Peterson."

"No problem. Just stay out of the way, and don't go near the suspects."

Jess trailed Mona across the grass toward the barn, an unsettling cloud hovering over her thoughts. So many things could go wrong before this was over.

As she entered the barn, a loud, indignant whinny echoed through the rafters and she grinned. Her old friend felt neglected. Slipping into the dim, cozy stall, Jess left the frightening outside world behind.

"Hey, Casey, how's my girl?"

She stroked the soft red-brown coat, and felt the magic flow through her, calming her thoughts, slowing her heartbeat. The mare's velvet muzzle poked inquisitively around Jess's body, tweaking her shirt, nudging her arm.

"Sorry, baby. I haven't been to the feed room yet, but I'll come back."

As she headed down the aisle, a car passed by the barn door, then Mona emerged from the feed room.

"Computer geek's here."

Minutes later, Jess shook hands with a tall, gorgeous, redheaded woman.

Mona grinned. "Sarah here is our expert on data retrieval. She can squeeze information out of thin air."

Sarah had a warm, throaty voice, and a great smile. She slipped into Jess's chair and got down to the business of shutting down the computer. Jess suddenly felt dowdy and awkward, and found herself wondering what Howard would think of this charming creature.

Watching the deadly serious work taking place in her personal space, she suddenly wanted to get away, ride through the woods, smell the fresh air, hear the birds, feel horseflesh beneath her legs. The impact of the situation bombarded her and, for an instant, she wanted to run. Hide. Leave the country, leave the terror behind.

Her shoulders sagged and she turned to Mona. "How long do you think it will be before you can arrest these guys?"

"If we catch any kind of break, it'll be soon. 'Til then, we just have to keep digging."

ᚸ

## *Thirty-Five*

Around one o'clock, Zada's Lexus pulled up in front of the barn, Dania hopped out, and the car pulled into a parking spot. Jess sighed and turned from the window to paste on a friendly smile she didn't feel.

"Good afternoon, Zada. Is Dania excited about the show on Saturday?"

The woman's tone was cool. "Yes, she wants to have a perfect ride for her Papa. *Insha'Allaah.*"

Jess thought her attitude a little odd. "I'm sure she will. Her natural talent is a gift few riders have, especially at such a young age. We both think she's national champion material. Faith wants her to come twice a week for lessons, through the winter."

Zada said nothing, but her features did soften a little with the praise.

Jess continued. "Buster is an excellent mount, but she needs a lot more experience on him before show season next spring. And she needs a good performance saddle. Our schooling tack is okay for practice, but she should have her own equipment if she's going to show seriously."

Zada fiddled with the edges of her pale blue *hijaab*, and Jess tried to assess the body language. Did Zada know anything about her husband's activities? *Not likely, if he's as clever as everyone thinks.*

Jess pushed a little harder. "If you'd like, I can take Dania to Enfield next week, and help her pick out some suitable tack."

"That will not be necessary. We are leav–. Miss Rayder, Dania's last ride will be on Saturday."

"Oh, my! Is something wrong? Are you unhappy with us for some reason?"

Zada's eyes glowed with condescension. "There are more important things than worldly pleasures. Dania must learn that her own desires are to be put aside. There is no room for sentimental possessions. She must prepare to be a wife and mother, to follow the will of Allaah."

"Good grief, Zada, she's only twelve! Why should she think about those things *now*?"

Zada's stature seemed to grow taller than her diminutive five feet. Displeasure and scorn settled over her elegant features, and echoed in her speech.

"You Americans will never understand. The will of Allaah is all that matters. Righteous women will be devoutly obedient, and marriage is the way to discourage immorality. It is written in the Holy Qur'an."

Jess grappled with the nasty retorts raging through her mind. She'd gain nothing by having an argument with the woman. Whether Jess agreed or not, she had to accept that Zada's cultural ideals were ingrained, a history and pattern spanning thousands of years.

"I see. Does Dania know?"

"Not yet. Please do not mention it to her. My husband will tell her when the time is right. *Insha'Allaah.*"

She turned toward the door without another word.

"But what about her new horse?"

Zada turned back, her dark eyes flashing cold fire.

"We won't be needing Buster anymore. Just destroy him."

Zada's words hung on the air like a fetid odor, and nausea rolled through Jess's stomach as she stared at the empty doorway. The wave passed, and a fine film of perspiration sprang to her skin. The woman had to be mad. She didn't *really* expect them to put the horse down–or did she?

Jess shivered. Howard's revelations about what drove these religious radicals had shaken her. The ideology made no sense, and the values seemed warped. *Poor Dania!* Jess closed her eyes, imagining the little girl's sorrow when she learned of her parents' decision. Sudden anger stormed through Jess's head. *Women are supposed to be the protectors of the young and innocent. Zada must be involved, otherwise, she'd be concerned with the consequences for her own flesh and blood.* Another horrifying thought leaped in. What if Hafez or Mustafa had orders to kill Buster after the show?

She dialed Mona's number with shaking fingers. An answering machine picked up immediately. *Dammit!*

"Mona, it's Jess. Call me as soon as possible on my cellphone."

She put the receiver back in the cradle, and her cellphone chimed. The words "blocked call" flashed on the tiny screen. She hesitated before answering, then relaxed at the familiar voice on the other end of the line.

"Hold on a minute, Mona. I'm headed outside."

She strode out of the barn, heading toward her house while she reiterated the scene with Zada.

Mona's tone sharpened. "Okay, thanks. We're about ready to implement some plans. I'll call you as soon as I hear from Hartford. In the meantime, stay alert and call me if anything else happens."

Jess's heartbeat thundered in her ears. Things were suddenly moving briskly, hopefully toward a positive conclusion. She looked toward the arena where Dania watched Faith take Buster over a series of jumps. Zada sat on the sidelines. There *had* to be a way to protect the horse. Mindless slaughter in the name of Allaah wouldn't happen on Jess's watch.

Mona called back an hour later.

"The lab has the information from both the phone and your hard drive. Call Howard and tell him we want a meeting this afternoon. Four o'clock, your house."

Jess phoned Howard's motel, but he didn't answer, so she left a message. In the arena, Faith appeared to be pacing off the distance between jumps. Taking a deep breath, Jess headed across the grass, wondering how they'd ever manage to work together again after this mess.

She leaned on the fence. "Ready for Saturday?"

"Yeah, I've designed a really fancy course–my best yet."

Her voice sounded calm, and Jess relaxed a little. Things might sort themselves out naturally, given some time.

She looked at Faith's course sketch. "Looks great."

"Thanks. What's up?" Short and civil, but not friendly.

Jess decided against revealing Buster's vulnerability, at least for the time being. Until she could count on Faith to stay sober, it would be necessary to carry the ball alone.

"The agents have called a planning meeting for this afternoon. Mona says something's about to happen."

Faith's skin paled and her tone softened. "What do you think they're going to do?"

"I have no idea, but I guarantee it'll be exciting." Tension knotted Jess's neck and shoulders, and she exhaled sharply. "I need to see a horse about a ride."

Steely Dan was full of himself as Jess headed across the field toward the trail. She hadn't ridden him for a while, and the challenge of controlling his exuberant energy provided a respite from her problems. When he eventually leveled out into a steady trot, Jess focused on the beautiful scenery. The dense stand of white oak and mountain laurel cocooned around her, making her feel safe and hidden from prying eyes.

During the first year at Easton, she and Faith had forged a rough trail through the state forest bordering the property. In those happy times, they'd ridden together almost every day. Sadness closed in on her. So many things had changed–would they ever be right again?

Off to the left, she caught a movement, and her pulse quickened, then realization slammed into her head. *The man in the woods! An undercover agent, for sure.* As she focused, the soft brown outlines of two deer melted away, and she exhaled slowly. High above the ground, a bluejay warned the world of her intrusion, then flew off. Danny's ears pricked forward to catch every sound, his nostrils flaring to grab every scent. As his powerful legs carried them along at a strong trot, Jess smiled at his enthusiasm for the ride. The trail began to rise, and she reined him back to a walk and scanned the ground for dangerous rabbit holes. At the top of the hill, she brought him to a halt and patted his neck.

"When this is over, we'll play every day, I promise."

The horse nickered softly and bobbed his head. Nature's soft silence caressed Jess's over-stimulated brain, and for the first time in weeks, she felt something akin to hope.

Jess spent a few extra minutes grooming Danny, wanting to savor the precious personal time a little longer. The horse danced around and pawed the floor, anxious to return to his stall. The evening feed was imminent, and Jess chuckled at his single-mindedness. In the background, she heard Faith talking quietly to a horse as she led him into a stall. Mona wheeled a feed cart down the aisle, tossing hay into each stall to the accompaniment of whinnies and snorts. At the far end of the barn, the late afternoon sun slanted across the concrete. Everything seemed so normal–no one would ever suspect the simmering intrigue.

Her optimism flagged. Deep inside, she knew the whole thing could fall apart in the flick of a tail.

# *Thirty-Six*

In the quiet privacy of her room, Jess sat on the edge of the bed and closed her eyes. *One step at a time. Focus individually on each part of the whole. Play the market, feel the pulse.* The technique she'd always used for psyching herself whenever the stock market wavered would work as well in the current situation. Research, assessment, action.

When she returned to the kitchen, Faith was regaling Howard with a horseshow story. His amusement sent a small ripple of jealousy through Jess's head. *She* wanted to be the one entertaining Howard, telling him about the hilarious things that happened at horseshows. He glanced up and smiled, and her throat contracted painfully. *Just give me the chance.*

Footsteps thumped on the wooden porch, and she opened the front door for the agents.

With a quick glance at Howard, she took the initiative. "Did you find anything good on the phone or computer?"

Peterson smiled. "Yes, we did. We're ready to move."

"What did you find?"

Professional cool replaced the agent's brief friendliness. "We're not at liberty to disclose that information."

Irritation broke through Jess's composure. "Wait a minute! You want our help, but you won't tell us what's going on? Why should we cooperate?"

Kerr intervened, his tone rough and aggressive. "Listen, Jess. We know you're used to being in charge, but this time, you're just gonna hafta be a player."

She opened her mouth to retort, but his hand slashed the air like a machete, cutting her off.

"No, listen to me! This isn't a card game. This is deadly. You're mixed up with people who want to repeat operations like the Trade Towers, the Pentagon, airplanes fallin' outta the sky. We have a responsibility to protect you. Now, if you're gonna be obstructive, we'll take you into custody right now, and detain you somewhere 'til we've finished our job."

His vehemence matched Mona's, and Jess's anger disappeared. The two agents had integrated their quest for vengeance into their jobs and, clearly, neither one would rest until they'd made a difference.

"I'm sorry. You're right–but it's been so frightening. We really do want to help."

Kerr threw her a curt nod, but didn't comment. Peterson cleared his throat.

"Mona will be here in a minute." He glanced at his notebook. "You had a conversation with Zada Mahfood. Could you go over it again with us?"

Jess recounted the exchange, and both agents took notes. Mona arrived a few minutes later, and the plan began to materialize. Howard wrote furiously, but said nothing. Faith sat like a statue, her blue eyes bright with fear.

Peterson explained the sudden shift into action. "Our agents have been monitoring Samir's calls. The pieces are moving into place for something, but we don't know what. On Monday, Hafez and Mustafa took a little detour on their way to pick up your show supplies."

Jess leaned forward. "You caught up to them?"

He grinned. "Yeah, these foreigners drive like maniacs. A cop pulled them over just north of here, so our guy was able to tail them the rest of the day."

"Where'd they go?"

He gave her an exasperated look, and she shrugged. "Never mind."

Kerr stood up and paced as he took over the conversation.

"Mahfood will be here for the horse show on Saturday, and we're sure he'll make direct contact with Hafez and Mustafa." He stopped and looked at Jess. "How many people are you expecting?"

"Around seventy-five. This is our big event of the year."

He nodded thoughtfully. "Good. We'll plant our counter-terrorism unit in the audience." He turned to Peterson. "How many are assigned to this operation?"

"Twenty."

Jess could barely breathe. *Twenty agents to keep tabs on <u>three</u> people?* The new information sent shocks of fear rolling through her.

Kerr continued. "What are your arrangements with Mahfood about paying for the horse?"

"I don't have any yet–the next payment isn't due for another couple of weeks. Frankly, I was hoping he'd be arrested before I had to see him again."

Kerr sat down. "Here's the plan. We want you to call him, ask for early payment, and set up a specific time to meet at the end of the lunch break. Tell him to meet you in the office. You'll be under close surveillance during the meeting–Mona will fit you with a wire. If you get into trouble, someone will be there immediately."

Jess's pulse thundered in her ears, and reality faded as she listened to the plan evolve, one that seemed better suited to a movie box-office hit.

Peterson's voice brought her back with a start.

"Our intelligence points toward a major move by these three, any time now. We are prepared to take action and arrest them, if necessary." He turned to Faith. "Your role is to keep the show running smoothly, and keep the riders and families focused on the event. It's critical that you act normal, be cheerful, and never try to watch what's going on in the background. These people are finely attuned to nuances and unusual body language. One worried glance at Mahfood, and the whole thing could go south. Do you understand?"

Faith nodded silently.

Howard spoke up. "What if there's shooting? Will the girls be protected?"

"We don't anticipate any gunfire, but we'll fit them both with bullet-proof vests, just to be safe."

Kerr snorted. "I'm sure you'll want to be in the middle of

everything, as usual, but I'm telling you right now, London–stay in the spectator section, and do *not* go anywhere near Jess or Faith."

Crackling tension snapped between the two men, then Howard nodded. "Not a problem."

"Mind if I have a look at your notes?"

Howard narrowed his eyes. "Yes, I do. Client privilege."

"I can get a subpoena."

"Go right ahead."

Jess watched in stunned silence as the two men maneuvered through the land-mined conversation. Did the agent think Howard would give up the plan to the enemy? Or was Kerr just playing out his own authority?

Kerr studied Howard's face for a minute, then pocketed his notebook and turned to Jess.

"Call me after you've talked to Mahfood."

## *Thirty-Seven*

Jess leaned her head back against the couch and stared at the ceiling. "This is like a bad dream."

Faith moved toward the door. "I'm going home. I'll see you in the morning."

Guarded concern edged Howard's tone. "Why don't you stay here tonight? You've both had a rough day."

She gazed at him for a moment. "No. . .this isn't about me right now."

Howard looked genuinely baffled. "I just thought the two of you could use each other's moral support."

Faith snorted. "Oh, yeah, right!" She grabbed the doorknob. "See you tomorrow."

The door closed behind her and Howard shook his head. "This kind of strain is the perfect trigger for a binge."

"I think she'll be okay. I suspect this nightmare has sobered her up."

"Let's hope so. Jess, listen. . .I have to go back to Idaho–"

She jumped up. "Howard, no! I need you here. . ."

"Calm down, I'll be back Friday morning." He smiled. "You'll manage just fine." His attention swiveled to the window. "Uh-oh. We've got company."

She moved quickly to see the cause of his concern. A sleek white State Police car moved slowly up the lane.

"Oh, crap. *Now* what?"

The cruiser passed the house and pulled up in front of the barn.

Howard touched her shoulder. "Come on, hon. Let's go see what he wants."

He covered the distance between the house and the barn in long confident strides, and Jess hurried to keep up. The patrol car door swung open, and Jess started to laugh.

Officer Carter climbed out of the car and grinned. "Hi. Remember me?"

"Of course! Did you come all the way out here to see if I fixed that taillight?"

He chuckled. "Nah, I'm on my dinner break, thought I'd come find your place. I read in the paper you're having a horseshow on Saturday. I'm gonna bring Kristy. She's been buggin' me ever since I told her about meeting you."

Jess's pulse twitched. More innocent bystanders in harm's way. She couldn't let that happen.

"Gee, we're filled up–"

Howard nudged her arm.

"–but, by golly, we'll find some extra chairs."

Carter checked his watch.

"Great! Well, dinner's over. Gotta get back on the road. Do I need tickets or anything?"

*Maybe extra life insurance?* "No, this is a freebie."

"Thanks. See you Saturday."

Jess nodded toward the cruiser. "Don't arrive in *that*, please. You'll scare all our guests."

He winked. "Must be a lotta guilty consciences!"

With a flourishing salute, he climbed into the car, and headed down the drive, ending the visit with one short whoop of the siren.

Jess's knees turned to jelly, and she reached for Howard's arm. A moment later, she rested her cheek against his chest, her body enclosed in his firm embrace.

His voice rumbled through the shirt fabric. "It's gonna be okay, Jessie. Just take things one day at a time."

Tears sprang to her eyes and she struggled to swallow the hard lump rising in her throat.

Dawn filtered through the window, casting its promising glow on the wall next to Jess's bed. She lay still, wishing she could retreat back into the safety of sleep. On awakening, her first thoughts had been about Howard. She gazed through the window, seeing the pale sky, knowing he was already airborne. The knowledge left her feeling vulnerable and alone. Closing her eyes, she tried to relive the few special minutes she'd spent in his arms, but the memory wouldn't stay long enough to enjoy. Instead, scenarios of how the FBI trap might work–or fail–pounded through her head, daunting her confidence. She was truly afraid for the first time since the whole thing had begun.

At the barn, morning chores were in full swing. Mona was hard at work, Faith would be arriving any minute. Jess stared at the phone on her desk. *I have to do this now, before I lose my courage.* How would she sound? Would Samir hear the loathing in her voice? They hadn't spoken since the night of the poker game. Would she be able to pull this off?

"Good Morning, Miss Jessica. How have you been?"

Samir's soft voice sent a chill through her chest.

"Fine, but busy. Samir, I need the next payment on Dania's horse. Would you bring it to the show?"

"I believe we still have some time before it is due, correct?"

"Yes, but the seller has had some bad luck, and she asked if you could pay a little early."

She held her breath, hoping Samir wouldn't press for details.

"I will bring a check."

"Thanks. I'll meet you in the office toward the end of the lunch break."

"I will be there. *Insha'Allaah.*"

*That was easy.* Her heart thumped. Maybe she could maneuver Samir into revealing something of his plans. His big weakness was his pride in Dania–it was worth a try.

"Oh, by the way–I'm sorry to hear Dania won't be continuing her lessons with us. She is *so* talented, Samir. Faith considers her to be national caliber, and capable of winning some very important titles. Not to mention large cash prizes."

The words echoed into a frigid silence creeping through the line, and Jess immediately regretted her rash action.

She took a deep breath. "Samir? Are you there?"

"Yes. I will see you on Saturday, *Insha'Allaah.*"

The line went dead, and a wall of fear moved in as the dial tone droned in her ear. What had she done? She'd triggered the wrong response from Samir. She stared at the phone in her hand. The Feds monitoring her calls were probably reporting to Peterson or Kerr at that very moment. She'd catch hell, and she deserved it.

Faith walked in the door. "You look like you've seen a ghost. What's wrong?"

"I just called Samir. . .Sometimes I feel like I won't make it through this."

"I know, me too. But after Saturday, we should be able to get back to normal. . ." Her voice dropped. "Whatever *that* is. Well, I have the pleasure of an audience with little King Mohammed this morning. I think after Saturday, I'm going to make some excuse why I can't teach him anymore. If I never see another A-Rab, it'll be too soon."

She turned and disappeared into the barn, leaving Jess alone with her own similar thoughts.

Rage flooded through Samir's head as he paced back and forth in his tiny office at the back of the shop. How could he have been so careless? Offering Zada the opportunity to go home for an extended visit seemed a good idea at the time. She was thrilled, confirming his suspicions of her unhappiness about living in the United States. His anger flagged a little–his motives hadn't been completely honest. No matter how deeply ingrained his allegiance to the cause, a fierce desire to protect those he loved still prevailed. In a short while, life in America would not be so easy for his family. His tender thoughts reverted to cold fury. Zada had not only dishonored him, she had put his beautiful Dania in harm's way. His wife would pay dearly for her loose tongue.

Pushing his personal problems aside, he concentrated on the work that lay ahead. Some minor adjustments needed to be made, and quickly. Jessica Rayder hadn't fallen neatly into his plans, and he'd been forced to find another, less convenient safe house. He picked up a folder and removed a large photograph, shaking his head as he gazed at the aerial shot of Easton Ridge. The perfect place, compromised because of a damned woman. With a flick of his lighter, the corner of the paper curled, and he dropped the photo into an empty metal wastebasket. He watched it burn, and the flames fed his fervor.

# *Thirty-Eight*

Mona stood just beyond the office door.

"Did you call Samir?"

*She's already heard.* Jess donned a mask of innocence. "Yes, he'll meet me in the office before the end of the lunch break."

Mona came into the room, her eyes narrowed slits.

"Anything *else*?"

Jess's facade faltered. If she wanted to stay out of Kerr's way, she'd better be up front.

"I told him I was sorry to lose Dania as a student."

"And why, exactly, did you do that?"

"I don't know. I thought maybe he'd talk about his plans, and your guys could get it on tape."

Mona stepped up close to the desk. "Jess, you're becoming a liability. We have too much invested in this operation for you to be rodeoing through it. I'm only going to tell you one time. Let us do our jobs–we're professionals, we know what we're doing. Don't do or say anything we haven't written into the script." She stared into Jess's eyes. "Understand?"

Jess nodded, biting back the urge to snap a retort. Mona was right.

The agent stepped back and pulled a small notebook from her pocket.

"You said there'd be about seventy-five guests on Saturday. Can you give me an idea of the mix? Will it be mostly adults? Women? We can't have only male agents mixed in, if the audience is all women and kids. That would look strange."

Jess was amazed at the logistical details of the plan. "Mostly women and kids. Some fathers, but not many."

Mona wrote something, then looked up. "Anything else I should know about?"

Jess started to shake her head, then remembered the surprise visit from Officer Carter. Was it important? Reminded of the repercussions from her last foray into independence, she let out a long sigh.

"There'll be an additional guest and his daughter. He stopped by last night. He's a cop."

Mona's usual restraint disintegrated. "For Chrissake! What was he doing here?"

As Jess related the story of the taillight, Mona gathered her emotions and stuffed them back into whatever dark hole they inhabited most of the time. When Jess finished, Mona pulled out her cellphone and punched auto-dial.

"Kerr? We have a situation. . .yeah, right. Anyway, a cop plans to bring his kid to the show on Saturday." Mona jerked the phone away from her head and frowned, then gingerly put the instrument back to her ear.

"Calm down. I'll find out."

She placed the phone against her chest. "What precinct is this guy with? Do you know his name?"

"He's a State Trooper. Officer Carter."

Mona rolled her eyes and put the phone back to her ear. "It gets better. He's a Statie. Name's Carter."

She listened for a few minutes, then nodded, said goodbye, and pocketed the phone.

Jess scowled. "What the hell difference does it make if a policeman comes to a horseshow on his off-time? I can't read your mind, so if you have guidelines about this plan, I'd like to know what they are."

"Jess, there's always a chance for casualties in an operation like this. We'd prefer to have *no* civilians around if a takedown happens. We could fill the audience with skilled agents, but it would send all the wrong signals if no parents or families are watching the show. If something goes wrong, a trained law enforcement officer would react, and that could blow this whole operation to hell. He cannot be here."

"But how can you keep him away?"

"We'll get in touch with his supervisor, get him called in for relief duty or something."

She left the office and Jess leaned back in the chair. In twenty-four hours, her world would become the stage for God-only-knew what. Visions of violence played through her head, a concept that had never occurred to her until Mona's warning.

How could a run of bad financial luck spawn the treachery that now festered inside the once-secure boundaries of her life? Why hadn't her intuitive skill for dodging bullets kept her out of trouble? She closed her eyes and exhaled slowly, trying to keep the painful answers from crowding into her tired brain.

Angry shouting outside the window brought her back with a jolt, and she leaped up to have a look. Faith stood facing eleven-year-old Ibrahim, who waved his arms wildly while he ranted. Faith's body language indicated something would give any second, and Jess raced outside, heading toward the two at a brisk trot. As she came closer, she cringed at the nasty tone in the boy's voice.

"You are a stupid woman! I want to ride the black horse! Do not tell me what to do!"

Faith's cheeks were crimson with anger. "*You* listen! *I'm* the boss here, and you'll ride the horse I tell you to. In fact, you're not going to ride *any* of my horses! How does *that* sound?"

Jess broke in. "What's going on?"

The boy turned his haughty gaze on her. "I pay a lot of money to come here to ride. I do not expect to use your old broken-down nags for my lessons."

Jess narrowed her eyes at the miniature replica of what she now considered the enemy.

"Well, then, Ibrahim, I think you need to take lessons somewhere else."

In Jess's peripheral vision, Nadia Mohammed hurried toward them, her features rigid, her dark eyes cold.

The woman slipped her arm around Ibrahim's shoulders. "What is the problem?"

Faith's tone was firm. "Ibrahim is a difficult child to teach. He's not ready to take lessons here. We're geared toward more advanced students, young people with strong desires to excel at the sport. Ibrahim's riding is recreational. I can recommend other stables that are more suitable."

The boy turned to his mother. "She only gives me boring old horses that have no fire. I want to ride the good ones!"

Mrs. Mohammed gazed at Jess. "I'm sorry you feel my son's interest in riding is beneath your standards. We came here as a favor to the Mahfoods. We understood you were in financial trouble and needed money. Obviously, your own pride is more important than your future." She gave the boy a gentle nudge. "Come, Ibrahim. We will go home."

Adjusting her *hijaab*, she looked directly at Jess. "The Holy Qur'an teaches the virtue of humility. No one should boast over one another, and no one should oppress another. *Allaahu akbar.*"

She turned and walked away.

Faith muttered under her breath, "Speak for yourself, Lady."

ꭗ

## *Thirty-Nine*

By mid-afternoon, Jess felt as though she'd been slogging through mud. Nadia Mohammed's knowledge about Easton's finances proved that a strong tie existed between the Middle Easterners who'd suddenly peppered Jess's life. Were they all an integral part of the plot? Or just convincing window dressing–a clever ploy to cast a sense of normalcy over a deeper undercurrent?

She tried to concentrate on all the details for the horse show, but her subconscious ticked off the hours as her fate moved closer. The numbers blurred on the accounting page in front of her, as her brain focused on Saturday's schedule. The youngest riders would go first, followed by a couple of the advanced students. Then, Alex and Beth would demonstrate the various riding gaits, just before the lunch break. Jess's breath caught. The beginning of the excitement–or terror. She tried to imagine the FBI's apprehension of the suspects. Would armed men crash into the office as soon as Samir handed over the check? Would there be shooting? She closed her eyes tightly. *All those kids! How can these guys protect everyone?*

She thought about Dania and sympathy sifted into her heart. The girl became a different child when she rode a horse. Open, curious, enthusiastic–happy. In the shadow of her mother or father, however, she withdrew behind her small *hijaab*, disappearing into the mysterious world of a Muslim female.

In a century where women in many countries excelled at most things–even surpassed their male counterparts in some–the antiquity of the Middle Eastern woman's submissive role glowed like a hot coal. In America, Dania had the opportunity to be anything she wanted, but if Zada and Samir kept her pressed into the cookie-cutter mold of the culture, she would never even recognize the freedom she'd missed.

Pain replaced the empathy in Jess's heart at the images evolving in her head. What would happen to Dania when her father was arrested? Would Zada be taken, too? The visions sharpened. A frightened little girl, shuffled between foster homes, or maybe even sent back to Yemen to live with relatives she'd never met. And how would that affect her? What lasting impression would she have of America? A bitter taste rose in Jess's mouth. The drama about to unfold would plant the seeds of hatred in yet another young Middle Eastern heart, and America's battle with terrorism would be a never-ending conflict.

Tires crunched on the gravel outside, and Peterson's black pickup pulled into the parking area.

An hour later, Jess leaned her head in her hands and closed her eyes. Peterson and Mona had drilled her and Faith relentlessly, taking them both through every step of the operation, over and over, coaching, haranguing, pelting them with questions, pushing them to the edge to find any weak spots. With each assault, Jess's courage grew, strengthening her determination to withstand the intense pressure. Even Faith's subdued attitude disappeared as she got used to the idea

Peterson grinned and snapped his notebook shut. "You did good, ladies. See you Saturday morning."

Jess watched the agents drive away. The silence in the office felt ominous, and she wondered, for a second, if she should use the opportunity to try to break through Faith's barriers.

Her partner's soft voice answered the question.

"I don't hate you, Jessie."

Tears sprang to Jess's eyes, and her voice cracked. "I'm so sorry, Faith. You have every reason to be angry with me." She turned, blinking the moisture away. "I get so involved in problems, I think I can beat them single-handed. . .and I've been worried about *you*."

Faith sighed, deep and long. "I've been a bigger part of the problem than I should have. We're partners, and I failed you miserably."

Jess gestured toward the chair by the desk, but Faith shook her head and smiled sadly.

"I think better on my feet." She began pacing. "When I went home that first night, I was so angry I wanted to kill you–I blamed you, and our financial mess, for *my* problems. Later, when I cooled down a little, I wanted a drink. *Really* wanted a drink."

She stopped and leveled a serious look at Jess. "It was a pivotal moment. I had a choice to make: the easy way–and flush my life down the drain again–or the tough road–find the strength to overcome my demons." She resumed pacing. "I had a helluva time for about an hour. I even poured a glass of wine. . .stared at it, touched it, smelled it. . ."

Jess ached with the pain of Faith's struggle, feeling it seep into her own heart.

"What did you do?" she whispered.

Faith's sad expression almost broke Jess's heart.

"I dumped it down the sink, then called Bill." She smiled at Jess's surprise. "Yeah, I needed a partner to talk me through the temptation–someone who'd been there. I had to swallow my pride."

"And?"

"Hardest damned thing I've ever done, Jessie. But he was so good about it, even offered to come over, but I said no."

Jess had a sudden worrisome thought. She tried to keep her tone level.

"What all did you talk about?"

Faith's cheeks flushed. "Don't worry–I didn't say anything about what's going on. I'm not as blonde as you'd like to think."

"I didn't mean–"

"Yes, you did, and it's okay–I can't blame you for not trusting my judgment." She exhaled sharply, and her tone softened. "I told him the financial mess was getting me down. . .and that I missed him terribly." Her chin trembled and she fell silent.

"Honey, will you stay with me tonight? Please?"

"No, I *have* to be able to function on my own. I can't be someone else's responsibility all my life–but I *will* call you if I need to."

Jess jumped up and slipped her arms around Faith and hugged her tightly.

"I *promise* I'll always be there."

Late that night, Jess lay in bed, staring into the darkness, thinking about all that had happened in the last twenty-four hours. It seemed an eternity since Howard had gone, and she couldn't wait for him to return. Surprising as it seemed, she needed his strength and support.

Her thoughts snapped back to the situation. What terrible plot might be in its last stages? American bloodshed in the war had reached a level no one could ignore, and it seemed logical that more blood would be spilled on American soil to emphasize al Qaeda's hatred of the infidel.

She shuddered and threw back the quilt. *I need a horse fix.* Controlling the tangible, manageable aspects of her life would be the only way to confront her feelings of powerlessness.

The crisp night air chilled her face as she walked across the field toward the barn. A sliver of waning moon hung below a cloud, casting an eerie glow over the landscape. Something crackled in the underbrush and her heart thumped. An opossum scuttled across the driveway and into the dark protection of the trees. Jess quickened her pace.

The large sliding doors at both ends of the barn were always left open a crack to allow fresh air to circulate through the warm building. As she approached the closest door, she suddenly felt she was not alone. Her step slowed. A hard knot rose in her throat, and she swallowed hard. She'd just flown in the face of Mona and Kerr's stern warnings. *What in God's name is the matter with me?*

Standing just outside the barn, she listened. Something was definitely wrong. At well past midnight, the horses should be sound asleep. Instead, sounds of restless feet and curious snuffling drifted through the open door. Someone was inside the barn.

A wave of fright crashed over her, and she darted past the door and into the dark shadows behind the building. From that vantage point, she could see the carriage house. The apartment windows were dark, but the silhouette of the van was visible in the thin moonlight. Hafez and Mustafa had returned.

She closed her eyes and took deep, measured breaths, willing her pulse to stop racing. She needed to get back to the house quickly, and without being seen. She looked again toward the carriage house, and her breath froze. At the back corner of the structure, a tiny light flared, illuminating a man's face for a moment. The flame died, and the small orange dot of a cigarette glowed steadily in the dark.

Jess could barely breathe. Terror paralyzed every muscle. A small noise behind her sent a blast of adrenaline careening through her system, and she crouched down. The glowing cigarette moved slowly toward the dark barn.

She listened, hearing only her pulse thundering in her ears. A minute later, she began to move through the trees toward the house. Feeling her way, she tried to move silently. Brambles tore at her bare ankles. Every step crunched on dry leaves and twigs. She stopped once and looked back, listening intently for any sign she'd been detected, but the night air was heavy and still. Another step found a rabbit hole, and she went down on one knee. Pain seared through her hand as she connected with something sharp. She finally reached the edge of the woods next to the house, and sank onto a fallen tree. Inhaling deeply, she willed her pulse to slow, and tried to stifle the sobs crawling up her throat.

The moon reappeared, brightening the arena and pastures. At that moment, two figures emerged from the barn. They each appeared to be carrying something. Their muffled voices drifted on the night breeze as they skirted the arena, then headed across the pasture toward the main highway. Terror bore down on Jess like a gale force wind. *They're moving the weapons*. A deadly plot was imminent.

When the figures were out of sight, she slipped around the side of the house and into the kitchen. A minute later, Mona answered the phone.

"Mona? It's me, Jess. They're moving the weapons. . .I just saw–huh? No, I couldn't sleep. I went out for some fresh air."

Mona thanked her for the heads-up, then said goodnight. Jess closed her eyes and pondered the agent's unsurprised tone. Without a doubt, Mona already knew, which meant agents were hiding out there in the dark. The noises in the woods–for sure, they'd seen her lurking near the barn. Nothing to do about it now. Tomorrow she'd probably be taken into protective custody.

𝕏

# *Forty*

The following morning, Jess leaned on the arena fence to watch Beth Caldwell work, but in minutes, her thoughts snapped forward to the plans. She glanced at her watch. In twenty-four hours, she'd be free again–or dead. The thought sent a wave of determination through her mind, then a spark of excitement. For the past few days, she'd been sleepwalking through the surreal activities–almost like watching a play. The final act was about to begin, and now she knew her part. Memorize her lines and don't miss any cues. This wasn't about what life handed out, but how one handled it. *I can do this.*

"Thanks for calling me last night."

Jess jumped, then grinned. "Sorry I woke you–I was *really* frazzled."

Mona leaned her back against a fence post. "You did the right thing, proved you're a team player–we weren't sure for awhile. I know this has been hard–you're on your own turf and used to being in charge. I've seen how good you are at what you do. You're very professional." She looked Jess directly in the eye. "I think you understand, in this situation, you're not a pro. But *we* are. We've covered every base, anticipated things you'd never imagine. We're ready to proceed in the quickest, safest way possible. But you *must* be conscious–every second–of the potential danger in this operation, and your role in it. We *need* you."

Jess nodded, comforted by her own new attitude about the situation. "I'm ready."

Mona pushed away from the post and grinned. "Well, I got stalls to clean."

Jess glanced back at the rider in the arena, then fell into step beside Mona. When they reached the door, she caught the agent's sleeve.

"Do you think Zada's part of the plot?"

"We're not sure. These guys are very cagey about who they include in their circles. Wives are usually excluded, but Zada's not your usual subservient wife."

"The hell she isn't! You should have heard her carrying on about wifely duties and obedience and morality."

Mona posed a grim smile. "She's a good actress, Jess. Her background and education belie the character she becomes for you."

Jess nodded thoughtfully. What had Shakespeare said? *"All the world's a stage. . ."* In the space of a few days, Jess had learned, all too well, that things weren't always what they seemed. Apparently, she'd lost her sharp insight about people.

"Are you going to arrest her, too?"

Mona clucked her tongue. "That's a need-to-know item. Not included in your script."

In the casino coffee shop, Samir concentrated on his friends' angry conversation. Because they wore the features of the Middle East, they felt scrutinized, suspected, and feared. They had a right to their indignation–most of them had lived in America all their lives, but now felt like strangers compelled to prove their worth.

Fury burned in Samir's chest. These were good men, devout Muslims. They should be afforded more respect. But what did Americans know about respect? They entertained themselves with filthy books and films. The women were careless of their bodies, wearing immodest clothing and displaying bare flesh to the world, painting their faces like harlots–even the young girls. No self-respecting Muslim man would allow his wife or daughters to shame him with such actions.

His thoughts turned to Zada, recalling her sobs of the night before. He felt no pity–she deserved everything he'd handed out. She would never step outside her boundaries again.

"Samir, when will you make the pilgrimage?"

He smiled at the elderly man beside him. "Ahh, Mecca. Soon, *Insha'Allaah*." He rose and bobbed his head. "I must go now. I will see you all again. *Allaahu akbar*."

He walked away, the group's echoed good wishes drifting behind him. Moving slowly down the marble concourse, he gazed at the surroundings that had been his personal getaway for so long. The beautiful trappings provided such an elegant camouflage for the relentless undercurrent of addiction. The Achilles' heel of the Western World. He smiled without humor. Jessica Rayder was one of the fallen. How he wished he could tell her what a helpmate she'd been to his mission. Unfortunately, she would never understand its importance, and her assistance would go unacknowledged. In fact, her very existence had become a liability.

He passed through the heavy glass doors and headed toward his car. When he reached the jammed parking lot, he pulled out the prepaid cellphone he'd purchased that morning.

"Mustafa? Yes, the weather looks very good for Saturday." He listened for a moment, then nodded. "*Quy-eese*. Be sure to feed the horse. *Ma'assalama*."

By mid-afternoon, all the students had been coached one last time, saddles and bridles were polished to a fine sheen, and the barn hummed with excitement. Jess listened to the happy young voices out in the aisle, and thought back to her own youth, her first horse, her first show–the excitement and fright pounding through her chest as she'd waited at the in-gate. Her eyes misted. The beginning of the dream. Captured by the euphoria of victory, she and Faith had made a pact to someday open their very own riding stable. *Those were the days. Not a care in the world except getting on that horse and beating Felicity Smarty-Pants.*

Beth Caldwell's pert face appeared in the office doorway.

"See you in the morning, Jess."

"Right. You get a good night's sleep. It'll be a big day."

Jess's thoughts sobered. Faith's girls were all good friends, with only a touch of friendly rivalry. Nothing like the nasty and devious undercurrent that could thread its way through a group of serious show-jumping competitors. Her heart lurched at the thought of putting the children in harm's way. If something went wrong and one of them was injured or killed, she'd never forgive herself.

*Suppose there is gunfire? Or hostages? Good grief, what better way for the terrorists to escape than to take a couple of little girls with them?*

"Dammit, I need to talk to Mona."

Jess leaped out of her chair, and it careened into the file cabinet. Out in the aisle, she assumed a pleasant smile and looked around. Lexie Troy walked toward her, leading Jazz Man.

"Hey, Lex, how's he doin'?"

The teenager's face blossomed into a big smile. "Really good. The vet says I can start riding him again next week." Her smile faded and she stuck out her lower lip. "But no jumping for another month."

"I'm sure sorry, honey, but you know you can ride Danny as long as you want."

The girl smiled again. "Thanks–he's, like, really a neat horse."

She headed out the door toward the paddock, and Jess remembered what she'd been doing.

"Anybody seen Mona?"

The agent emerged from Buster's stall. "I'm down here. What do you need?"

Jess motioned for her to follow, then walked briskly toward the barn door. Outside, she lowered her voice.

"I *have* to know how you're going to protect the students."

Mona's mouth twitched into a patronizing smile, and Jess stepped up close. "No crap, Mona. You've let me know I'm no pro, but I have a responsibility to these kids and their parents. You tell me right now what the plan is, or there won't *be* any plan."

The agent's features hardened. "Don't even try blackmail, Jess–it won't work. I'll fill you in, but know this: it's not because I'm afraid you'll take your ball and go home."

Jess stood her ground, unblinking, and the old instincts returned: if the opposition can read your face, it's over. As far as she was concerned, if they couldn't protect the kids, the agents were her opponents.

Mona's confident tone lent credibility to her answer. "Once the riders and families begin to arrive, Mustafa and Hafez will never be left alone, and Samir will be surrounded in the spectator section. If they make any threatening moves, we'll stop them."

"Why can't we have protective vests for the riders, like I'm going to have?"

Mona snorted. "Why don't we just take out an ad in the local newspaper? 'Terrorist Cell to be Caught.' Jess, I'm telling you one more time–don't start making your own plans. You have to trust us. The kids will be safe."

Jess's hostility faded, and she exhaled slowly. "Boy, I hope so."

Mona touched her arm. "I promise." Her gaze moved across the field. "Looks like you have company."

Howard had set up shop on the breakfast bar. His open briefcase sat on one of the stools, and stacks of papers lined up neatly across the countertop. His rolled-up shirtsleeves revealed tanned, muscular forearms, and Jess's stomach gave a little jump.

She whistled softly. "Looks like Legal Central here." She climbed up on a stool, and hooked her heels over a rung. "What's up?"

"I've been working on a statement for the press. You and Faith need to rehearse it, be sure you both say the same things. Obviously, the FBI won't want you to give away any of their planning secrets, but–"

"Howard, you have to be kidding! We have to talk to the press?"

"Jess, did you think something this big would go unnoticed? This place will be crawling with reporters and television cameras within a few hours after the horse show. You need to be prepared."

He handed her a sheet of paper. "Here are some logical questions they'll ask, and some innocuous answers. I've put in a call to Peterson. I want his approval on these, and any guidance he might give us."

Jess scanned the list. "You've certainly thought of everything."

"Considering the seriousness of what you're doing, I can't afford *not* to."

ꭗ

## *Forty-One*

Snuggled deep into her warm bed-nest, Jess dozed, listening to the weather.

*". . .storms in Texas and Oklahoma. Here in Hartford, the wind is steady at five miles per hour, temperature is fifty-one degrees, and we're looking at the chance of heavy rain sometime after mid-day."*

She looked out the bedroom window, dismayed by the gloom on the other side of the glass. Even that early, the sky should have been a little brighter. The show would start at nine and, with any luck, finish before the weather turned nasty.

*"It's six o'clock. At home, Americans are rising to face another sorrowful anniversary of the September Eleventh attacks on our nation. Around the country, memorials are planned, and President Bush has called for a national minute of silence at 8:45 this morning. God bless America."*

A soft country-rock tune whined through the speaker and, with a heavy heart, Jess rolled out of bed.

Waiting impatiently while the coffee brewed, she watched the mahogany liquid dribble into the pot, her mind taking a painful journey through the past few days. A lump rose in her throat and her eyes misted. After today, Howard would return to his forest refuge to surround himself with the positive things he'd built into his life, and she would return to the shell of an existence she'd worked so hard to attain. How in hell had she ever imagined she could make him part of it?

The coffeemaker finished its task, she poured a mug, then walked out to the porch to collect her thoughts for the day ahead.

On the horizon, a strip of sky brightened beneath low clouds, and a moment later, the sun leaked through a cleft in the billowy gray blanket. At the end of the road, headlights turned into the drive, and a couple of minutes later, Faith stepped onto the porch.

The strain of the past few days etched her features. "Well, Jess, you ready for this?"

"Ready as I'll ever be. . .You know, I think about this nightmare and how it happened, and all I can see is a trail of my screw-ups, bungled chances, and poor judgment calls." She shook her head. "God, I must have done *something* worthwhile at some point in my life."

Faith grabbed her, hugging fiercely. "You have! Don't do this to yourself–especially not right now. We need you to be strong. You're the glue that holds this plan together." She stepped back, her eyes bright with tears. "You're gonna be a hero, Jessie. I'd say that's a pretty worthwhile accomplishment."

A car turned into the lane, followed by Mona's truck, and Jess let out a long, slow breath.

"Looks like the players are taking up their positions. Let's go."

A small spurt of adrenaline pumped through her system, and her confidence rose. Today she'd have the chance to use her biggest and best bluff ever. The Poker Face of the Century.

Over the next fifteen minutes, students began to arrive, and the barn echoed with noisy enthusiasm. Youthful laughter ricocheted off the rafters, horses whinnied and snorted, and someone boosted the volume on the barn radio, filling the air with the strains of good boot-stompin' country music. Faith plunged into her mentor's role, and Jess directed the guys putting up the food tent.

Hafez and Mustafa went about the morning feed routine, and Mona cleaned stalls after each horse was taken out to groom. Jess assessed Mona's diligence. She certainly knew how to play the part. *I wonder if she feels any remorse for deceiving us. Or sadness that she won't be coming here anymore.* In the fervor of the past week, Jess hadn't considered what emotions might be tormenting Mona. With the exception of that one brief glimpse of her personal dedication to wiping out terrorism, Mona had simply been a stranger in the midst of Jess's chaos–a stranger who, under the wrong circumstances, could mutate from friend to foe in the blink of an eye.

Jess glanced around her office, so familiar, so secure–the stage for the most important thing she'd ever do. She wondered if hidden cameras and microphones had been placed to document her meeting with Samir. Her stomach pitched, and she looked at the clock. Seven-thirty. In less than five hours, she would be the catalyst in one more strike for freedom.

Through the office window, the sky had brightened, patches of blue interspersed the light gray clouds, and thin sunshine cast pale shadows over the arena. A group of parents drank from cups of steaming coffee, and chatted amiably, oblivious to the peril lurking in the depths of Easton Ridge. Would those parents string her up for putting their children in harm's way? Jess closed her eyes and whispered a prayer of deliverance.

Mona's voice intruded. "Okay, Jess, time to get dressed."

She held up a clothes bag, and motioned toward the bathroom door in the corner. Inside the cramped room, she unzipped the bag and pulled out a dark blue vest. Jess's breath caught again at the notion she might be in enough danger to need body armor. Mona fiddled with the garment, unhooking the four Velcro® straps that kept it together, then held it up and squinted at Jess's figure.

"This should fit. Peel off your shirt."

She wrapped the bulky vest around Jess's chest, then hooked the shoulder straps.

Jess exhaled sharply. "Wow, it's really heavy–I had no idea."

Mona grinned. "Only seven pounds, but it'll stop a .44 dead in its tracks."

The rough fabric against bare skin sent fear blasting through Jess's head. This was for real–seriously deadly. Her life could depend on her skill at the bluff.

Mona hooked the side straps tightly, to the point that Jess almost couldn't breathe normally. The thick Kevlar® pad rubbed uncomfortably along the bottom of her rib cage, and the tiny bathroom closed in, wrapping her in the only brief safety she'd feel for the next few hours. Muted sounds from the show ring trickled through the cracks around the door, reminding her why she was closeted.

She took a deep breath. "I'm ready."

Mona's smile was less than reassuring. "Relax, Jess. You're tight as a tick. You'll be fine. This is just a precaution in case something goes haywire." She shook her head emphatically. "But it won't–trust me. Here, put your shirt back on."

Jess's agitation grew. "How can you be so sure? These people are animals–they'll do whatever they have to. You said so yourself."

Mona laid her hand on Jess's shoulder. "They are, and they might. But we're right on top of them. They'll never know what hit 'em. We're the pros, remember?"

*Except when you make a mistake*. Jess shuddered, thinking about Howard's story of an operation gone bad.

A few minutes later, she headed for Casey's stall, frightened by the compulsion to talk to her horse one more time before the day began.

"Hey, Sweetie, ready to go out?"

Casey's whiskery muzzle tickled Jess's chin, and she giggled. The amusement caught in her throat and her eyes burned.

Resting her face against the mare's warm cheek, she whispered, "I love you."

Hafez and Mustafa were in the arena, setting up the jumps when Jess led Casey out of the barn. She watched them for a minute, noticing their mechanical movements and tight faces. They seemed nervous, as though they were in a hurry to finish.

A steady stream of cars paraded up the lane, quickly filling the parking area. She glanced at her watch. 8:00. A quiver of anticipation and excitement raced across her skin. The chase was about to begin.

In the paddock behind her, the students were exercising their horses and letting off nervous energy. Inside the barn, Beth Caldwell's shrill voice rang out.

"Alex! Did you take my crop?"

Lexie's response was typical. "Like, why would I take *your* crop?"

Jess grinned, listening to the teenage spat sparked by the undercurrent of nerves. She led Casey through the pasture gate, then turned her loose. The old lady immediately dropped to her knees to roll in the dust.

As Jess headed back toward the barn, she focused on the spectator section. Faces she didn't recognize appeared throughout the crowd. The newcomers were a mix of young and middle-aged women, plus a couple of older men with gray hair. Grandfatherly types. The picture clearly illustrated what Mona meant. The whole crowd looked normal, a blend of ages and genders. No one would suspect that armed FBI agents peppered the audience.

In the back row, she caught a glimpse of Howard's silver hair, his head bobbing as he talked to the mother of one of Faith's students. The woman laughed, obviously charmed by his engaging conversation. Jess's throat constricted with her desire to be the object of his attention, and she looked away. At that moment, Samir emerged from the dark innards of his Mercedes, and stood still, surveying the scene like a monarch assessing a kingdom.

An emotion akin to hatred seethed in Jess's brain, startling her with its intensity. She hadn't seen him since the poker game and, in the face of this imposing attitude, her original perception of a small, ingratiating man disintegrated. Instead, she saw a huge man with a plan–a deadly scheme, carefully thought out, a blueprint for death. Her jaw tightened. *Not if I can help it, you bastard.*

She glanced back at the arena. All the jumps were in place, and Mustafa and Hafez had disappeared. She took a few steps away from the barn door, scanning the area to find their whereabouts. By the carriage house, they'd spread their prayer rugs on the ground. On their knees, heads pressed against the ground, they remained still. Jess turned away, fighting the new, terrifying emotions clawing their way into her thoughts.

"Boy, this thing is uncomfortable!"

Jess jumped, then frowned. "As compared to what? A bullet in the chest?"

Faith's eyes widened, and she threw a frightened glance over her shoulder. "Shhh!" She squeezed Jess's arm, took a deep breath, then headed for the arena, striding confidently toward the announcer's stand. Jess turned to go back into the barn, glancing once more at the carriage house. She froze in mid-step as Hafez threw two duffel bags into the back of the van and closed the door. Then, the two men started toward the barn.

Jess hurried inside, looking up and down the aisle for Mona.

The men's silhouettes appeared in the backlit door at the far end, then they disappeared into the feed room. Jess heard voices in the office, and walked briskly across the aisle. Mona and Kerr were deep in conversation when Jess stepped into the room.

Mona turned, a frown knitting her dark brows. "What is it, Jess?"

She lowered her voice. "I just saw the men loading their stuff into the van."

"Yes, we know. Thanks. You'd better go on outside. Your party's about to begin."

Jess left the room, uneasiness edging into her chest. *Something's going on I don't know about*. She moved down the aisle, giving everyone a heads-up that the show was about to begin. Faith's voice echoed over the PA system.

"Please take your seats. We'll start in a couple of minutes."

Jess hurried outside and scanned the far side of the audience, wanting one more glimpse of Howard. He looked directly at her, sending a small wave and an encouraging smile. A ripple of emotion stopped her breath for an instant, then she smiled back.

Faith's voice drifted on the crisp September air. "Good morning, everyone. Welcome to the fall gala at Easton Ridge."

She stood very still in the center of the arena, scanning the crowd. Her voice grew stronger.

"We can never forget the tragedy of September Eleventh, 2001." Her voice cracked, she swallowed, then continued. "Every one of us was affected by what transpired that day, and as we remember, our hearts and souls will stand forever frozen in time. Our show today is dedicated to the memory of those who died on that date, and to those who still fight for our freedom from terrorism."

She moved to the flagpole beside the announcer's stand and, for a moment, gazed up at the flag waving lightly in the morning breeze. Slowly, she lowered it to half-mast. Turning back to the silent crowd, she spoke softly into the microphone.

"It's 8:45."

Not a sound could be heard. Even the normal murmurs of nature seemed to cease in reverence for the moment. Through lowered lashes, Jess watched the audience. Every head had bowed, but one.

Cold black eyes gazed defiantly across the arena, arrowing straight into Jess's heart. She raised her head and met Samir's gaze, wanting to send him a message, but not daring to. She looked away and focused on the half-mast flag that filled her with renewed courage.

# *Forty-Two*

Faith's enthusiasm sparkled in the fresh morning air.

"Ladies and gentlemen, enjoy the show!"

Minutes later, she walked toward the barn, face flushed, eyes sparkling. "C'mon, ladies! First level, on deck!"

She gathered the flock of little girls, who looked very much like tiny beetles in their black velvet riding hats, knee-high shiny boots, and flapping coattails. The three beginner lead-line students guided their ponies into the ring.

With the first part of the event well under control, Jess returned to the barn to check on the next round of riders.

"Alex, will you and Beth see that the B-group is ready to go out? I need to hit the restroom."

The teenagers grinned, delighted to be in charge. They immediately set about fussing after the younger girls, tweaking chin-straps, adjusting jackets and, in general, acting like mother hens. Jess chuckled and headed toward the office. As she approached the door, Mona came around the corner, a peculiar expression changing her sharp features.

Her voice oozed sarcasm. "Wasn't *that* a nice touch."

Jess glowered. "Think what you like, Mona, *that* was Faith's battle cry."

An emotion flickered across Mona's face. Remorse? A glisten of moisture slipped onto her lower eyelashes, and she looked away. Jess stepped into the bathroom and slammed the door. Mona's raspy voice trickled through the barrier.

"Don't get your knickers in a knot. It was very moving." A hesitation. "But I don't remember any discussions about a patriotic speech being part of the plan."

Jess leaned on the sink and dropped her head. *I can't wait to get this woman out of my life!* She opened the door and leveled a hard look at the grim-faced agent.

"Then perhaps that was an oversight on your part. Don't you think it would seem odd if we didn't acknowledge that today is the anniversary of the most horrifying tragedy in American history?"

Mona dropped her gaze and her shoulders slumped as she let out a long, slow sigh. "Yes, it would." She said nothing for a moment, then looked up. "Sometimes I'm like a dog worrying a bone–this is one of those times."

Jess realized Mona's earlier reaction was a knee-jerk, the instinct to cover up her feelings.

"Mona, I honestly didn't know she planned to do that. Sometimes, Faith surprises me–she *does* have a mind of her own."

Mona nodded. "Just see that *you* remember where you are and what you're doing today."

**10:00 A.M.**

Jess watched Zada's subdued demeanor, the antithesis of her usual strong and self-assured attitude. Her gaze never left the ground, and when Samir addressed her, she nodded and bowed slightly. *It's almost like she's been beaten up–she's afraid of him.* A sick feeling grew in Jess's stomach as the reason became clear. Her comments to Samir had inadvertently placed Zada in a dangerous position–that of a Muslim wife who'd betrayed a confidence. She'd obviously paid dearly for her transgression.

Jess turned away, unwilling to deal with the wide range of feelings raging through her head. Turning to the refuge of the barn, she immersed herself in the throng of eager young riders on their big day. Surrounded by the happy excitement of the morning, she pushed away all thoughts of Zada, and what the next two hours might bring.

A child's voice accompanied a soft tug on her shirttail.

"Can you help me with Archie's bridle? It's twisted."

Jess grinned at the small face peering up at her. "Now, how in the world did you do *that*?"

Listening to the long, detailed explanation, she followed the girl to the crossties, where a sturdy roan hunter pony stood patiently waiting to be untangled. Concentrating on the puzzle of the intertwined leather lines, Jess felt more serene than she had in days. Her fingers worked the soft leather, coaxing it back to the correct position, her hands brushing against warm horseflesh. For a precious few moments, only the present mattered.

Jess squeezed the little girl's shoulder. "You go, girl!"

Waiting by the barn door, Dania stood in front of Buster, clutching the reins against her narrow chest, and murmuring to him in Arabic. Her sorrowful expression sent a stab of sympathy through Jess's thoughts. *Samir must have told her.* Jess could think of nothing that would ease the pain, but she stepped up beside the child anyway.

"How's Buster this morning? Ready to make you a champion?"

Dark eyes regarded her for a moment.

"Yes, Ma'am. We will win for Papa. *Insha'Allaah.*"

The girl was subdued, beaten, sorrowful–a small rubber stamp of her mother. Jess wanted to reach out, pull her into a hug, tell her how sorry she felt about everything that had happened. Of course, she could not. Dania would never enjoy the bright future Easton Ridge had planned for her.

"Good luck, Dania."

Jess turned away, unable to bear the child's pitiful courage. A movement down the aisle caught her attention and she saw Mustafa emerge from Buster's stall and hurry toward the equipment room. What was he doing down there? He was supposed to be at the arena, waiting to set up jumps. Zada's horrible directive echoed in Jess's head, and panic moved through her chest.

She darted across the aisle. The roomy, newly-bedded stall smelled of fresh wood shavings, and everything appeared normal. She looked around carefully, inspecting the wooden walls, checking the ledge of the mesh-covered window, but finding nothing. The bedding. Something could be hidden there, but what? Using the toe of her boot, she brushed the shavings aside, clear down to the packed clay floor. Nothing. She exhaled slowly. *What could he have been doing in here?* She looked into the black rubber feed bucket. Empty. Buster hadn't left even one grain of sweet-feed behind. Water bucket–full to the brim.

She shook her head. Maybe she should find Mustafa and *ask*

him why he'd been in Buster's stall. *Yeah, right.* She was being paranoid. The Mahfoods had no good reason to destroy the horse. What would it prove? A shiver chilled her skin. A cruel warning of the terror to come?

As she stared at the water bucket, a red shimmer appeared. She focused on the pearly film spreading over the surface of the water. Leaning closer, she peered into the bucket. In the bottom, a small white tablet bubbled slowly.

Nausea rose in her throat–she'd almost missed it. In thirty minutes, Buster would be back in his stall, tired and thirsty. Then, dead. She reached for the clip holding the bucket, then stopped. *No, better check with Mona.*

She left the stall and hurried down the aisle, scanning the length of the barn. Mona stood just outside the main door, smoking a cigarette and watching the show. Jess tried to walk normally, repressing her desire to sprint.

"Mona, can you come in for a minute?"

The agent stubbed out her cigarette and nodded. "Problem?"

"Big one."

The two women moved into the barn just as Mustafa emerged from the equipment room and started toward them. Jess stopped and turned, raising her voice a little.

"After the show, we're going to move horses around. A couple of the stalls need some repair work."

Confusion flickered through Mona's eyes, then comprehension.

"Okay, what do you want me to do?"

Mustafa walked past them, his gaze directed at the floor. When he was well out of earshot, Jess closed her eyes, suddenly lightheaded.

"You okay?" whispered Mona.

Jess nodded, glancing again at Mustafa's retreating figure. She walked over to Buster's stall and lifted the latch. A moment later, Mona released a sharp breath.

"What the hell is *that?*"

"I don't know, but I guarantee it won't improve the quality of Buster's life. I started to dump it, but I was afraid one of them would see me."

Mona thought for a minute, staring at the deadly water bucket.

"We can't move it. I'll just have to make sure no horses get put into this stall. Leave it to me, I'll think of something."

A burst of cheering and applause floated through the open doors.

Jess shook her head. "I have to get back outside. Please, *please*, make sure no horses get to that bucket."

# Forty-Three

**11:00 A.M.**

Buster flew around the jump course, sailing over each obstacle as though it were merely a bump on the ground. Dania's face glowed with pride and joy, her skill taking her to an emotional level only enjoyed by talented athletes. The final jump was a two-foot hogs-back–a real challenge for a beginner. Jess held her breath as Buster straightened out and gauged his take-off. Dania's head was high, her eyes straight ahead. The horse launched his body and took flight, clearing the highest rail by inches.

The audience rose as one, applauding and whistling, and Jess blinked back the tears as she watched Buster trot toward Faith in the center of the arena.

"Ladies and gentlemen, Dania Mahfood, our show champion for Level One. Dania has only been taking lessons for five weeks." Faith grinned up at the child. "As you've seen, she is a talented young lady, and we have big plans for her here at Easton Ridge."

Faith pinned a large purple rosette to Buster's bridle, then handed Dania a gleaming silver trophy. As the girl and her horse trotted their victory pass around the arena, Jess's thoughts saddened, knowing Dania was enjoying her last smile of freedom in America.

Jess scanned the crowd, noticing several empty chairs. Her heart thumped twice under the sweltering body armor, and she glanced at her watch. 11:10. A wave of panic followed, and her gaze moved to the now empty spot where Howard had been sitting. Where had he gone? She needed to know he was close by. Anxiety began to creep in, pressing heavily on her earlier determination to make the plan work.

Hafez and Mustafa moved the last jump out of the way, then Alex and Bethany entered the ring. The two young ladies were perfectly turned out in their matching burgundy hunt jackets and tan breeches. Polished black boots gleamed in the faint sunlight as the girls went through their paces, moving in perfect time to Faith's commentary.

Jess's focus returned to her own role. In less than an hour, she'd see the fall of Samir and his murderous cohorts. Wicked pleasure warmed her thoughts as she imagined the three men behind bars–or worse.

Music filtered through the loudspeaker, adding a festive air to the occasion, and the crowd began moving toward the food tent. The audience had thinned considerably, and Jess wondered where the undercover people had gone. Her pulse quickened. *I hope to God they'll act quickly if Samir and the boys get frisky.*

Faith appeared. "You okay?"

Jess's smile felt wooden. "I think so. Everybody did a great job this morning. Congratulations–you've worked really hard."

Faith's eyes misted and her chin trembled. "Thanks. . .Jessie?" She swallowed hard. "If anything goes wrong–"

Jess quickly slipped her arm around her friend's shoulders and squeezed hard. The lump in her own throat made speech difficult.

"It's going to be fine," she murmured, hoping she sounded convincing. "Don't you worry–these people have everything under control. We're more than covered."

Fifteen minutes later, Jess checked the crowd again. Howard had returned to his seat, but now Samir was gone. Zada and Dania sat quietly in the spectator section, balancing plates on their laps. The black Mercedes was still in the parking lot. To Jess, the air felt still and ominous, but a relaxed atmosphere seemed to surround everyone else.

Behind her, Mona's voice was low. "Time to get into position."

Jess nodded and took a deep breath. The vest pressed against her chest, reminding her that every move, every nuance, would count toward the success of the operation. A rivulet of sweat trickled down between her breasts. Her hands grew clammy, and every breath came with effort. She stepped into the shadow of the doorway, throwing one more glance toward Howard. Their eyes met, and she prayed she'd see him again.

The distance between the barn door and her office seemed the longest walk she'd ever taken, each step bringing her closer to the unknown. About fifteen feet from the office door, she spotted Samir walking briskly away from the carriage house. *He did meet the nephews, just like Kerr said he would.* Her confidence soared. Everything should go according to plan. She moved quickly into the office.

A minute later, she glanced out the window and horror engulfed her. Hafez's van disappeared down the driveway toward the highway. *They're getting away! Oh, my God, I have to–.* She closed her eyes and took a deep breath. *Calm down. The agents have eyes. They'll handle it.*

The office door closed quietly, and she snapped back to attention. Samir leaned against the doorjamb, a patronizing smile directly contradicting the malice in his dark gaze.

"Good afternoon, Miss Jessica."

She assumed a neutral expression, willing her thoughts to stay clear of her eyes.

"Hello, Samir. Are you enjoying the show?"

He smiled and pushed away from the wall. "Yes, of course. And my Dania is the star, no?"

"She performed beautifully. We are very proud of her."

Jess's breath caught as Samir reached inside his suit coat. "I have a check. Will that be acceptable?"

She nodded, her pulse pounding in her ears. "Yes, of course."

*Probably not worth the paper it's written on.* She looked at the check for a moment, her heart racing as she waited for the agents to make their move.

Samir cleared his throat. "I would like a receipt, please."

Fright rose in Jess's throat, and she chanced a quick look through the window. *Where are they?* Nothing but the ordinary scene of spectators returning to their seats. A hot flush crawled over her skin beneath the vest, and her breathing almost ceased.

"Oh. . .Sure."

She willed her fingers to stop trembling while she wrote.

He accepted the receipt and smiled. "This is such a nice place.

My family has enjoyed it."

He turned toward the door.

Jess couldn't move. He was going to leave, and no one was going to stop him. *No, they'll get him outside, or after he leaves the property.* That hadn't been the plan. but obviously, she'd never known the real plan.

Samir turned back, his smile gone. His cold gaze speared through her.

"Allaah will prevail, Jessica. Know it in your heart, and you will find peace. *Allaahu akbar.*"

He bowed, opened the door, and disappeared into the barn.

Tension braided through her emotional turmoil, launching an attack on her dance with reality. In the big picture, she'd been a chess piece. Anger rolled like thunderclouds through her chest. She exhaled sharply and leaned on the desk, shuddering with the reaction. The shuffle of feet outside the door notched up her pulse, and another surge of adrenaline flooded her system.

Faith scurried in and closed the door, her face a grotesque mask of fear.

"Jessie, what's going on? They've all left!"

"Yes, I know. And I'm sure as hell going to find out why!"

She moved to the window again. Faith crowded up against her arm like a frightened child.

Across the arena, the audience had settled in for the second half of the show, but the crowd had thinned. The undercover people must have left the grounds. Jess focused on the food tent. Zada stood with Dania, who'd already changed out of her riding clothes, but Samir was not with them. The Mercedes was no longer amongst the parked cars.

Jess grasped Faith's arm, trying to appear confident. "You go on out and get started. I'll find out what happened."

Faith didn't look reassured, but nodded. When she'd gone, Jess paced the room, gathering her wits and playing out scenarios. Her solitude didn't last long. The door opened, and the three agents entered.

Jess drew herself up to her full height and folded her arms across her padded chest, narrowing her eyes as she faced the team.

"Exactly what the hell is going on? Why didn't you guys arrest him? I saw the other two barrel out of here just as I was getting ready to meet Samir!" Her voice rose, and she struggled to control her anger. "I almost lost it!"

Peterson moved closer, holding up his hand in a conciliatory gesture. "Calm down. Everything is fine." He smiled. "In fact, everything is better than fine."

The other two agents nodded, but their calm expressions fed her fury.

"No! You tell me what's going on! You have us jumping through hoops, watching our backs, frightened half out of our wits–and you say *calm down*? Bull–shit!"

Kerr's usual surly attitude simmered just beneath the surface of his speech. "Listen, Jess, you girls did a great job, but your part is over. Everything went according to the most recent plan. All along, our preference was to keep the situation away from a public venue, reduce the risk of collateral damage. We didn't have time to tell you about the change." He paused and looked her straight in the eye. "Your safety depended on it."

Her anger ebbed, and she felt ill. She turned away, hearing the disgust in her tone.

"Fine, then just get the hell out of here and leave us alone now."

Their feet shuffled as they left the room, but a second later, Mona's voice drifted into Jess's battered thoughts.

"It'll be soon–then you'll understand."

Unable to remain standing for another moment, Jess dropped into a chair. The huge flush of adrenaline had seeped into every fiber of her body, and its sudden departure left her drained. Her brain went on strike and she sat like a statue, staring at the floor. In the barn aisle and outdoors, she heard the traditional sounds of a horse show in progress. Loudspeaker. Applause. Laughter and shouting. Voices. The sounds of her world. Sounds that slowly moved into her thoughts, and began to ease the strain.

As her physical strength returned, the finality of her personal drama clarified. It was over. She could put the fear behind her now. Life could resume as usual. Or could it?

Coming so close to the enemy had given her a new perspective on what was important–and what was not. Her breath caught as she considered the possibility that Samir and his fellow fanatics would succeed in their malignant quest to annihilate the American belief in freedom. What if the FBI had misjudged the terrorists? It wouldn't be the first time rebels had slipped through the net. A Damoclean sword hung over everything Jess had ever cherished.

Another thought occurred to her, and a shiver ran across her shoulders. She and Faith might be liabilities, details to be purged. Howard's lesson in terrorism resonated through her brain. Samir's cell was only one of many. Destroy it, and another would take its place, like the tide washing away footprints in the sand.

She closed her eyes and took a deep, shuddery breath. The Kevlar vest chafed her ribs, reminding her that the immediate danger had passed. She slipped into the bathroom and peeled off the hateful thing, flinging it to the floor in the corner. Catching a glimpse of herself in the mirror, she cringed at the dark circles under her tired eyes. When was the last time she'd really slept? Who knew? Who cared? Tomorrow, she and Faith could start over.

A horse whinnied, and she grinned. Tomorrow, she had a date with Danny.

*Oh, shit! The poisoned water!* She dashed out into the aisle and headed toward Buster's stall. She snatched open the door, and stopped short. Horror flooded her chest. The big horse's head swung up quickly, and he peered at her curiously. He flicked his tail at an imaginary fly. Water dribbled from his lips.

)(

# *Forty-Four*

No! No! No!"

Jess's wail echoed through the huge barn.

Buster's calm attitude disappeared, and he skittered nervously around his stall. Jess tried to get close, but he evaded her. She squinted, trying to see better in the dim light.

"Why is it so damned dark in here?"

She stopped short. At midday, the stall should have been bright from the sun through the window. *Where is the window?* She stepped back into the aisle to look at the nameplate on the door. *McKenzie.* She almost threw up. Buster was in the wrong stall.

She pulled open the heavy door of the adjoining stall, and moved to the corner. The water bucket was empty.

Behind her, Mona's voice sounded matter-of-fact.

"I took care of it."

Jess's pulse thundered in her ears, and she felt wobbly in the knees. "Thank God."

The agent smiled. "You did real good today. You'd make a good undercover cop."

The teasing comment cut through the tension, and Jess relaxed. "Thanks, but I think I'll pass. Now can you *please* tell me what's going on?"

"A couple of agents are sweeping the other arena and the carriage house."

Jess cocked her head. "You think they might have left some incriminating evidence behind?"

Mona's expression sent a prickle of apprehension up the back of Jess's neck.

"No. . .well, they *could* have, but it's not likely. They're highly-trained operatives–they don't usually make those kinds of mistakes." She glanced down at her hands, then continued. "We want to make sure they didn't rig up any explosives."

"Oh my God, should we move the horses out?"

"No, the barn's clean. Our team moved in as soon as the suspects drove the van out of here. Your house is okay, too."

Jess's thoughts staggered at the idea. She gazed around the beautiful barn that had been her life for the past six years. A place filled with hope. A flashback smashed into her brain. The Trade Towers, billowing black smoke, spewing debris and humanity. Adrenaline poured into her system faster than her nerves could handle it, and she started to shake.

The days, hours, and minutes of fear swooped down, battering her without mercy. The light began to fade, and voices echoed somewhere in the far reaches of her mind as she sagged toward the ground. Strong arms circled her body, and she leaned against the sturdy woman who'd been beside her from the very beginning of the nightmare.

Samir peered through the tiny crack at the side of the window shade. Heavy humidity hung in the late afternoon light, casting a dreamlike quality to the trees and overgrown shrubs in the neglected front yard of the old farmhouse. It might have been a nice place at one time, but not as elegant as Easton Ridge. Irritation needled through his thoughts. Jessica Rayder's arrogant, typically American independence had interfered with his plans. No wonder she was an unmarried woman. What man would want to play second fiddle to that sharp mind and unfeminine personality?

Samir's gaze moved from the yard to the dilapidated fence surrounding a pasture of waist-high brown weeds. At the near corner of the field, an ancient oak towered, lifeless except for the thick green tangle of kudzu crawling over its trunk. Long, suffocating vines dripped from the bare limbs, reaching out and hooking every available part of the rusty farm machinery parked below. At the far corner of the property, tall grass and weeds almost obscured two abandoned trucks and an old wood-sided station wagon. He squinted, trying to make out details of the vehicles, but they were well camouflaged.

He clucked his tongue and stepped away from the window. These Americans had no pride of ownership, no concept of the wealth in their own country. In his homeland, one-tenth of this property would be worth a fortune, but available to few. He stared down at the red beads in his hand, his fingers moving lovingly over each smooth orb. Soon he would be an instrument of Allaah, showing the arrogant, self-centered infidels of this country who was boss, showing up their weakness against the will of the Almighty.

Hafez appeared beside him. "I fed the horse, as you instructed." He grinned, revealing crooked yellow teeth punctuated by black spots. "By now, the lady will be screaming her lungs out."

Samir turned away, repulsed by the man's bad breath and sour body odor. Soap and water cost nothing–there was no excuse for a filthy body. He took a measured breath. It couldn't be helped. Someone else chose the workers. They were well trained and zealous, but still basically peasants with nothing to lose in the fight for the Sword of Islam. They would be martyrs and heroes–the ultimate reward for true believers.

Moving the window shade aside with one finger, Samir scanned the yard again. The peculiar light of late afternoon had disappeared, and dusk approached. He glanced at the Rolex gleaming from beneath the edge of his black windbreaker, seeing only the time–not the fruits of a successful life in America.

He turned back to Hafez and Mustafa. "When did you talk to Mounir?"

"Just before we left the farm. The members were in place."

Samir frowned. *The team leader should have called by now.*

"Something is wrong." He began to pace the room, his fingers feverishly rolling the prayer beads. "We will wait ten more minutes."

His two companions said nothing.

He moved to a different window, and peered at the other side of the property. Hafez's van was parked next to an old barn that leaned precariously. Samir's Mercedes was inside, out of view. Nerves on edge, he moved into the kitchen and surveyed the back of the property. In the waning light, he could make out the dim outlines of an ancient privy and a low-roofed shed.

Though not as large as Easton Ridge, this remote farmstead provided good security, hidden deep in the midst of property lines camouflaged by mature trees and undergrowth. But more important, it gave him with the means for a contingency plan.

He returned to the living room and faced the men. Their expressions did not change while he spoke.

"The plan is compromised. Something has happened and we must leave. Prepare yourselves."

He pulled a cigar from his shirt pocket and unwrapped it while he walked toward the kitchen. The draft from the screen door sent the fine cellophane fluttering to the cracked linoleum floor.

Jess watched the last car disappear down the driveway. The final hour of classes had been a blur, and weariness saturated every muscle. She wanted to crawl into her bed, burrow under the covers, and let unconsciousness claim her. She sighed. Sleep wouldn't be the refuge she craved. Her dreams, both asleep and awake, would be dominated for a long time by images of the day's drama.

An arm slipped around her shoulders, and Howard's voice warmed the hug.

"I suspect you won't have any trouble falling asleep *tonight.*"

She managed a weak smile. "You must be a mind-reader–I was just planning that very event."

"Are you okay, Jess? You can't imagine how hard it was for me to stay in the audience, especially when Samir came out of the barn and drove away."

"I know. I just kept waiting for the agents to storm into the office, thinking any second it would be over. I don't know how I kept my thoughts from showing." She shrugged. "Maybe I didn't. Maybe he just didn't notice. Or care."

She leaned into Howard's shoulder and closed her eyes. "I am so glad it's over."

"I'm not so sure it *is* over. There'll be some sort of wrap-up. The Feds aren't just going to say, 'Okay, thanks, goodbye'." He squeezed her shoulder. "C'mon, let's help Faith clean up the arena."

Inside the ring, Faith was hefting poles and standards. Her face lit up as they approached.

"Wow, was that exciting or what?"

Howard grinned. "Which event are we talking about?"

She laughed. "*All* of them! The A-Rabs are outta here forever, and my girls did a fabulous job today."

Jess shook her head in wonder. Faith's excursion into fear seemed to have carried her to a new level of confidence. *I wish I felt as free and refreshed.* A twinge skipped through her heart. The frightening episode was over, but she'd never be the same–too many raw nerves and emotions had been exposed during her guided tour through terrorism. For the first time in her life, she felt vulnerable and unsure of herself.

The physical work of clean-up energized her and, with three of them working together, they cleared the arena in twenty minutes.

Mona emerged from the barn, her brisk stride and sharp expression seeming out of place in the new, relaxed atmosphere.

"How's everybody holding up?"

Howard shook his head. "Mona, we're done here. These girls need some rest. If you have questions, they'll have to wait until tomorrow."

"I'm sorry, but you *all* need to stay right here for a while, for your own protection."

Faith's voice rang with frustration. "Mona, I want to go home! *Now*!"

"When the situation is clear, I'll let you know."

Jess frowned. "What situation? What are you talking about? Our part is finished."

"Sorry, Jess. This is the way it has to be. I can't tell you anything else."

On the back stoop of the house, Samir took a deep drag on the exquisite Habano, then removed a small picture of Dania from his pocket. He gazed at the lovely face, her dark eyes filled with childish delight. *Habibi, ana behibek. Allaahu akbar.* His heart contracted painfully and he exhaled slowly, pressing the picture against his chest and gazing up at the pitch-black sky. A new moon hid somewhere up there, completing the cover of darkness. Behind him inside the house, he heard shuffling feet, and the low voices of his companions as they prepared to leave.

Dry grass rustled in the heavy silence. Samir's senses snapped into high alert. He held his breath, waiting. Another soft crunch and rustle. In his peripheral line of sight, he caught a movement. He slowly reached for the gun in his waistband. A black-masked face came around the corner, and a fat raccoon lifted its nose as it caught the human scent. Samir exhaled sharply. The animal stared at him for a second, then scuttled into a hole beneath the house.

Pulse jangling in his ears, Samir returned to the house. "*Yalla.* We go now. Hafez, you first."

Hafez stepped through the front door, and a brilliant flood of light outlined his silhouette. A bullhorn roared through the night. *"This is the FBI. Raise your hands where we can see them!"* Hafez stumbled backwards into the house.

Samir held up his hand. "Be calm. I have a surprise for them. I will return in a moment."

He slipped out the back door and looked at the black sky. *"Allaahu akbar."*

ẌX

## *Forty-Five*

Jess woke with a start and blinked at the dim light. Confusion rambled through her head as she tried to remember why she was sleeping on the couch. Howard's and Mona's voices drifted on a chilly draft, bringing clarity to the moment. The ache of tension grumbled through every muscle in her body as she struggled to sit up.

Mona came into the room, a frown creasing her forehead. "Where's Faith?"

"Asleep in the bedroom. What's going on?"

The agent dropped into an armchair, and leaned her head against the back. "It's over. We got 'em."

Weariness fell away like a chunk of iceberg, and Jess leaped up from the couch. "Yesss! Hallelujah!"

A second later, Faith stumbled into the room, her cheeks flushed with sleep and confusion. "What's all the shoutin' about?"

Jess felt giddy. "Tell us what happened, Mona–how did you catch them?"

"I still can't give you any details, but I'm sure you'll hear about it before too long." She smiled wearily and stood up. "Faith, you ready to go home? One of my guys will follow to see you get there safely."

Jess's heartbeat skipped. "Why does she need an escort? You just said it was over."

"We can't be too careful–you never know."

After they'd gone, Jess looked at Howard. His face showed traces of weariness, and she felt sudden remorse. She'd thought only of herself and her own exhaustion, forgetting the fact he'd been with her every step of the way, probably feeling the same fear about the future.

She stepped up and laid her hand on his arm. "Thank you for being here, for supporting us."

He stroked her cheek, his eyes warm with appreciation. "I couldn't have done otherwise."

All the things she wanted to say lodged in her throat, refusing to move, keeping their own counsel.

His voice softened. "You get some sleep. I'll see you in the morning."

She gazed into his eyes, trying to ask him to stay without actually saying it.

He smiled, and she knew he'd gotten the message. "I want to talk to Peterson and Kerr, find out what the hell really went on here this afternoon."

In the velvet silence of pre-dawn, Jess lay in her bed, staring at nothing. The turmoil of the past few days had commandeered her dreams, leaving her as exhausted as when she'd fallen into bed. She drew in a long breath, thinking about Howard, imagining how his warm body would feel spooned against hers under the quilt. Thoughts of making love with him sent desire stirring through her belly. Would he be a tender lover, considerate and attentive to her needs? Maybe his calm demeanor hid a passion that transcended any fantasies she could summon. Warmth crawled across her inner thighs, and she lay very still, savoring sensations that had lain dormant for years.

A creak in the hall sent her pulse leaping. She held her breath, straining to hear, senses on high alert. Silence. House noises, nothing more. Exhausted relief chased the adrenaline from her chest, and she closed her eyes and sank back into restless dreams.

An hour later, she woke with a start to a room bright with morning light. The shadowy fantasy interlude of the predawn hours fled with the brilliance and she felt foolish. Shuffling down the hall, she moved into the kitchen and turned on the small television. The lighthearted banter of a cereal commercial filled the room while she made coffee. Her emotions bubbled to the surface, feelings spawned and nurtured in the wee hours. Howard was a page from a story yet unwritten, a tale that might never unfold if she didn't take a chance.

The commercial break switched to the television news desk.

*"A large-scale terrorist arrest took place in Bridgeport, Connecticut yesterday afternoon, when FBI agents stormed a garage where five suspected terrorists were reported to be hiding. Agents found several shoulder-mounted Stinger rocket launchers, and a partially empty crate of explosives."*

Jess's cup hit the floor, spraying hot coffee over her bare feet. She stared at the screen and fought a wave of nausea. Were those the weapons hidden in her loft? The aftermath of Easton's involvement ballooned, more than her stunned brain could handle.

She refocused on the newscaster.

*"Brynn Tennant has more details from the scene. . ."* A sharp-faced young woman appeared, her worried expression accentuating the tense description of major news. *"John, we're here in the neighborhood where the FBI raided this garage yesterday. . ."* She gestured toward a run-down corrugated tin building, roped off with yellow crime scene tape. *"According to our sources, the FBI has been tracking this particular sleeper cell for months. Search teams found weapons capable of bringing down an airliner in a landing or take-off pattern. LaGuardia is just sixty miles away. Seized evidence indicates the huge international airport was the target. Agents aren't saying how they found out about the planned attack, but it may be related to another incident in New Haven County."* The television station switched back to the main news desk, and the young announcer stared earnestly at his audience. *"An abandoned farm south of Prospect was raided just hours after the arrests in Bridgeport. Tom Finn has details."*

Samir's dark image appeared on the screen, and Jess gasped.

The newscaster's voice echoed in the background. *"Samir bin Fahad Mahfood is believed to have been the cell organizer for yesterday's thwarted attack. Mahfood was a U.S. citizen living in Hartford for over twenty years."* Samir's image faded, replaced by the dark faces of Hafez and Mustafa. Jess's thoughts snapped back to Easton, and the knowledge that these animals had wandered freely amongst the horses, been within easy range of the kids, plotted deadly schemes right under her nose. The reminder of her close association with Samir sent a cold chill through her stomach, then a vicious stab of malevolence tore through her thoughts. *Good, I'm glad they caught the bastards! I hope they rot in jail.*

The picture changed to a new scene–showing a smoldering, burned-out farmhouse surrounded by double rows of yellow streamers. The camera panned to a gutted van, also cordoned off with crime tape.

*"Mahfood and his companions set off suicide bombs when FBI agents moved in. The house was completely engulfed in flames before firefighters arrived, and forensics teams are now sifting through the rubble for evidence. It's not certain if the group was headed for the Bridgeport location, but authorities have hinted that these men were involved in a major plot. Back to you, John."*

The Hartford newscaster solemnly assured the audience that the day's programming would be interrupted as new details became available. Jess stared at the screen, mindlessly watching a commercial for an investment firm that promised to protect the future. *There are no guarantees. There is no way to protect the future.* Radicals peppered the world, their only mission being to strike a blow against freedom.

Since the morning she'd watched the Trade Towers attack, seen the massive hole in the Pentagon, and footage of a shattered airliner, Jess had buttressed her emotions, safeguarding her grip on sanity, forbidding the terror to invade and put down roots. While experts expounded about Post Traumatic Syndrome and the need to accept and deal with the reality of the attacks, Jess had fortified her psyche and plunged on. Avoided reading about it. Never thinking about it. Making it go away by sheer determination to remain unscathed.

Hot tears rolled down her cheeks, blurring the images on the television into strange art-deco murals, animated in slow motion. The dam broke and years of disappointment and suppressed sorrow poured out.

The dampness of old concrete crept into every joint, and Samir shifted uncomfortably, trying to ignore his aching knees and the dank, musty odors in the cramped old bomb shelter. He clenched his jaw. Jessica Rayder was responsible for this–he knew it as sure as he knew his own name. Twenty years wasted–destroyed by a stupid infidel woman. He closed his eyes and rage filled his head, his heart, every breath. Worse than the aborted plan, he had failed Allaah.

He sat very still in the dark, straining to hear what might be going on above ground. His watch glowed faintly. Three a.m. He needed to leave soon. In a couple of hours, the FBI would discover there were only two bodies in the house. He flicked his lighter and glanced up at the trap door in the faint light. He grabbed the handle, then extinguished the flame.

Pushing the heavy steel plate up about an inch, he listened. The sounds of voices in the distance drifted on the damp, acrid night air. Slowly, he pushed the door up a little more, listening carefully for any signs of people close by. The floodlights at the front of the burned-out house cast an eerie glow on the tree branches along the road, and even deeper shadows over the small shed covering the bomb shelter. He eased the door open just enough to slip out onto the ground, taking care not to let the lid clang shut.

He lay still in the tall grass, breathing heavily, willing his heart to stop pounding. He raised his head and looked across the pasture at the abandoned truck. Fifty yards. Did he dare try to make a run for it? If he crawled that far, would his knees hold up? Allaah would keep him safe, if that was His will. Another surge of rage coursed through Samir's head, pushing his faith away, and he began to slither through the tall grass toward the tiny car he'd hidden the day before.

# *Forty-Six*

In the quiet refuge of her bedroom, Jess fumbled into some clothes. The tears started again and her throat ached with rising hysteria, as too many thoughts crowded into her head.

"I need to get out of here."

Walking quickly across the dew-covered grass, she inhaled deeply, hungry for fresh air–anything to clear her head. The early morning sky was gray with rain clouds and thunder rumbled in the distance. A minute later, she slid the large door aside and chuckled at the chorus of whinnies echoing off the rafters. The mingled scents in the warm barn lifted her spirits as she moved down the aisle toward Casey's stall, listening to the ordinary sounds of morning. *It's over. We're free.*

Her step slowed as she approached the stall door, a sudden heaviness cloaking her. She focused on an object stuck into the wood, and horror rose in her throat. A short, thick-bladed knife stood out in stark relief against the door. A long, dark red drool stained the wood beneath it. Terror convulsed her as she leaped forward to snatch open the door, then her screams echoed through the cavernous barn.

A second later, she collapsed into the blood-soaked sawdust, and threw herself onto the still-warm body of her oldest friend.

Numb with disbelief, Jess sat back against the stall wall and stared at Casey through swollen, burning eyes. Who had done this? Panic sparked through her pulse, and terrible images flooded her head. Terrorists coming back to clean up the operation. She *had* to call someone. Why had she let Howard leave? She struggled to her feet, and hurried out into the aisle, latching the stall door behind her, out of habit. Heart pounding, she glanced around, then flipped open her cellphone and headed out the barn door. Two large raindrops splattered on her hand, and she looked up at the dark clouds preparing to deliver a deluge.

A crashing pain at the base of her skull nearly blinded her, and she dropped to her knees. She fought the closing darkness, gulping deep breaths, trying to clear the brilliant spots from in front of her eyes. A familiar menacing voice filtered through the clanging in her ears, and nausea boiled up in her throat.

"You are a bitch! Unclean, infidel whore!"

She looked up and tried to focus on Samir's face, black with hatred. How he could possibly be there? Before her thoughts could collect, he savagely kicked her in the belly, and she fell face first into the gravel. A loud clap of thunder shattered the air, and a boot smashed into the side of her head. She closed her eyes and darkness descended.

"No! You stay awake!"

He grabbed her by the hair and she screamed as he yanked her up into a sitting position.

He stepped back. "You have destroyed everything I have spent my life building. Now you will pay."

Blood ran down the back of her throat, the taste so vile she gagged. Staring through her tears, she struggled to comprehend his words.

"I'm going to kill you, Jessica. But first, you will suffer."

He picked up a large dead branch covered with dry leaves, then pulled a lighter from his pocket. Glowering at her with black, merciless eyes, he flicked open the lighter.

"You're going to watch your horses burn, and listen to their screams."

Jess's arms felt as though lead weights bound them to the ground. Grief overwhelmed her, and she rolled onto her side. The sky opened up and the rain came in earnest, mingling with her tears of despair, the thunder muffling her sobs. Samir turned on his heel and walked slowly and purposefully toward the open barn door.

Casey's lifeless body flashed in front of Jess's eyes, and the futility of all her heroism smashed into her brain. Images of Howard's face, and the memory of his embrace flooded her thoughts. A bolt of lightning jagged through the sky, and touched the top of one of the massive oaks by the house. The upper branches burst into flames.

*No! By God, this isn't over!*

She gathered her feet under her and crouched, ignoring the pain screeching through her body. She waited for the sudden dizziness to fade, then looked around. A pitchfork leaned against a fence, about ten feet away. Samir had almost reached the door. Watching him carefully, she crabbed sideways toward the fence, and reached for the pitchfork. Samir ignited the leaves and a cry froze in her throat.

Fueled by terror and adrenaline, she drew a deep breath, then pushed herself into a staggering run. Thunder rolled, camouflaging the sound of her feet on the gravel. The eerie glow of the blazing branch flared inside the barn. Horses whinnied with fear at the smell of smoke and another surge of adrenaline rammed through her. She held the pitchfork in front of her body like a jousting lance as she closed in.

Samir's maniacal laugh curled through the air. "*Allaahu akbar!*"

Jess plunged forward and buried the pitchfork in his back, relishing the crunch of bone and gristle as the tines penetrated his spine. His scream mingled with the cries of terrified horses. Tears and rage almost blinded her as she gave another superhuman shove and rammed the fork deeper, until the base touched his jacket. He pitched forward onto the fiery branch, and the flames crackled on contact with his blood.

Jess sank to her knees, sobs rolling up from the depths of her anguish.

ꭗ

## *Forty-Seven*

Low voices and the hum of machinery filtered into Jess's fractured dreams. Terrifying images ebbed and waned in her head. She recoiled from Samir's snarling face as he crawled toward her, the tines of the pitchfork grating on the concrete floor. She smelled smoke.

"No! Don't!"

A soft hand grasped her shoulder, and a soothing voice cut through her terror. "It's okay, Jessica. You're safe now."

The crisp fluorescent light and odor of disinfectant were reassuring, and Jess's pulse slowed. A kind, smiling face shimmered into her line of vision. The nurse's features were framed by curly gray hair, topped with a perky white cap. Jess tried to lift her head, but a sharp jab of pain ran through her face.

"Careful, you've a nasty wound on your cheek. We're about to sew you up."

The nurse turned to someone out of Jess's line of sight. "She's awake. You can talk to her for two minutes, then you'll have to leave."

In seconds, Jess's battered body and shattered mind sank into the glorious tones of Howard's voice.

"Oh, Jessie, thank God, you're okay." He grasped her hand and raised it to his lips. "I should never have left you alone."

She started to shake her head, then gasped at the blast of pain careening through it. Her voice croaked when she tried to speak, and Howard touched her swollen lips with his fingers.

"Shh, it's okay. I'm here now."

Tears trickled down her temples and her throat ached, but she managed a weak smile.

The nurse returned. "The doctor's here, you'll have to wait in the hall."

Howard leaned down and gently brushed his lips across Jess's forehead. "I'll be back."

Jess woke up, the change in her surroundings momentarily confusing her. Soft recessed lights reflected against peach-colored walls, a sharp contrast to the bright light of the emergency room. The din of catastrophe had faded to quiet privacy. A soft knock on the door preceded a small dark-skinned woman with a soft southern drawl.

"You awake, honey?" She came into the room and smiled. "I'm Debra. Boy, you look like you tangled with a 'gator."

"Pretty close. You oughta see the other guy."

Warm brown eyes twinkled. "Yeah, I heard. I guess you're some kinda hero or somethin'."

Jess frowned, then winced. Even her eyebrows hurt.

Debra chuckled. "Let me get your blood pressure, then I'll turn on the tube and you can see for yourself."

A few minutes later, a car commercial promised the best value possible, then the screen flicked to a news desk.

*"Recapping today's big story, Samir Mahfood, a suspected terrorist who was thought to have died last night in a suicide bombing, was killed early this morning."* The screen abruptly switched to another scene, and Jess gasped. A long shot of Easton panned to the highway, where a half-dozen police cars mingled through emergency vehicles, fire trucks, and television vans. The camera swept back to the barns, and zoomed in. Yellow police tape ran across the back door of the barn, around the corner, and across the driveway to the arena. Inside the cordoned-off area, a black van marked "county coroner" sat close by the main doors. A man emerged from inside, carrying a pitchfork wrapped in clear plastic. Jess's stomach heaved and she closed her eyes, the reporter's words penetrating her brain.

*"This beautiful horse farm is the scene of a grisly killing. We don't have all the details, but sometime in the early morning hours, suspected terrorist ringleader Samir Mahfood came here, and was*

*killed by the owner of the farm. The FBI hasn't released any details, but we do know that Mahfood was originally thought to have died in last night's explosion during a raid in Prospect, Connecticut."* The camera flashed to the barn doors again. Two men slid a black body bag into the back of the coroner's van.

"You don't want to watch that."

Jess's tears sprang up at the sound of Howard's voice. He picked up the remote and switched off the television, then took her hand.

"How're you feeling now?"

"Exactly like shit."

He laughed, and she couldn't help chuckling too, though it hurt like the devil.

A sharp knock on the door, and Mona stuck her head in.

"Doc says we can talk to you now."

"Yeah, might as well get this over."

Mona stepped into the room, followed by Kerr and Peterson.

Howard dropped Jess's hand, and took two long steps toward the group. His level tone emphasized the hostility simmering beneath the words.

"Throughout this entire operation, you assured Jess and Faith they'd be safe, that all your planning was air-tight. Made a big deal that there was little risk of retribution, and how terrorists work hard to keep low profiles, their mission more important than revenge. This should *not* have happened. Do you have *anything* to say?"

Kerr's jaw tightened and his skin flushed dark red. His mouth formed a hard, thin line as he returned Howard's stony stare.

Howard stepped back. "I trust you'll find the opportunity to express your regrets to these women. For my part, I *will* copy you on my report to the agency director."

The silence grew, the air thickened with tension, and no one said a word. Finally, Mona cleared her throat.

"Can we get on with this?"

Jess painfully scooted up in the bed, smoothed the covers across her chest, and took a deep breath. "Before we start, please tell me what happened."

Peterson stepped closer. "When the hideout house finally cooled down enough to get a team inside, we started sifting through the rubble. It wasn't long before forensics discovered there were only two bodies, but we didn't know whose they were. We immediately called the sheriff at the end of your driveway and told him to get up there to stand guard." He cast an apologetic look at her. "We were a little late."

Jess leaned her head back into the pillow and closed her eyes, fighting the band closing around her throat, trying to erase the image of Casey's body. A sob erupted, and she swallowed hard. Howard touched her shoulder, and she opened her eyes again, blinking away the tears.

Mona's face reflected genuine sympathy. "We know this is hard, but you need to tell us everything that happened."

Howard's fingers squeezed gently, and Jess launched into the horror for the second time that day. Twenty minutes later, the door closed behind the team, and she exhaled long and slow.

Howard brushed a strand of hair off her forehead. "You did good, hon. You get some rest now."

"I can't–too many thoughts are fighting for first place." She bit down hard on her lower lip, hoping to quench the sobs waiting to explode. "Where's Faith?"

Sorrow flashed over Howard's features. "She…said she'd see you tomorrow."

Jess's pulse quickened. "What is it, Howard? Is she okay?"

He nodded. "Yes…She and Mona, uh, took care of Casey this morning."

The pain descended like a winged demon, and every hurt, every sorrow, every missed opportunity rose to meet it.

# *Forty-Eight*

The next morning, Jess pushed tasteless scrambled eggs around the plate, idly watching the muted television. Every channel carried news of the debacle, touting Jessica Rayder as a hero. Somehow, they'd unearthed a photograph from her days of wheeling and dealing in Hartford. The screen flashed a shot of the burned-out farmhouse, then switched to a live interview with Samir's next-door neighbors in Hartford. She turned the volume up as an elderly man glanced nervously at the camera, then down at the large black microphone.

*"We're stunned, absolutely stunned."* The gray-haired woman next to him nodded solemnly, then spoke. *"They were such nice people. And that little girl–she's so beautiful and smart. She used to talk to me while I was gardening. She was taking riding lessons, and had just gotten a new horse. She was so excited. . ."*

Jess stared at Dania's small, solemn face. "How do they get those pictures so fast?"

Pain tore through her heart, thinking about Dania and what she must be going through, knowing her father was dead. What would her life be like as she grew up with the knowledge he'd been planning mass murder? The answer hit Jess hard. Dania would view Samir as a hero, a freedom fighter for Allaah. She would never look back and yearn for her brief life in America.

When Howard arrived to take Jess home, he'd changed into a business suit.

Jess cocked her head. "Why are you all dressed up?"

He grinned. "The front of the hospital is a sea of reporters. If we get caught, I'd at least like to look good on TV."

"I suppose this nightmare will go on forever."

"The Feds should wrap it up in a day or two, but I wouldn't be that optimistic about the media. They'll beat a story to death for as long as they can garner attention with it. Hell, they'll be sneaking through the woods to take pictures of you while you clean stalls. You're a national hero, hon, and that's what news is all about."

The doctor stepped into the room and smiled. "Well, you're looking more chipper this morning." He pulled a pen from his coat pocket, made a note on his clipboard, then looked up. "I'm discharging you, but I want you to take it easy. Give your body a chance to recover." His smile faded and he looked directly into her eyes. "Thank you for your courage."

Jess stared in embarrassed silence as he left the room, then glanced up at Howard.

"I want to go home."

Half an hour later, good wishes and congratulations followed her down the hospital corridor, and she smiled woodenly. Behind her, the orderly pushing the wheelchair asked if he could have an autograph. She closed her eyes. *Please, just let me get out of here. I want my life back.* Pain crushed her chest. *What's left of it.*

The elevator doors opened and the man steered the chair down another hall.

"Where are you going?"

"We're slipping you outta here through the ambulance entrance. The TV crews are all hanging around the front."

Automatic doors swung open, and they breezed through the emergency room. Through the glass doors ahead, Jess saw Howard's rental car, and breathed a sigh of relief. No one else was in sight.

Even with Howard helping, Jess could barely navigate from the wheelchair into the front seat. No part of her body didn't hurt. She patted the pocket of her jacket, feeling for the bottle of pain medication. If she could just disappear into dreamless sleep, she'd be happy, but she knew there'd be no such reprieve.

Howard didn't say much on the drive home and, for that, Jess was grateful. She glanced sideways at him, seeing the strain of the past few days, and wishing she had the strength to pursue more personal desires. She looked away, watching the countryside slip by. If she were meant to be with Howard, it would happen. For now, she could only think about the present.

"Ah-ha! There they are!"

Jess jerked out of her reverie and focused on Howard's attention. Ahead, dozens of vehicles were gathered at the entrance to Easton Ridge. Police cars with rotating blue lights sat on either side of the driveway.

Despair squeezed into her thoughts and she drew a deep breath. "I can't do this right now."

"I know. I'll placate them, then we'll set up a short press conference for later."

As they approached the driveway, news people on foot leaped into action, grabbing cameras and microphones, surging toward the car. Howard shook his head at them and turned in the drive. A patrol car pulled in behind him and stopped, blocking off any further traffic. Howard pulled up a little farther and turned off the engine.

He winked and flashed a charming smile. "Wish me luck."

Jess watched him in the sideview mirror. Men and women spilled out of their vehicles, moving quickly to set up equipment, vying for prime positions to capture everything on film. When he reached the crowd, Jess rolled her window down a little so she could hear. The reporters oozed forward, surrounding Howard like an amoeba.

His voice was loud and firm. "Miss Rayder is fine, but won't be available for interviews. I'll answer your questions, but here are the ground rules. No one goes into or near the barn or horses, and the house is off-limits." The reporters all started talking at once, and he raised his hand. "Does everyone understand?"

Thirty minutes later, Jess eased onto the couch, praying for the pain medication to kick in quickly. Howard had done an outstanding job with the news people. They had thoroughly researched Faith's riding accomplishments, and Jess's own stellar investment career. She felt naked and vulnerable before the world. She closed her eyes and dozed, vaguely aware of Howard's movements in the kitchen.

Low voices drifted into her consciousness, and she opened her eyes slowly. Mona stood a few feet away, looking uncomfortable.

"Hey, Jess. How you feelin'?"

"Pretty rough, and I don't feel like answering any more questions right now."

"That's not why I'm here. I'm helpin' Faith with stalls."

Shame and gratitude poured into Jess's head. Mona wasn't so bad–their unlikely relationship had simply gotten off to a rocky start.

"Thank you, I appreciate it."

Howard came into the room carrying a large flower arrangement. He set it down on the coffee table and grinned. "There are three more in the kitchen. Where do you want 'em?"

Before she could answer, the telephone rang and Howard walked over to pick it up. Mona sat down next to Jess, and handed her the card from the flowers.

Jess smiled at Frank's scraggly scrawl. *"Get well soon, Miss Jessie. Anytime you're ready to buy Easton, I'd be honored to sell it to you."*

Howard held out the portable phone. "It's a Doris Troy."

Jess's stomach pitched. For sure, this wouldn't be pleasant.

The woman's pompous tone confirmed it. "How could you put those children in danger? I'm stunned at your lack of responsibility."

Jess closed her eyes, trying to find words to placate the woman. A thump blasted through the base of her skull and, suddenly, she was aware of every bruised muscle and stinging wound.

"Doris, put a sock in it." She pressed the disconnect button and grinned. "Damn, that felt good!"

Mona stood up. "Well, I need to get back to headquarters and start filling out reports." She started toward the door, then turned back, a tentative expression softening her features. "You know, I could come in every day until you hire some help." She looked a little embarrassed. "This has been the best undercover duty I've ever had."

Jess didn't respond. Could she bear having a constant reminder of the past week?

Mona reached for the doorknob. "You don't have to make a decision right now, but you have my number."

Faith showed up shortly after Mona left.

She shook her head and rolled her eyes. "Wow! I almost got

trampled trying to get in here!" She grinned. "I've always wanted to say 'No Comment'!"

Jess felt a surge of love and hope she'd despaired of ever finding again. Howard disappeared down the hall toward the bathroom, and Faith sat down on the couch, her blue eyes glittering with sympathy and tenderness.

She slipped her arm around Jess's shoulders. "I'm *so* sorry, Jessie."

Jess sank into Faith's arms and finally let go.

In the space of ten minutes, she felt drained of all feeling. Taking a ragged breath, she looked up and saw her friend's sad expression. Jess felt as though she, personally, had abandoned a frail bird in a storm. Sorrow drew down the corners of Faith's eyes, and her small mouth quivered with emotion.

"Jessie, I've signed myself in to Black Rock Rehab Center. I'm leaving in the morning. Mona will cover the stalls until you're on your feet again."

Jess gasped, sending a stab of pain searing through her bruised ribs. "*Tomorrow?* But what about Brandford? It's next–"

Faith shook her head. "The counselor and doctor have agreed to let me out on a day work pass until after the show. I'll be here a couple of afternoons to work with Lexie and Beth. After that, we'll just have to reschedule the fall session for November, like we planned." She looked down at her hands. "I'll lick this, I promise."

Jess's voice came out almost a whisper. "And I'll help you. I promise, too."

Howard returned, and Faith rose. "Howard, thank you for everything. I hope we meet again sometime."

The front door closed quietly behind her, but to Jess, it seemed as though the door to the past had slammed shut, and the door to the future had locked.

Howard sat down beside her. "Want to talk about it?"

She leaned her head against his shoulder. "No. It'll consume my thoughts for a long time. Right now, I just want to be with you."

He slid his arm around her shoulder and pulled her close. His cheek rested against her hair, his breath soft and warm. Why couldn't she put everything on hold, see if there was a future with him?

His voice rumbled with emotion. "Jessie, you have a lot on your plate right now. You'll need every ounce of strength you can muster to get through whatever lies ahead. . ."

Tears burned her eyelids, and she sniffled.

"But somewhere down the line, you'll need to take some time for yourself, decide what *you* want." He cleared his throat. "When that time comes, I'd like to know."

She could think of no response that would cover all the unasked questions, so she said nothing. Instead, she listened to his heart thump steadily beneath the soft oxford-cloth shirt. She imagined resting her cheek on his bare skin, tracing her fingers along the outline of his ribs, spending the rest of her life in his arms.

He loosened his grasp, and sat back to gaze at her. His eyes held a reflection of her own smoldering thoughts.

"Jessie, I have to go home now. I'll call in a couple of days."

He leaned forward and brushed a kiss across her forehead, then rose, picked up his briefcase, and walked out the door without looking back.

As soon as the door closed, Jess's reserves crumpled, and emotional agony joined her physical pain.

)(

# *Forty-Nine*

At dawn, Jess struggled to open her eyes, emerging from a deep, dreamless sleep more tired than when she'd fallen into bed. Too much excitement, too much adrenaline, too much emotion blended with copious doses of pain medication, taking a heavy toll on her battered body and mind. The silent emptiness of the house seemed overwhelming. Would anything ever be normal again? Routine, maybe–but not normal.

She rose with effort and walked haltingly down the dark hall toward the living room. Through the front window, she saw the dim outlines of the patrol cars at the entrance to the farm and, a short distance down the road, a van. Her heart thumped and she instinctively stepped back from the window in fright. Could other terrorists be waiting for the chance to finish what Samir had started?

She moved into the kitchen, trying to think about other things. A moment later, she returned to the window. Early morning light replaced the murky shadows, and she could see more detail. The call letters of a Hartford television station stood out clearly against the white van. Reporters. Another lettered truck pulled up, followed by a white sedan. Relief swallowed the haunting images of fear, then the magnitude of the circumstances crashed down on her. In a seemingly random string of events, her life had changed forever and, for the first time, she didn't have a plan.

Ten feet from the barn door, Jess stopped and squeezed her eyes shut. *I can't do this yet.* Scenes of horror raced through her head, looping again and again back to Casey. A vise of pain in her throat nearly suffocated her, and hot tears escaped to dribble down her cheeks. She turned away and faced the glow in the east as the sun edged over the horizon, a fiery jewel in an opal sky. The promise of a new day, a new beginning.

Morning barn sounds drifted on the air–the clank of a stall latch, Mona talking to one of the horses, the clip-clop of iron shoes on concrete–reminders of a dream come true. Jess had her life back and, though the future would be littered with fragments of the past, maybe with time, she could get beyond them.

She took a deep breath and swiped at her tears, then stepped into the cool dim barn. Mona stepped out of the feed room and waved.

"Morning, feel any better?"

"Not much, but thanks anyway."

Mona stood still for moment, then nodded and grabbed the handle of the cart to resume the morning feed.

Jess listened to her heart thumping in her ears, then slowly started toward the two end stalls, painfully aware of the absent joyful greeting. The dark streak on Casey's stall door had blackened overnight, blending into the wood grain, its meaning known only to an unlucky few. Jess's breath came in ragged gulps, and the enormity of her loss crushed her chest. She stopped, dizzy with the physical assault on her senses, and her breath shuddered as she grappled with the pain.

Taking two more steps, she confronted the empty stall. Every speck of sawdust had been removed, and the packed clay floor dusted with lime. The faint odor of disinfectant obliterated any hint of death–or life.

Her voice squeaked with sorrow. "Oh God, Casey. Can you ever forgive me?"

She'd failed everyone who'd ever loved her, and this was her punishment.

A soft nicker rumbled into her heartache and she looked up. Blurred by her tears, Steely Dan's large dark eyes peered through the iron bars of the next stall.

Later, bolstered by Danny's unconditional love, Jess sat down at her desk and stared at the blinking red light on the answering machine. Twelve messages. She hit the play button and listened in disbelief. One by one, people introduced themselves and asked if riding lessons were available at Easton Ridge.

Mona walked in. "Sounds like business is picking up."

Jess shook her head. "It's the end of the season. . .we usually lose a few riders for the winter session. This is unbelievable."

"No, it isn't. Notoriety has advantages. Every television station is carrying the story that Hafez and Mustafa worked here. Add the news about Dania's riding lessons–you guys are celebrities."

Jess hadn't considered the positive aspects of being in the news. "Do you think these are all legitimate inquiries?"

"Probably most of them. You might get a couple of gawkers with morbid curiosity about the scene of the excitement." She stood up and grinned. "Ride the wave while you can." She turned toward the door.

"Mona? Can we talk?"

The woman hesitated for a moment before turning back, her body language proof they were both on the same page. Their eyes met, and Jess exhaled slowly before speaking.

"I really appreciate everything you've done here. We've had a couple of rough spots between us, but I admire your hard work and real concern for the welfare of the horses. . ."

Mona smiled without humor. "But at some point, you'd like me to disappear and let you get on with your life."

Jess nodded. "We both know the past few days will always hang between us. I want to put it behind me, move on, and recapture some semblance of normalcy."

Disappointment briefly shadowed Mona's features, and Jess knew the agent's undercover work hadn't been her only involvement at the farm.

Mona recovered her usual self-assuredness. "I understand. Actually, my thoughts have been running about the same. In my job, getting personally involved is risky. Kerr already gave me hell for defending some of your actions." She smiled. "When you're ready, just say the word."

Jess nodded, then took a deep breath. "One more thing. . .where is she?"

Mona looked confused for a second, then sympathy rushed into her dark eyes. "Near the entrance to the state forest."

"Thank you," whispered Jess.

Mona pulled on her work-gloves. "You've done a great service for your country, Jess. Don't *ever* forget that."

# *Fifty*

Jess sat back and closed her eyes against the dull throb creeping into the base of her skull. *I should go home and lie down.* The telephone rang, scraping across raw nerves, bringing quick tears to her eyes.

A smooth voice thrummed through the receiver, asking for Faith Angelo.

"She's on vacation. May I take a message?"

"This is Kenneth Sharpe from Beauregard Saddlery in Wisconsin."

Five minutes later, Jess put the phone down and smiled. *Faith will be thrilled.*

She took a deep breath, then let it out slowly. Already, the excitement and intrigue seemed in the distant past. She wanted to bury herself in solitude, think about Howard, perhaps feel a little sorry for herself. But Fate and the future of Easton Ridge muscled in and took charge of her thoughts. Hiring barn help was the number one priority.

Easton's new notoriety had generated a half-dozen inquiries about employment. She would spend the day weeding out the least suitable candidates, then doing background checks on the others. If nothing else, she'd learned that *no* help was better than *bad* help.

The flood of new students would generate plenty of money–and more expense–but she could definitely handle problems like *that.* With careful scheduling, there would be few days without lessons, once Faith returned full-time. Jess simply needed to come up with a balancing act to support the fast growth.

She opened the green ledger book just as the phone rang.

Naomi Morton sounded cheerful. "Hey, Jess. How're you holdin' up?"

"Better than yesterday, which probably isn't saying much."

"Listen, I know you've had a lot goin' on, but now that the little girl and her mother have left the country, we need to sort out the deal with Buster."

"Yes, I know. The problem is, he's too strong for most of our students. Any of the older girls could ride him, but they all have their own horses."

"I can take him back. He's valuable enough I'll easily find another buyer." A pause. "Technically, the Mahfoods are in default on the sales contract, so I have the right to keep the down-payment." Her tone became matter-of-fact. "I'll just come by tomorrow and pick him up. Around ten okay with you?"

"I'll be here."

"How's Faith doin'?"

Jess hesitated. Word traveled fast in the horse community, so it would be unrealistic to think no one knew about Faith's problem.

"She's going to be just fine."

Late that afternoon, Jess drove down the driveway toward the main road. As she approached the gate, car doors opened, and reporters spilled out, scrambling toward her.

"Oh nuts, how am I going to do this?"

A deputy climbed out of a patrol car and started toward the knot of news people. Jess slowed as the group blockaded the road. One man charged up to the window, and the others followed, all shouting and jostling for position. Jess caught the deputy's eye, and shook her head. He immediately strode up, verbally pushing everyone back from the entrance. Jess's car slipped through the opening, and she accelerated onto the highway. She threw a quick glance in the rear-view mirror, and gasped. The reporters were hurtling back toward their vehicles. She punched the gas and flew down the highway and around the bend. Safely out of sight, she made a sharp right turn onto a farm road, and slipped into the cover of trees. She chuckled and headed off through the back roads, knowing the news people would never find her. How she would handle the return trip, she wasn't sure. *I'll just cross that bridge when I come to it.*

An hour later, she pulled off the highway and drove slowly along a winding driveway lined with birches. After about a quarter-mile, split-rail fence replaced the trees, and Black Rock Rehabilitation Center appeared against the green backdrop of the Algonquin State Forest. A large red barn lay to the west of the house, and several horses grazed in the pasture beside the lane. Her research into the place had turned up a bonus. Black Rock not only counseled and comforted alcoholics through the drying-out process, but also took in abused and abandoned horses. Patients at the facility had the option of working in the barn and with the animals, as part of their therapy. A perfect situation for Faith.

Jess stepped onto the wrap-around porch and rang the bell.

Faith opened the door, and her face lit up with delight. "Hey, I wasn't expecting to see you 'til tomorrow!"

Jess hugged her tightly, blinking away the moisture burning her eyelids. Faith extricated herself, and gestured toward the parlor.

"Come on in, tell me what all is going on."

"Beauregard Saddlery wants you to endorse their jump saddle."

Faith's beautiful eyes widened, and she gasped, her face blossoming into a radiant smile. "Oh wow! It's the best one on the market!"

"There's more. The owner said he'd give us several demos to use in the riding program."

"That's fabulous! I can't wait to get back. . .I hate myself for screwing everything up. I–"

"No–don't. We aren't going to live in the past. We both need to take life just one day at a time."

Faith lifted her chin and squared her shoulders. "You're right–so, what else is going on?"

Jess spent the next twenty minutes detailing the list of new clients and Naomi's plan to take Buster back.

A young woman poked her head into the room. "Dinner's ready."

Faith nodded, and stood up. "I'm so glad to know things are getting back on track." She cocked her head, a mischievous twinkle accentuating her smile. "Since you have all this unscheduled time, you could take a little trip." She winked. "See ya tomorrow."

Jess left the halfway house, thinking about Faith's idea. What a perfect opportunity: no clients, no shows–free time she could spend with Howard. She tuned the radio to the all-music station, slipped onto the highway, and picked up speed. Settling back for the drive, she let her thoughts roam through optimistic plans. Something caught her attention in the rearview mirror, and she swore under her breath. A dark green Camaro roared up behind her, blue and red lights flashing through the grill.

*Calm down. You weren't speeding*. She pulled over, took a deep breath, and watched in the side mirror as a uniformed state trooper strode toward the car. A second later, she grinned at Officer Carter through the open window.

"*Now* what? I got the taillight fixed."

He laughed. "Yeah, I can see that. I recognized your car and wanted to tell you how bummed I was about not making it to your show. I pulled some extra duty." He shook his head. "My daughter was ticked."

"I can imagine."

"And then you turn out to be the hero of the century. Man, I have all the bad luck!"

The young cop's disappointed expression turned sympathetic. "Boy, you really took a beating." He suddenly acted embarrassed, then cleared his throat. "We're all really proud of what you did."

Jess nodded, unable to think of an appropriate response, so she gestured toward the Camaro. "New patrol vehicle?"

He brightened. "Yeah, repo'ed drug car. Kinda hard for me to be sedate in a machine like that."

"I noticed–I thought you were going to run me down."

He grinned. "I had to catch up to you. Well, anyway, it was nice seeing you again. I'll try to bring the kid over sometime next spring."

Jess caught a movement in the sideview mirror, and groaned. "Oh God, is this ever going to end?"

Carter turned toward the reporter and cameraman hurrying toward them. "I'll take care of this. Stay right here."

He strode forward, adjusting his hat. Jess watched the pantomime, the angry expression on the reporter's face, the trooper's firm stance. A minute later, the news crew walked back to their vehicle, and Carter returned to her side.

"I'll follow you back to your place, but you know, sooner or later, you're gonna have to talk to 'em."

He stepped back from the car and saluted, then sauntered back to the snazzy unmarked patrol car. Jess pulled back onto the highway, painfully aware that her personal privacy had disappeared with the adventures at Easton Ridge.

# *Fifty-One*

The weather changed abruptly overnight, bringing a cold sting to the early morning air, and nudging reluctant foliage to begin the change into brilliant colors. The promise of winter's imminence urged every living thing to make ready. The barn swallows had gone, but the local chickadees and jays made more frequent raids on the feed room, scavenging spilled grain like treasure seekers. The horses seemed to have grown instant fuzzy coats.

The temperature drop during the night left the grass crisp with frost. Jess crunched across the field, watching the steam curl away from her coffee to mingle with her breath. Inside the cozy barn, the radio played in the background, and the reassuring sounds of horses drifted on the warm air. She started toward the feed room, followed by a loud chorus of excited whinnies. For the first time in several days, she laughed out loud. The creatures inhabiting her world were so comfortably predictable. Pushing the grain cart down the aisle, she gazed at each horse with love. Reaching the end of the row, she slipped into Danny's stall. The big horse plunged his nose into the grain, and an ache grew in her heart.

"I know I've neglected you, and I'm sorry. I promise we'll start playing together again soon."

He raised his head and nickered softly, deep in his throat. He moved to the wall and stuck his nose through the bars of Casey's old stall. His nostrils flared as he inhaled, searching for the scent of his friend. A moment later, he swung his head around and gazed at Jess with huge, sad eyes, and she thought her heart would break.

Jess hit "play" on the answering machine, and sat down.

Howard's voice surged into her heart, and tears sprang up from nowhere.

*"Hey, Jessie, sorry I missed you. . .uh, just wanted to know how you're doing. . .well, call me if you want to. . ."*

She whisked away the drops on her cheeks and nodded. *I want to, but not yet.*

The sound of a truck engine outside sent a flash of adrenaline sprinting through her veins. Through the window, she saw Naomi's truck pull past. The lump of fright stuck in her throat. How long before she could leave the fear behind?

Naomi jumped down from the cab, and Jess grinned.

"Isn't a six-horse rig a little overkill to pick up one nag?"

Naomi threw her a smug look, then strode to the rear of the trailer. An instant later, Jess gaped as Naomi led a sleek, gray Thoroughbred down the ramp, and handed Jess the lead-rope.

"You take this one. I'll bring the other two."

"What's going on?"

Naomi disappeared into the depths of the trailer, and Jess turned to look at the calm, kind eyes of the mare. The horse bobbed her head and whinnied, and Jess looked back at the rig just as Naomi emerged, a lead-rope in each hand.

Two horses followed her quietly down the ramp, then lifted their heads, nostrils wide to test the new scents, ears swiveling to catch every new sound.

Naomi chuckled, obviously tickled by Jess's astonishment. "I got to thinking about your situation. These horses are past their prime for hard work, but perfect for schooling. I'd like to donate them to your riding program."

Jess found her voice. "Naomi, they're beautiful, but you can't just give away your animals."

"Yes, I can. I know you'll take good care of them and, besides, I can use the tax deduction. I had a very good year." She winked. "I made *way* too much money."

As they led the horses into the barn, Jess thought about the wonderful, generous gesture and a brief undercurrent of anxiety surfaced. The last time she'd accepted "free" help, she'd gotten into a pile of trouble. But in this case, she'd known Naomi Morton for years–the breeder's reputation was spotless, and she was well-known for her support of the horse industry.

Jess's voice quavered. "I really appreciate your generosity."

Naomi turned and gave her a sly look. "It's not completely altruistic, my dear–it's an investment. After all, you *are* grooming my future buyers."

Throughout the morning, several boarders stopped by the office to say hello, each offering their own version of hero-worship. Jess tried to be gracious, but wanted nothing more than her old life back. Just before noon, Lexie and Beth popped into the room, bubbling with excitement.

Beth's eyes widened with horror and morbid interest. "Oh! You look awful! Were you scared?"

Jess chuckled. "Terrified, actually. You girls here for a lesson?"

Lexie's ponytail bobbed vigorously. "Yeah, Faith wants us to, like, double up. Oh my God, I so can't believe we're actually going to Brandford!"

Jess nodded, remembering the feeling like it was yesterday. "You and Danny do good for me, you hear?"

Faith appeared in the doorway, eyes bright, hair neatly pulled into a black velvet headband. Her smile radiated serenity.

"C'mon, ladies, we have some catching up to do."

Jess listened to the exuberant chatter fade into the inner barn. It had all been worth it–the future was the only thing that mattered. Faith's, hers, Easton's.

A low cough brought her back. Frank stood by the door, hat in hand, stiff-shouldered, a sheepish smile playing across his whiskery jaw.

"Mornin' Miss Jessie. Thought I'd drop by and see how yer doin'."

Jess smiled, but wondered at the surprise visit. "Pretty good. Taking it one day at a time. Come on in and sit down."

He shook his head. "I'm not gonna stay. . .just wonderin' if you still wanna buy the place." He smiled hopefully. "I'll make you a real good deal."

So much had happened in the short time since she'd last talked to him. Too many different emotions and decisions, desires and needs, realities and fantasies.

She smiled sadly. "Ah, Frank. . .I can't think about it right now. Easton is in a big transition, and adding another piece to the equation wouldn't be smart." She saw his disappointment. "How about I call you after the first of the year, when I know where we stand?"

The old man's shoulders drooped, and Jess wondered if she'd ever again *really* know what was best.

She watched through the window as his truck drove away, then turned her gaze to the teens working their horses. Faith watched them, her posture confident and relaxed. Jess's throat tightened, thinking about Faith's battle. Would her partner ever be able to take over, make it on her own? Sadness moved into Jess's heart. She'd eventually move on. At some point, she'd have to relinquish her feelings of responsibility for anyone other than herself.

By late afternoon, she had interviewed five stall cleaners, and hired three on probation, pending reference checks. Faith and the girls had gone for the day. One lone boarder remained, lunging her horse in the round pen. Mona was bringing horses in for the night. Jess sighed. *Time to go home*.

The phone rang and she automatically picked it up. In a split second, her blood turned to ice in her veins, and she couldn't breathe.

A soft voice laced with desert wind oozed through the receiver.

"Good afternoon, Miss Jessica. This is Sheikh Abdul ibn Mohammed."

# *Fifty-Two*

Jess struggled with flashbacks, the ache in her chest overwhelming. Then, her head cleared. She could live on the edge for only so long before she either let herself be swept into eternal fear, or faced it squarely.

"Yes?"

A tiny hesitation roared through the receiver, then Mohammed spoke, softly and with great care. "First, I wish to tell you of my horror at the news of yet another terrorist plot in your country. I hope to convince you of my innocence in this travesty. *Insha'Allaah*."

"That's pretty far-fetched, considering your family ties with Samir."

"Ah, but he is only a distant cousin in the tribe, and from a different clan. He left our country many years ago. I did not know him, which is why I asked for his company at the casino. Miss Rayder, every family has its. . .how do you say? Bad apples."

Jess nodded at the time-tested adage, wondering, at the same time, why she should believe Mohammed's story.

"Miss Rayder, I am also calling about *Sharata*. . .my racehorse?"

Jess blinked. She'd completely forgotten about that part of her winnings. Before she could respond, Mohammed continued.

"I know you have no use for her, but my trainer believes she has Kentucky Derby potential. She is also my favorite filly. I am an honorable man, and I would like to buy her back."

Jess spoke briskly. "Just keep her."

"I cannot do that. If you do not wish to sell her, I'll have her shipped to you from Lexington next week."

Jess exhaled sharply. "Mohammed, I can't use a racing Thoroughbred here, so okay–how much are we talking about?"

The next morning, Jess gazed out the living room window at the magnificent landscape, amazed at how quickly the leaves had colored. But, before long, they'd fall, leaving the stark outlines of bare branches against the streaky eastern sky.

She topped up her coffee mug, turned off the pot, and flicked on the television just as the weatherman smiled his way into Connecticut homes. *"Chilly this morning, in case you haven't been outdoors. Winter's on its way early. We're expecting some light snow this afternoon, with accumulations overnight of up to an inch. Temperatures will remain in the mid-thirties through the weekend."* Muting the sound, Jess thought about the conversation with Mohammed. She wanted to believe he'd been an innocent bystander. She yearned to take comfort in her life-long trust in the inherent goodness of most people. But during the post-attack years, as security levels vacillated between red, yellow, and orange, the country's imagination deepened, stretching even the most trusting individuals to question their beliefs.

Suddenly, Mustafa's dark face stared at her from the television screen, bringing the nightmare back in full force. *Do I want to know what this is about?* Her reflexes were ahead of her reticence and, a second later, she was sorry.

*"—led to Mustafa al-Ani, a member of the terrorist cell that blew themselves up on September Eleventh. Al-Ani had been working as a baggage handler at LaGuardia Airport since April of 2000."*

Another familiar face appeared and Jess's pulse jerked. The newscaster continued.

*"Hafez al-Nabi had been driving a food-service truck, delivering meals and beverages to various airlines at Bradley International. Both suspects had full access to secured areas of the facility. Airline schedules for both airports were found at the Bridgeport warehouse. Several arrival times had been circled, supporting the FBI's belief that the group planned to shoot down one or more loaded flights as they landed. Police dogs combed the parking lots around the LaGuardia facility, finally*

*locating a van rigged with explosives in the packed short-term parking lot. The vehicle had an airport security pass displayed inside the windshield, and is believed to belong to one of the suspects employed by the Port Authority."*

Jess pressed the power button and the screen darkened. In this frame of reference, she could almost justify getting tangled up with Samir. If she hadn't, would she be watching news of death and destruction at this very moment?

Twenty minutes later, she snapped a lead rope onto Danny's halter and led him out the back door. He danced and pranced, testing the chilly breeze and snorting.

"Come on, Big Boy. I need you for moral support."

She walked past the carriage house without giving it a glance, past the empty round pen, and through the gate. Danny dropped his head into the thick grass and snatched two mouthfuls before Jess tugged on the lead, urging him to follow her. She could see the dark entrance to the trail against the undergrowth at the edge of the trees on the far side of the field. Her heart thumped and her pace slowed. Danny grabbed another clump of grass. Each step on the frosty ground sent waves of pain rolling through her chest. Was she ready for this?

A few minutes later, she stood before a large mound of gray fieldstone. A sickening twist of nerves curled through her stomach. Danny stretched his long neck to nose the edge of a clear plastic bag wired to one of the rocks. Jess dropped to her knees and a sob erupted from deep inside. Through the sparkling, dew-covered plastic, two little girls smiled up from a yellowed newspaper clipping, and Jess and Casey's first blue ribbon was tucked into the lower corner of the bag.

Ж

# *Fifty-Three*

By afternoon, the normal rhythm of a busy riding stable hummed in the background, and Jess buried herself in several projects that needed immediate attention. The new barn staff arrived together, and she spent two hours going over procedures, barn rules, and employment issues. Faith arrived for lessons, and added her two-cents' worth. Life marched on, leaving no time for self-pity.

At four o'clock, Faith came into the office.

"I'm headed back now. I'll be here real early to load horses." She shifted from one foot to the other. "Are you going with us?"

Jess shook her head. "I can't, Faith–you'll do just fine." She picked up a fat folder. "Here's the paperwork, including duplicates of everything, in case you need them."

Faith looked as though she might try to convince Jess to change her mind, then her expression softened.

"Okay, hon. See you in the morning." She picked up the folder and started toward the door, then turned back. "I love you, Jess."

Mona showed up late that afternoon, her face bright with enthusiasm.

"Jess, I really appreciate your confidence in me." She looked embarrassed. "You can't imagine how much I love being here."

Jess recognized Mona's open honesty, and thought, for the first time since they'd met, how hard the agent's job must be. The possibility of dying in the line of duty *had* to be a daunting shadow over every day. Jess knew virtually nothing about this woman who'd given so much of herself.

"I realized you were the only person I would trust to take

care of things while I'm away. The staff is too new for that much responsibility."

Mona's eyes reflected gratitude for the compliment. "Your timing is perfect. I'm on after-assignment light duty, and I also have some vacation time that I *have* to use, or forfeit."

"I guess I lucked out that you didn't have a trip planned."

Mona's face shadowed, and her smile faded. "I don't have that luxury." She hesitated, then shook her head. "My mother's in a nursing home in Farmington. I stay pretty close to home."

Jess felt instant remorse that she'd never wondered anything about Mona's personal life. Trying to cover her discomfort, she gestured toward the stalls. "We have some new horses, if you feel like riding. The gray mare and the chestnut gelding are pretty sedate, but that bay mare needs some work."

Mona chuckled. "I always like a challenge."

"Now *that's* an understatement."

"Does Howard know you're planning to visit?"

Jess whirled around. "How did you know?"

Mona rolled her eyes. "Pu-leeze, Jess! You two had lightning bolts snapping between you the whole time. It was like watching an old-time movie." She chuckled. "I'm not as big a hard-ass as you think."

The following morning, Jess watched the farm truck and horse trailer turn onto the highway. A twinge of guilt hovered in the recesses of her mind. She should have gone with Faith, offered to lend a hand, but selfishness reared its snakehead, supported by rationalization. Faith had been doing major horseshows for many more years than Jess. Other than possibly needing moral support, Faith could handle it. Jess's shoulders drooped, and she faced the cold truth–she'd stepped out of the realm. The joy had gone, the excitement faded–now it was just a job.

As she stared at the end of the driveway, a van turned in. A knee-jerk thump bounded through her chest, then she exhaled as she read the large letters on the side: FedEx. Ten minutes later, she stared in disbelief at the Chase Manhattan cashier's check for $100,000.

"Jeez, it's either chickens or feathers around this place!"

A small piece of paper fluttered to the floor. The precise script intrigued her, but the message struck deeper.

*"Dear Miss Rayder,*

*For what it is worth, I thank you again for believing me. In return, I offer the message of the Holy Qur'an: for guidance and mercy to bring forth all mankind out of the depths of darkness into the light. Peace be on you.*

*Sheikh Abdul ibn Mohammed."*

The message seared straight to Jess's heart. With a history of centuries of discord in his own part of the world, this man could still feel hope, and see the possibility of a future where all people might know peace. Maybe her own beliefs weren't so distorted, after all.

She folded the check in half, tucked it into the back of her desk drawer, and strode into the aisle. All the familiar sounds and smells wrapped around her, and she smiled. The future could only get better.

National security had advanced from orange to red since the FBI raid, and Jess nodded her endorsement as the airport parking garage guards searched the trunk of the car in front of her. In times past, she'd have chafed at the delay, but her brush with the enemy changed the way she thought about everything. Nothing to be taken for granted, or sloughed off as unimportant–evil could be on your doorstep at any moment.

She'd heard news reports that air travel had dropped since the incident, and now she saw it for herself. The usually jammed concourses were surprisingly uncrowded, except for armed National Guardsmen with dogs. A shiver ran over her shoulders. Would life in America ever again be as she remembered it? Anger followed the anxiety–by striking fear into the hearts of U.S. citizens, the terrorists had already won a victory.

She gazed out the small window at huge pillows of white cumulonimbus clouds rolling past the jetliner. The plane hit an air pocket, and her stomach lurched. Then, apprehension threaded through her anticipation. She hadn't called Howard, wanting to surprise him. Maybe that was a mistake. What if he wasn't home? Just her luck, he'd be on his way to New York, or even to

Connecticut, to surprise *her*.

Another horrifying thought crashed into her head. What if he lives with someone? Or is married? She squeezed her eyes tightly, fighting the thoughts. *No, he's not the kind of guy who would–Hell, I don't know anything about what kind of guy he is!* Suddenly, she couldn't believe she'd acted so impulsively, without thought to unforeseen consequences.

The clouds disappeared and, far below, the checkerboard of Midwest farmland appeared. She closed her eyes and turned off her brain.

Jess shaded her eyes against the brilliant sunshine outside the Spokane Airport terminal. An exotic shade of blue spanned horizon to horizon, and the promise of snow drifted on the crisp air. She inhaled deeply, then smiled as her earlier trepidation faded. New air, new surroundings, new opportunities.

Settling behind the wheel of a rented car, she consulted a map of the area. Coeur d'Alene lay thirty-seven miles east of Spokane, just across the Washington-Idaho border. Eagerness jerked through her heartbeat–in less than an hour, she'd be in Howard's arms.

Unlike the teeming freeways in the East, the highway through Spokane held sparse traffic at midday. Modern buildings rose like shiny new pennies from the downtown area, and just past the urban center, lush green residential areas sprawled in all directions. Within minutes, the highway ribboned away from the city into a wild and beautiful landscape–the rolling foothills of the Rockies. Jess gazed in wonder at the scene, so different from the compact geography of central Connecticut.

Her cellphone chimed.

"Oh please, don't let there be any problems in the barn."

Heart thumping, she fumbled through her shoulder bag, keeping her eyes on the highway while she maneuvered to the side of the road.

Howard's voice was the sweetest sound she'd ever heard.

"Hey, Jessie. How are you?"

She grinned. "I'm great!"

"You sound great–wish I was there."

She could barely keep from giggling. He'd be so surprised

when she showed up on his doorstep.

She composed her tone. “What’s the weather like out West?”

“We’re supposed to get some snow, not much–just enough to make it pretty. . .”

Jess held her breath, wondering at the hesitation in his voice.

“. . .I really miss you, Jess. All that stuff seems like months ago.I almost jumped in the Cessna this morning, but I know you need time to get everything sorted out. ”

“It won’t be much longer, Howard–I promise.”

ЖК

# Fifty-Four

Jess crossed the border into Idaho, increasingly mesmerized by the towering evergreens on either side of the road. The colors and contrasts in this part of the country were breathtaking and inspiring. She tore her attention from the scenery and started watching for exit signs. The woman at the car rental counter had said to take the Spirit Lake exit to get to Howard's lodge. The sign appeared and Jess headed north on a narrow two-lane road.

The picture postcard on her refrigerator hadn't done the place justice. Set against a panorama of dark green forest, the magnificent turn-of-the-century log lodge glowed in the sun, a white spiral of smoke drifting lazily from the chimney.

By the time she'd parked the car, she could barely breathe from excitement. She closed her eyes briefly, preparing herself. *In my entire life, I've never felt like this. Never.* She climbed out of the car, took a deep breath, and started toward the entrance. A wide plank porch wrapped around three sides of the structure, complete with rough-hewn rocking chairs and milk-can spittoons. *Just like in the movies.* She stepped from the porch into the rustic entry hall of the lodge. After the brilliant outdoor light, she was momentarily blind in the dim room.

A cheerful voice greeted her. "Hello. Are you here for a room?"

Jess turned toward the female voice, and her stomach pitched. The most beautiful woman she'd ever seen stood behind the registration desk. Long, shiny black hair cascaded over both shoulders, framing a finely featured face with dark eyes, delicate eyebrows, and an aristocratic nose. Her perfect mouth smiled a welcome.

*Oh man, I've really screwed up! There's no way Howard's not involved with this one.*

The woman's pleasant expression changed to one of confusion. "Is something wrong? Are you lost?"

"Jessie!" Howard's laugh roared as he covered the short distance between them. "You devil!"

He scooped her into his arms and whirled her around, sending a dizzying flash of joy through her heart. When he set her down, she giggled, struggling to catch her breath.

"I almost blew it when you called." She gazed into his eyes, sparkling with delight, a look that filled her with courage. "I've missed you, too."

He kissed her soundly on the forehead, then turned to the woman at the desk. "Noji, this is my friend Jessica from Connecticut. Is the Roosevelt cabin available?" He turned back to Jess and grinned. "I can't believe you're really here."

The wind had picked up a little, and Jess shivered as she followed Howard along the path toward a beautiful rustic cabin built of heavy logs, and nestled in a stand of fir trees. Howard unlocked the door, and stepped aside for her to enter.

"This is the premium cabin–reserved for special guests only. There's a folk-tale in these parts that Teddy Roosevelt stayed at the lodge on a hunting trip in the late 1800's. Unsubstantiated, but it adds interest to the brochure."

Jess gazed around the room, suddenly wanting to stay there forever, forget the heaping plate of responsibility waiting for her back home.

A fieldstone fireplace covered an entire wall, topped by a three-inch-thick oak mantel. Hurricane lamps sat at both ends, and a Thomas Kinkade painting hung high on the chimney face. By the granite hearth, a brown bearskin rug covered the floor in front of a deeply-cushioned sofa–a cozy spot to soak up the heat from a blazing fire. A chandelier crafted of antlers hung from the peak of the cathedral ceiling. A loft overlooked the living room, and Jess could see the corner of a four-poster bed.

No television. No phone. The place was perfect.

Howard moved toward another door. "You know how to build

a fire?"

"Sort of."

She followed him out onto the porch to the woodpile. The silence of the mountains comforted her, and she closed her eyes and inhaled the sharp, sweet air. In this place, she could find peace.

While Howard worked on the fire, Jess wandered through the rest of the cabin. A small kitchen contained everything necessary to cook full meals. An old oak table and four chairs sat next to a large window with a view of the side yard. She gazed at the blazing fire, feeling as though she'd traveled through time.

Howard slipped his arms around her from behind, his voice husky in her ear. "I'm not letting you out of my sight again."

She leaned into him and closed her eyes. "Sounds good to me."

They watched the fire in silence for a few minutes, then Howard cleared his throat. "I have some stuff to do, and I'm sure you want to rest up a little." His tone became tentative. "Do you want to have dinner in the lodge restaurant, or here?"

Without hesitation, Jess turned in his arms and kissed him, savoring the tender lips she barely remembered, feeling his moustache soft against her skin.

"I want to stay right here."

Freshly showered, toasty warm, and fully relaxed, Jess stood at the bank of windows overlooking the side yard. The late afternoon light faded quickly, and small flakes of snow drifted on the air. At the edge of the trees, a doe stepped into view, seeming to stare right through the window. After a moment's hesitation, the animal dropped her head and nosed through the underbrush. Jess gazed at the scene, her throat tightening as she imagined spending her life with Howard in such a setting. The beautiful lodge in the mountains, Howard in a heavy plaid wool jacket, trudging through the snow hand-in-hand, the solitude of the outdoors. Her eyes burned. How could any of that happen? All these years, she'd thought she had everything she'd ever want. What would have to change? What would she be willing to give up?

Over the soft crackle of the fire, the wind whistled around the eaves of the sturdy structure. Alone with her quandary, the afternoon stretched out, giving her room to advance and retreat, duke it out with her desires, and hope the answers would be the right ones.

Heavy boots stamped on the wooden porch, then Howard bumped through the door, his arms laden with grocery bags. The wind caught the door and slammed it back against the wall.

"Damn! This storm is way ahead of schedule."

Jess hurried to close the door against the whirling snowflakes, and Howard carried the bags to the kitchen.

He hoisted a wine bottle. "First things first."

While he uncorked the wine, Jess peered into the sacks. "You have enough food here for an army for a month."

He wiggled his eyebrows. "You think you're going home? Think again."

Warmth flooded her heart and reality hit her. *I'm in love.*

Howard handed her a glass of wine, then raised his and held her gaze. "To the future."

# *Fifty-Five*

Jess opened her eyes, instantly aware of Howard's warmth next to her. Snuggled beneath the heavy goose-down quilt, she focused on the feel of his bare skin against hers, remembering the passion of the night. Warmth crawled along her inner thighs, and she sneaked a look at his sleeping countenance. He was the handsomest, sexiest, nicest man she'd ever known.

Her gaze drifted to the high window in the loft bedroom. Through the small panes, the electric blue sky promised a magnificent day. *As though anything could be better than last night.*

Howard stirred, then rolled toward her, slithering his arm across to cradle her against him.

"Mmm. Good morning, beautiful."

She pressed her body against him, wanting nothing between them, sinking into her emotions.

She kissed his chest and murmured, "What are we going to do today?"

A wicked chuckle rumbled through his answer. "Indoors or out?"

"You're the resort owner–you tell *me*."

"Later, I'll take you down to the lake. After a heavy snow, Coeur d'Alene is the most beautiful sight you'll ever see." His hand slipped down to cup her breast. "But I'm not ready to get up yet."

Jess awoke with a start, the thick aroma of bacon tickling her nose. She gazed up at the brown logs rolling toward the peaked ceiling, seeing the differences in each one, admiring the meticulous skill that had gone into building such a structure. The cozy loft felt like a secure cocoon, and she nestled deeper into the bed, content to never move again.

Howard's voice echoed from the kitchen. "Chow's on! Rise and shine!"

Jess's heart contracted with happiness, and suddenly she couldn't wait another minute to feel his arms around her again.

Minutes later, she snuggled into his hug, delighting in the sound of his voice, only a heartbeat away.

"Boy, you are some greenhorn, layin' in bed all morning." He stepped back and smiled mischievously. "You sure you really work at that fancy horse barn of yours?"

Jess laughed with genuine amusement. "I'm not sure of anything anymore."

Howard moved into the kitchen and Jess sat down at the table. Through the windows, the world resembled the soft white shapes of the clouds high above the earth. Howard returned to the table and she stared at a plate heaped with eggs, bacon, hash browns, and toast.

"Good grief, is this for both of us?"

Howard grinned. "Hell no, you gotta keep your strength up. We have a long day ahead of us."

Jess studied him for a moment, loving the feeling of being pampered. "You're the boss."

When the dishes were cleared away, and the fire secured, Howard shrugged into his jacket.

"Come on, I want to show you something."

Outside the cabin, Jess stopped to inhale the sharp air, savoring every new smell and each new visual delight. Howard took her hand, leading her off the porch and around the side of the building. A bright blue snowmobile rumbled to life at the turn of a key, and Jess chuckled as she climbed on behind Howard.

"I've never been on one of these things."

"Hang on."

She slipped her arms around his waist and leaned her head against his back, thinking about all the "nevers" she'd experienced lately. The vehicle moved forward, then picked up speed, and Jess felt as though they were airborne. They flew across a field and down a slope, Howard expertly zigzagging between the trees. At the bottom of the hill, he guided the vehicle onto a road grooved with one set of tire tracks. A few minutes later, he pulled up in front of a small barn, and the snowmobile sputtered and died.

Jess stared. "What's this?"

"My riding stable."

Jess sat quite still for a moment, then climbed off into the snow. Howard's face formed a collage of emotions. Pride danced around the edges of uncertainty, as he waited for her response. Suddenly, the hilarity of the situation overtook her and she burst into laughter.

Howard's smile changed to a mock scowl.

"What's so durn funny?"

Jess leaped into his arms and kissed his cheek. "You are. Why didn't you ever tell me about this?"

He chuckled. "I wanted to make sure you were interested in me, and not just my horses." He extricated himself from her clutches and stepped back. "Well, come on, but don't get your hopes up. This is just a bunch of nags for the customers to use."

The structure looked like something out of an old Will James story. The flat roof slanted toward the back of the building, the front edge forming an overhang that shaded the stall doors. Weathered gray rails fenced individual turn-out paddocks in front of each of the five stalls, and five curious faces hung over the fence, warm breath curling into the cold air.

Jess slipped her arm through Howard's and leaned her head on his shoulder. "They're beautiful. Just beautiful."

In the quiet moment, the shaggy horses turned back to snuffling through the snow for any missed bits of hay, and the brilliant beauty of the morning closed around Jess, confirming her thoughts that change was in the air.

"Feel like a little trail ride?"

Jess's throat tightened. She hadn't been on a horse since her last ride on Danny. Fighting the tears, she gazed up at Howard and nodded. He reached out and brushed a tear off her cheek.

"Careful, hon. You'll turn into an icicle out here."

Jess took a deep breath and gathered the reins. The large, shaggy palomino blew dust from his nostrils and shook his head. The bulky western saddle felt strange, so different from the sparse, sleek form of a jump saddle. Howard sat easily on a large brown and white pinto with one blue eye. The horse pawed the ground impatiently.

Jess gazed at Howard, seeing yet another side to the man who now filled every thought of the future. His brilliant eyes sparkled in the morning sun, and laugh lines crinkled around his grin.

"Head 'em up and move 'em out!"

The horses moved easily through the drifts, and Howard turned toward a dark opening in the trees. Within minutes, Jess heard the sound of water. As they moved closer, it became a roar, and as they left the dense tree cover, the sheer beauty of the place took her breath away. Spray from the hidden falls rose in the air, clinging to every branch and twig, instantly freezing into crystal sculpture.

Howard dismounted and tied his horse to a small tree. Jess slid to the ground and handed him the reins. About thirty feet away, a wooden viewing platform hung over the water, surrounded by railings and wire mesh. Howard slipped his arm around her shoulders and guided her toward it. A moment later, she felt the power surging through the wooden structure, humming through the rocks on which it was built. She looked down at the frothing white abyss, both horrified and exhilarated. Glistening spray rose and swirled, then disappeared into the billowing mist, carrying her fears away with it.

"Jess?" Emotion and anticipation defined Howard's face. "Now I've shown you *my* world. What can I do to convince you to be a part of it?"

Words couldn't explain everything in her heart, or her fear of the rocky road ahead. She answered him with a kiss, soft and tentative, but promising.

The road south to Coeur d'Alene looked like an artist's fantasy. The highway ran alongside a river for miles, providing glimpses of rolling water, then areas frozen solid. The heavily blanketed boughs of the towering pines bent down with the weight of the snow, and every so often, the wind would flip a branch, dumping an avalanche of white stuff onto the road.

The serenity of the landscape soothed Jess's inner turmoil, and her thoughts turned to Howard's question–and reality. Ending the financial mess hadn't solved anything–the past few weeks would always dilute whatever happiness she might find at Easton. Her chest tightened. The time had come for change, and no matter how much she hated the thought, she could do nothing to alter that. And, if there were any chance for happiness with Howard, she'd need to do what had to be done.

The dark ribbon of highway wound through the white wonderland, distorted by sudden tears that threatened to spill over.

Howard took her hand. "Things'll work out, honey. They always do."

The lake came into view and Jess's spirits lifted. "Oh, what a view!"

He chuckled, squeezing her hand. "I know. I've been coming down here for years, and I never get used to that first glimpse, especially in winter."

A mile or so down the road, he pulled off into a scenic overlook and parked. Jess gazed at the sparkling turquoise water surrounded by brilliant white snow under an electric blue sky.

"The lake is thirty miles long, with over a hundred miles of shoreline. I like it best this time of year, when no one is around."

"You're quite the hermit, huh?"

"Sometimes." He threw her an almost shy smile. "But it gets lonely out in the woods."

Jess's pulse skipped and she sighed deeply. She couldn't make any commitments yet, no matter how much she wanted to.

"Things got really crazy after you left Connecticut. The phone rang constantly, and we picked up fourteen new students for the winter session. Faith got a work-release so she could take the girls to Brandford."

"How'd they do?"

Jess beamed with genuine delight. "Fabulous. Lexie took the junior champion trophy on Danny, and Beth took reserve–" She grinned. "–a feeling I know all too well." She gazed out the windshield at the serene setting. "Things should level out once we start again. Faith seems committed to getting back in control."

Howard's thumb traced the outline of Jess's knuckle. "You know, I have a good staff here. I could come out to Connecticut, just do the lodge at the peak season."

She quickly covered his hand with hers. "Howard, you can't do that–you've worked too hard." She took a deep breath. "I've come to realize that the dream has changed–nothing will ever be the same for me at Easton. When the time is right, I'm going to give Faith the rest of the poker money. Frank is willing to sell the place, and if she wants to own it, she'll have a down-payment."

Howard was silent, then cleared his throat. "That's a pretty generous gift. Don't you need something for yourself, for your new plans–whatever they might be?"

She chuckled. "Oh, I'm fine. I sold a horse before I left home." She gazed at him for a moment, then smiled. "Didn't you say I could show folks out West a thing or two?"

XXXX

# More Great Equestrian

"...filled with surprises, clever twists, and constant entertainment."
*–Midwest Book Review, March '05*

"...Sparks fly and suspense builds..."
*–Western Horseman, May '05*

"Definitely a must-read!"
*–The Romance Studio, April '05*

"...an exciting journey of how cutthroat the show world can be."
*–Horsemans Yankee Pedlar, Jun '04*

**FEATURED SELECTION IN Equestrian's Edge Book Club**

**Can Love Triumph Over Ambition? Ambition Overcome Prejudice?**

In the risky world of showing high-ticket Arabian Horses, two professionals–each with a great deal to lose–find out the hard way.

Young veterinarian, Liz Barnett, has moved her equine practice from Kentucky to rural California, excited by the chance to partner with an established clinic, as well as show her beautiful Arabian horses.

Hunky horse trainer, Kurt DeVallio, has spent the past ten years struggling with the deaths of his wife and infant son, and a horse-drugging frame-up that destroyed his professional career.

When circumstances force these two together,
they learn that "winning" has many meanings.

**Available from Amazon.com & Quality Bookstores**
***Published by Equine Graphics Publishing Group***
***under the Parallel Press imprint***
**http://www.equinegraphicspublishing.com**

# *Fiction by Toni Leland*

"Leland knows how to tell a good romance tale..."
*–Midwest Book Review, June '05*

"...a fascinating tale of horses, business, and romance."
*–Coffee Time Romance, June '05*

"...a great, fast-paced read."
*–Amazon customer, May '05*

FEATURED SELECTION IN

Equestrian's Edge Book Club

**Romance is the last thing on equestrienne Bethany Webb's mind** as she gazes across the lush green fields of Highover Gate, her prestigious world-class training facility - the dream of a lifetime. Before the day is over, Beth's future is snatched right out from under her in one wet, terrifying instant.

Ambitious and handsome Brett Hall's only objective is to unseat the national champion in Three Day Eventing. As Hall steadily gains on his goal, a chink in his armor allows his heart to peek out - a weakness that seriously undermines his focus.

Hearts Over Fences glows against the backdrop of Olympic-level equestrian sport - a world filled with drama and excitement - and a large measure of ambition.

**Available from Amazon.com & Quality Bookstores**
***Published by Equine Graphics Publishing Group***
***under the Parallel Press imprint***
**http://www.equinegraphicspublishing.com**

## *The Author*

Toni Leland began writing fiction at an early age, but didn't become serious about it until 1999. Since then, she has published three equestrian-oriented novels: *Winning Ways* (romantic suspense), *Hearts Over Fences* (contemporary romance), and *Gambling With the Enemy* (mainstream thriller), plus two juvenile chapter books: *Christa Meets a Mini* and *Christa Joins a Horse Club*.

Additionally, Ms. Leland has sold short stories and poetry to several anthologies. Leland's lifelong involvement with horses and horse-folk gives her fiction a realism that makes it not only enjoyable, but educational.

Visit her at http://www.tonileland.com

Printed in the United States
204282BV00003B/7-9/A